AURA

OF

NIGHT

HEATHER GRAHAM

AURA OF NIGHT

mira

mira™

ISBN-13: 978-0-7783-8681-0

Aura of Night

For questions and comments about the quality of this book, please contact us at CustomerService@Harlequin.com.

Mira
22 Adelaide St. West, 41st Floor
Toronto, Ontario M5H 4E3, Canada
BookClubbish.com

Printed in U.S.A.

In memory of Lisa Manetti,
brilliant author and storyteller, amazing and beautiful friend;
a woman whose smile and infectious laughter made all around her friends—
and friends with one another

AURA

OF

NIGHT

PROLOGUE

"There's such a rush! You can't begin to imagine the rush, the adrenaline racing through your system. Though I suppose every man is different. You know that," Rory Ayers said, sitting back in the hard metal chair. The accused crossed his arms over his chest heedless of the clanking chains he was wearing. Ayers's trial wouldn't come up for a few months, but he was being held without bond, charged with kidnapping at the very least and—by his own confession—multiple murders.

Every man was different, yes, Special Agent Ragnar Johansen thought.

But in this case, every murderer was different.

The Bureau and the prosecutors were still trying to unravel the horrors of the "Embracer" killings, which had been committed by at least two killers.

But possibly more.

"The Deirdre thing—" Ayers began.

"You mean the attempted murder of your own daughter?" Ragnar asked.

Ayers waved a hand in the air. "Not my daughter! I told you, her mother was pregnant when I married her."

"You made that choice."

"She had the money."

"But you raised her daughter."

"That never made her mine. And I had to do what I did. Your people were sniffing around Jim Carver, and I had to do something. That idiot. He was supposed to be my disciple. I told him his damned letters to the press were ridiculous."

"Still, in the end, you were trying to please him. But you kidnapped the wrong woman. Kind of sad, the way you capitulated to everything he wanted. I mean, you claim you're the original."

"The original 'Embracer'—as some labeled me." Ayers shrugged. "I couldn't help the way Carver turned out. The breakout from the bus! They'll throw the book at him for that one." Ayers's accomplice had managed a dramatic escape from custody, but Ragnar and his team had recaptured him.

Ragnar sat back, shaking his head. "I believe that 'the book' is being rightfully thrown at you. But the DA might be convinced to take the death penalty off the table if you cooperate and help us discover the identities of all your victims."

Ayers sat back, laughing. "The death penalty? Oh, please! I'm not going to get the death penalty. Too many good people out there are crying the death penalty is barbaric."

"At the moment, Mr. Ayers, the federal prosecutor is seeking the death penalty."

"I will live a long life. And you just never know when my circumstances might change. I'm a rich man, even in custody."

"Hmm. Well, I've heard that even for rich men things can be tough."

"Not when you can pay the right people."

Sadly, that could be true. Ragnar had done undercover work once in a federal penitentiary, and he knew there were "brotherhoods" who offered protection for the right price.

He smiled icily. He also knew there were those in prison who despised men like Ayers.

"The thing about prison is it can be hard to contain all the personalities," he said. "And some people who have been put away in maximum security consider themselves to be above others. Their crimes had just cause while yours... Well, some of those men have daughters. And when they learn you tried to murder a girl you raised..." He shrugged as he let his words fade out.

Ragnar was glad to see the tic in the pulse in the man's vein at his throat—a giveaway that he had irritated him.

And his words of warning might have been truth.

But Ayers managed a smile. "You still just don't know the half of it!"

"And you could help yourself by telling me the half I don't know," Ragnar said.

"Send the pretty agent in—you know who I mean. The one Jim wanted so badly." He started to laugh. "I'd have enjoyed the sister just fine. Megan. Beautiful girl. All that blond hair with the red lights like sunset! Those eyes...emerald pools of terror!"

Only experience and great effort kept Ragnar from betraying his own anger. Agent Colleen Law and her sister, Megan, had been targeted by the serial killers, but had managed to escape them.

"Well, Megan held it together. That's kind of why you're here, isn't it? And I'm afraid Agent Law is gone, and you can't fantasize about what you'd like to do with her if she were the one questioning you."

"Gone?" Ayers seemed truly disconcerted. "You mean, she quit? She moved? She kicked the can?"

"No, she's not in the area. That's what I mean."

"Where is she?"

"Gone," Ragnar said flatly.

"But she'll come back?"

"No."

"Ah, too bad. Not that I would have told her anything anyway, but it would have been so nice to chat with her awhile. So, they send in the bruiser. They think you'll intimidate me with your size. Well, you can't do a thing to me while I sit here. Not a thing."

"I don't need to do a thing to you. You're in here now. The law will take care of you. And you will get the death penalty unless you try to negotiate a life sentence."

Ayers just stared at him. He seemed a little too comfortable, almost lounging in the hard metal chair. And then he started singing. A really wretched rendition of Frank Sinatra's "New York, New York."

Ragnar raised his eyebrows in question.

The man just kept singing.

Ragnar stood, ready to leave. He wasn't getting anywhere.

He called the guard and headed toward the door.

"You don't know the half of it!" Ayers screamed after him.

Ragnar ignored the man. Ayers screamed the words over and over again.

Then when the guard came and Ragnar stepped out, Rory Ayers started singing again.

Horribly and loudly.

The door slammed closed behind him. Ragnar thanked the

guard, then collected his weapon from the man on duty, an officer he'd come to know named Brendan Kent.

"That is one sick puppy," Kent said, shaking his head as he handed Ragnar his weapon. "I'm damned glad the man is locked up tight, and I hope it stays that way."

"I believe it will."

Kent shook his head again and sighed. "The things people can get away with if they get lucky in court. I sure as hell may not make the money, but I'm damned glad I'm not a defense attorney."

Kent was a man of about thirty with light-colored hair who seemed pleasant most of the time.

"Yeah, I don't think that route would have been for me either," Ragnar said. "Then again, we have defense attorneys for a reason. Remember, we're all innocent until proven guilty."

"Not much to prove with him—the bastard admits it!"

"Yeah. I'm not seeing a bright future there," Ragnar said. "Anyway, thanks. I'll be back."

"I'm glad that even talking to him is your job and not mine. Or guarding him. Thankfully, they switch duties around, so no one is stuck escorting him to interrogation and his legal meetings again and again."

"Right. Thanks."

Ragnar left the correctional facility.

A few other people were leaving at the same time. A local detective he'd met briefly, and two men he figured to be attorneys. They tended to dress in similar suits and carry laptops and folders in the same briefcases. One of them was an older man, haggard, and looking as if he were ready to call it quits; one was younger and had a hard and determined look on his face.

Ragnar observed that while they had exited the facility at the same time, the lawyers didn't seem to be together. They didn't talk or confer but headed toward different rows of cars.

Ragnar lifted a hand in farewell to the detective, who returned the gesture with a nod. He thought he might have met or seen the older attorney in action, but the man was walking with his head down and Ragnar couldn't be sure. The younger attorney strode as if he were deep in thought, and he must have been: he walked into the rear of another car on his way to a navy sedan.

Ragnar had heard a young attorney from the public defender's office had been one of the first to work with Rory Ayers. He'd probably gotten the gig because none of the others had wanted to deal with it. Yet, on such a case, experience would be needed just to avert the death penalty.

Defending criminals wasn't Ragnar's problem. His job was finding proof against them, getting justice, and trying to bring some peace to families, friends, and survivors.

That's why he'd been there today.

But he was glad to be leaving. And he was glad Mark Gallagher, Colleen Law, and Mark's dog, Red—his partners on the case they believed had ended with the incarceration of both Carver and Ayers—were far away.

They were out of the country on a honeymoon. The powers that be in the Krewe of Hunters unit had insisted they take one.

Ayers might be talking out of his ass.

They knew he and Carver had killed certain women. And Ayers had attempted the murder of his own legal child, a young woman who'd been saved by the curious and unique talent that was Colleen Law's acute and inexplicable sense of hearing.

And now...

He'd almost reached his car when he suddenly stood very still.

You don't know the half of it.

Jim Carver had said those same words right before they'd discovered Megan Law had been kidnapped, and the killers were trying to lure Colleen to them as well.

You don't know the half of it…

New York, New York…

Megan Law worked in New York City. It had been Megan's strange talent of understanding the true meaning in a person's words that had led them to knowing that another killer was, indeed, out there.

Megan Law might have known what Rory Ayers meant now.

Megan…

Ragnar thought about the friction between himself and Megan, and he also thought about catching her when she had passed out cold, but only after the incident had been over. She'd held her own until the end.

All that blond hair with the red lights like sunset. Those eyes…emerald pools of terror.

He remembered Megan's eyes, and the way she had looked at him, as she'd come around.

Two things struck him. He could have used her unique ability today, hidden away in the observation room, listening to Rory Ayers.

And a second thing, so much worse…

New York, New York.

He gave himself a shake, hurried to his car, and put through a call to Jackson Crow, the Krewe's director of field operations.

It was early in the day. Luckily, he had gone to the correctional facility at just about the crack of dawn, which meant the day stretched before him. New York City was a two-and-a-half-hour drive from the DC area depending on traffic and the driver, and Ragnar sure as hell knew how to drive.

He needed to reach NYC. Make the right phone calls as he drove to get there.

He didn't have Megan's ability to read the secret meaning in words.

Even so, his sense of urgency grew with every passing minute.

He needed to reach Megan. She could be in danger.

CHAPTER ONE

"The only thing we have to fear is fear itself."

That had been said by President Franklin D. Roosevelt, and it had to do with the Great Depression.

Megan Law had learned from her sister, Colleen, that there were, in truth, many things to fear, but the president had been right about the emotion itself being the greatest thing to fear.

Because fear was paralyzing. Colleen had always warned her about that. Fear itself could prevent an intelligent person from seeking the logical way—or best way—out of a situation.

Megan closed her eyes for a minute.

Fear. Terror.

She could feel it all over again, could see the coming darkness. She'd blithely been trying to help, chasing after a runaway puppy. And then she had fallen, and she had assumed the puppy's owner had come to help her up...

Until the darkness. And the overwhelming, *paralyzing* fear.

Megan opened her eyes and let out a long breath.

She loved books—all kinds of books, and everything about

them. That's why becoming an editor for a publishing house had long been a goal, one she had achieved soon after her graduation from college.

She loved reading an author's words and finding the places where they hadn't really said what they'd intended.

She loved the human mind and unraveling the twists and turns that *meaning* could take as it made its way from the mind to the page. She was good at it.

She was sadly discovering she wasn't quite as good at creating all the written words herself.

Maybe it was the subject matter.

She had been kidnapped by the man—or as it turned out, men—known as The Embracer. Her publisher had begged her to write a book about the experience. An important book. One that might help women deal with their own fear and trauma.

It could also make a lot of money.

Their small press had flourished with their science fiction line. But they now wanted nonfiction, a firsthand account of the horror.

Publishing houses changed. They grew. And this was a great way to begin a nonfiction line with a book so important and so timely.

Megan was one of their own.

She was happy to be a team player, but the experience of being taken and held by The Embracer had been painful and terrifying. She had survived it without injury, keeping as strong as she could, full of the hope that her sister—an FBI agent with the Krewe of Hunters unit—would rescue her before she became a victim.

And she was alive to tell the story.

She was alive because of her family and their very strange

abilities. She had screamed to Colleen's mind, and Colleen had heard. Despite Megan's fear and knowing what happened to the victims of The Embracer, she had managed to pull some sense into place when the darkness had slowly lifted, and she had realized where she was and what had happened. She hadn't passed out cold until it was over, until help had come, and she had woken up in the arms of a blond giant of a man who then held her tight when she had almost fallen flat to the ground...

She gave herself a stern mental shake.

Start at the beginning.

But at the beginning of the events? Or her own involvement?

She started to type. Special Agent Colleen Law and her partners—Mark Gallagher, Ragnar Johansen, and Red, a most unusual dog—had left Megan at the train station in Virginia. She'd needed to get back to New York for a meeting. They'd seen her through to the platform.

But then there had been the man's desperate sounds of worry and fear. A cry: "He's just a puppy! Oh, God, someone help me! He'll be roadkill!"

Well, Megan was a dog person. No way she was letting a puppy be roadkill. And she'd left her spot at the station even knowing the train was due. As far as the transportation schedules along the mid- and northeastern seaboard, there was always another train coming.

A puppy was at stake.

So she had run to help the man, back out in the parking area, and...

Megan was suddenly interrupted by the sweeping arrival of one of her colleagues.

"Oh! I don't know what to do with this!"

Megan looked up. Nannette Benson had walked into her office, shaking her head, and sunk into a chair, her tablet in her lap. "Oh, Megan!" she muttered, shaking her head again. She was tall and slim and energetic with dark eyes and hair and a quick, flashing smile.

Nannette was ten years older, thirty-nine to Megan's twenty-nine, and a senior editor. From all Megan had seen, Nannette was an exceptionally good one. She was usually kind to her authors. She knew how to stay on the right side of the fine line between helpful criticism and flat-out insulting someone.

"Is it me?" Nannette asked. "I mean, I like the story, I like the concept! But here...listen. 'Sierra fled, running toward the strange, tall grasses that bordered the Alonian city of Ja with its strong defenses. If she could lose the beast in the grasses, the savage ra creatures would protect and defend her.

"'She was there...almost there. She could see the grasses moving. She sensed that the ra creatures were near the edge of the colorful grasses that towered above her.

"'And then...'"

"Then?" Megan asked Nannette.

"'She tripped. She didn't know if it was the ground itself that caught her up, perhaps the root system of such massive plants. But something, perhaps her own panic, tangled her feet and she tripped!'"

"Okay?" Megan said, sitting back, hoping to be helpful.

"It's so cliché! A trip. I mean, in every slasher movie someone trips!"

"I see. Well, I don't know where she's going from there, so..."

"Oh, well, Harkon, the Alonian hero, rushes out of the grass to do battle with the beast. Then, you know, the ra come out of the tall grass, too, and Harkon rushes the heroine through the grass to the fortress. Cliché." She sighed. "I guess I need to think on this, but how is it going with you? I'm so sorry! I know you don't want to do this and you are trying to make others happy, and…wow. I'm sorry. I shouldn't have come in here whining with my own worries!"

"No, no, it's okay. If you like the writing, but feel there's something else the author could do instead with the action, just give them a suggestion and see if they're willing. You know how to guide them toward ideas that might improve their work."

"You're right, you're right. What about your real-life adventure?" Nannette asked. "Nonfiction or not, it's a book. Make it exciting."

Megan arched a brow. "Exciting. Someone was crying about a puppy—"

"Dogs or kids. You'd be right there," Nannette said, nodding. "You *are* a dog person. And too kind. I can see it in real life, and there are lots of dog lovers out there. They'll understand you were trying to help save a puppy! But chasing a puppy led to what happened?"

"So, I ran into the parking lot trying to help. It looked like a man was trying to usher the little thing in one direction, and I ran around so I could help and…"

"And?" Nannette asked.

Megan grimaced.

"I tripped."

"Tripped?"

"Yeah. I tripped. He'd laid a trap. A rope was caught between the tires and I tripped. I thought he was coming to help me, but instead there was suddenly a black bag over my head. I smelled something strange and sweet, some kind of a knockout drug, and I wound up in the back of his car all trussed up. Next thing I knew, I was in a cabin. And two men were fighting. One had wanted to kidnap and kill my sister, and while we're not identical, we have a similar look."

"You tripped?" Nannette said. "You…tripped?"

"Yeah. For real. I tripped."

"Oh. So, it does happen in real life and not just in slasher flicks?"

"I'm afraid so."

Nannette looked so confused. Megan smiled and said, "Oh, no! Now I'm not just a victim, I'm a cliché!"

"Oh, sweetie, you? Never a cliché. I think you're right. I guess people do trip. Except I think the heroines have got to get up and join the fight. And this book they want from you…well, it is important. You survived. It's important for people to know how to survive in a situation like that. Megan, you are young and beautiful, and young and beautiful tends to be…"

"Prey. Thanks. I'd rather be young and tough-as-nails like my sister. I mean, I think my sister is beautiful, too, but she's savvy."

"Megan, you're smart, too. You're different."

Megan laughed. "We *are* different. Two of a set of fraternal triplets, and we're still different. We both knew since we were kids what we wanted to do with our lives. Colleen…"

She broke off. She didn't think she should explain her sister had supernatural hearing and had saved a woman's life when she'd been just a kid.

Nor should she explain they did share one strange skill—the sense to see and hear the dead when the dead needed to be seen.

"Colleen just always knew what she wanted to do when she grew up. And I knew what I wanted to do, too. So. Anyway, I'm sad to say I did trip. So, in your story, maybe the monster knew she would seek the help of the ra creatures and set a trap. That way, she's not an idiot for running—and tripping."

"Perfect!" Nannette said. "Of course, she can be a little kick-ass, like your sister."

Megan smiled and nodded again. She hadn't actually managed to do anything against the bad guys who had taken her. She had been knocked out and then tied up and then—when she wasn't tied—she'd been in a chair with a man holding a gun to her temple. She hadn't been kickass. Colleen was. And still, what would Colleen have done had the gun been to her temple? She knew now her sister blamed herself for what had happened to Megan, and she also knew Colleen would have died in her place without blinking an eye.

But Colleen and her partners were agents. They had played it out, and they had prevailed.

"Megan, are you all right?" Nannette asked.

"Oh, yes, fine, thank you."

"I know what was on the news," Nannette said. "I saw the pictures of the agents. Man, that blond one! I'm tempted to call him Thor or Odin or something like that!"

"He is of Norwegian descent," Megan said.

Nannette grinned. "Bring him up here, huh?" she said teasingly. "Special Agent Ragnar Johansen. I mean, the dog is cool, but bring the Viking!"

Bring the Viking? Like hell!

"Well, you know, he's a government cop. He works with my sister, not me."

"Too bad!" Nannette said. "I wouldn't mind waking up in *his* arms!"

Megan forced a smile. She waved a hand in the air.

"Let's get back to the novel you're working on. Who is the author?"

"Kelsey Mariner."

"Ah! Sounds like Kelsey. It will be great," Megan said. She enjoyed the author's work. The woman had a feel for creating a world with such imagery that the reader could feel as if they knew it, as if they were there. She created believable alien beings—terrifying creatures, funny creatures, and humanoid beings living in social circumstances that touched upon the same problems people discovered daily in both society and their private lives.

In fact, Megan very much wished she was working on Kelsey's book, battling beasts with the help of ra creatures, rather than trying to relate her own experiences.

"Whatever suggestions you give her, I know she listens to you. From what you've told me, she's always ready to do anything to make a project better. The book will be wonderful," Megan said.

"Oh, Megan, the book will be great. Kelsey knows how to write sci-fi. I'm just hoping I can keep this one fresh," Nannette said. "Thank you, you've helped. I'm sorry it was at your expense, but…a trap! I think Kelsey will love the idea. I'll call her, and we'll chat before I send my notes, and hope we're on the same page. So! I'm going to let *you* go back to work." Nannette started to laugh. "I hope you think I'm a good editor."

"I do."

"Great. Because I'm going to edit your book. Now, I know that sounds strange. I'm fiction, and fiction that doesn't touch much reality. But I was with a Big Five before, and I worked on nonfiction there. I edited a stock market book—beyond boring, a political book… Lord, did I hate that—and several memoirs. I'm looking forward to working with you." She laughed. "Wait until you see my revision letter!"

"I'll be waiting with bated breath," Megan assured her.

Nannette grinned and gave her a wave.

Megan gave her a smile and a wave in return.

Then Nannette was gone, and Megan stared at her computer again.

She had decided to start with the train station, then layer in the Embracer events that led to her abduction.

She paused, knowing there were many things she couldn't put in a book—like the fact Jim Carver was in prison because a detective had seen him drag a distraught woman back into his house.

Except the detective couldn't testify or go through normal channels; he'd been killed in the line of duty several years earlier, but he knew members of the Krewe could be reached. They saved a woman's life because of that detective. He still haunted the streets, because the case that had killed him had never really been solved.

Megan had met Sergeant Alfie Parker when she'd been at her sister's. She'd been asked down to DC to listen and decipher what was really being said—or not said, but meant.

Sergeant Parker had fascinated her and had broken her heart. She had wanted to do more for him, get Mark and Ragnar and Colleen to help him.

They'd promised. But his was an old, cold case. And they were involved now—well, Ragnar was involved—in finding out the truth behind a trail of bodies that might have been victims of one the "Embracers."

She started suddenly, giving herself a shake.

There was someone at her door again. She felt their presence before she saw Nannette had returned.

Smirking.

She stood there, staring at Megan, her face flushed and filled with amusement.

"Megan, you have a visitor," Nannette said.

She moved aside.

Megan was glad she was sitting. If she'd been standing, she might have fallen from sheer surprise.

Ragnar Johansen was in her doorway.

Ridiculously tall, blond hair a bit shaggy, eyes as icy a blue as ever colored Nordic waters.

"Ragnar?" she said, or rather, his name formed with the breath that escaped her lips.

In fact, it came out as more of a question.

"Megan," he mumbled, glancing at Nannette, smiling briefly, but his expression clearly showing he needed to speak with her alone.

What about? She hadn't heard anything from Colleen.

"Um, come in. Have a seat," she told him.

Ragnar turned politely to Nannette. "Thank you," he said.

Nannette backed away, still staring at him.

He smiled—a smile Megan knew. It was an expected smile. A polite smile. It went no further than the curve of his lips.

"Well. Uh. Lovely to meet you!" Nannette told him. She was all but stumbling over her words and her own feet as she walked backward.

"And a pleasure to meet you, too," Ragnar said.

Again, that smile. Others might find it charming. To Megan, it appeared to be more of a snarl.

Not always. There had been those ridiculous moments between them…

Better left forgotten.

When he closed the door in Nanette's wake, the smile disappeared.

"To what do I owe this great honor and pleasure?" Megan asked dryly. "The court date isn't for months. Both men are being held without bond—"

"You're in danger," he said flatly.

She hated the icicles that seemed to form in her veins. She tried with everything in her to keep her face expressionless.

"I'm in danger? How?"

He sat in the office chair across from her desk, shaking his head. Then he leaned forward. "We thought it was over. Really over."

"You got them both. Well, really, you got all three of them. And if there was something we missed, Mark or Colleen—"

"Are not available."

"Honeymoon. Right," Megan muttered. "But if we don't tell them—"

"They'll be angry, yes. But then…"

"Then, what?"

He leaned back. "I don't *know* anything."

Megan shook her head. She could usually fathom what someone was really trying to say.

Somehow, he was eluding her.

"What are you talking about?"

Ragnar let out a long breath. "All right. You know we interview those we apprehend when they're incarcerated. This time, it seemed especially important. We have bodies, and we don't know who they were. I've spoken with the DA. He tends to favor life in prison, but he wants to go for the death sentence for Ayers. I've tried to get him to negotiate in the interest of those still desperately looking for loved ones. Most need the truth. They need to bury their family or friends and mourn them. Not knowing can be torture."

"I understand that, but——"

"When I interviewed him, Rory Ayers started up the same way Jim Carver did the day you were in the observation room listening. 'You don't know the half of it.' He said it over and over again when I was leaving. And he started singing."

"And that means I'm in danger?" she asked skeptically. "Anyone might be in danger from psychotics like that man, but why would it mean I'm specifically in danger? He doesn't know I was in the observation room that day. The man was an idiot who thought I was Colleen."

"Right. But he claims Jim Carver was the idiot. He would have been perfectly fine with you…as a target…and he described your eyes and your hair before singing 'New York, New York.'"

Megan leaned back, stiff and cold.

She'd been so thrilled Mark and Colleen had been able to take a real honeymoon. They were both so dedicated to work, and what had happened had been harrowing in the extreme. They deserved some time away, together.

She was alive because of her sister's talent and her sister's partners…

Including Ragnar, she reminded herself.

She looked away. He always seemed nonchalant about his appearance, but today he wore a suit, and he wore it well. His height was impressive in itself. There were taller people in the world, but Ragnar had seemed larger than life from the time she'd first seen him. He was tightly muscled without being heavy. Physically, he was a beautiful specimen of the human race, and she knew that too well.

He was a good investigator. He was…

Maybe just too good in too many ways.

"Megan, are you listening to me?"

"I am. So, you drove up from the DC area to protect me? That's a long drive. You know we have cops in NYC, and we have *the* largest field office for the FBI."

"Yes, New York has the largest field office."

She frowned, looking at him.

"You've already spoken to them?"

"As soon as I left the interview."

"If you were that concerned, why didn't they send an agent?"

He was silent, unreadable, then said, "They did."

"You've had me watched?"

Megan had to argue.

She had to.

She didn't want to be afraid again.

Fear was paralyzing.

"Okay, okay," she said, "so you were worried when Rory Ayers started singing 'New York, New York' because he had spoken about me, and he knows I work in New York. But, Ragnar, he's locked up tight! Along with Jim Carver. I can guarantee you, after the breakout from the prison bus Carver was part of, they'll both be watched closely. I can't believe I have anything to fear from Rory Ayers."

"I don't think you have anything to fear from Rory Ayers," Ragnar said flatly. "They will watch him. And he will go to prison, and he'll be locked away for years and years—probably until his death, no matter how that may come."

"Then what are you worried about? Ragnar, this is already making a mess of my life. I don't want to remember all this, but I do believe a book might be important to warn others. I love what I do. And yes, I'm in my office writing and not editing, but I'm going to meetings for my writers, I'm making sure they get the copy, the art, and the promotion they need. And I am reading over the manuscripts because, obviously, this book won't go to press until the men have faced trial. If Rory Ayers is locked up tight, then really, I want to keep something of a life—"

He'd leaned forward and before she could finish he interrupted her.

"Megan, I'm trying to make sure you have a life, period!"

"But…" Her conviction was wavering. There was a tap at her door, and it opened a crack.

This time, it was Tasha from the mail room.

Most of the time, her authors wrote her through email and turned in their manuscripts the same way.

But she still received letters and some snail mail invitations to writer events and conferences. Even gifts relating to a story now and then.

"Oh! I'm sorry!" Tasha said. She stared at Ragnar.

Tasha was young, and when an editorial assistant job opened up, she'd be first in line for it, having just graduated NYU.

Ragnar stood and inclined his head politely.

Tasha bustled past him. "I didn't realize—sorry, sorry, anyway! Let me just set these down."

There was an assortment of cards and letters along with a brown cardboard box.

The box looked the worse for wear, but people reused boxes all the time. And it might have gotten beaten to pieces in transport.

"Thank you, Tasha."

"Of course."

Tasha wasn't looking at her. She was staring at Ragnar, smiling, entranced.

It was really annoying.

"Tasha, this is Special Agent Ragnar Johansen," she said wearily. "Ragnar, Miss Tasha Colter."

"Oh!" Tasha said. "You're working. I... Nice to meet you, sir."

"Likewise," Ragnar said.

He smiled until Tasha was gone, sat down, and stared at Megan again. She almost felt the hard ice in his eyes, making her colder still. He could look at a person in a way that was beyond chilling. *Stop!* she told herself. She'd always known she'd run into him again. He would still be working with her sister and Mark. And Red.

"You sent someone from the New York field office to watch me. They could have told me all this. So, why are you here?"

"I think you should come back to DC with me."

The ice in her system seemed to become a furious burn for a moment.

She shook her head.

"That's not possible. I need to be here. I can't spend the rest of my life hiding because a whacked-out killer sang a song."

"Maybe you could help again, and it could all end more quickly."

"All what could end?" she asked desperately.

He let out a sigh. "I believe the men we now have were part of a group. I believe they know—and can somehow communicate with—others out there who are part of their sick club. I believe Rory Ayers will have someone come after you, and he will live vicariously through the thrill of knowing you were taken in the end."

She didn't want to listen to any of it.

She didn't want to believe any of it.

She kept staring at him, absently fingering the mail on her desk. As she did so, she knocked the box over. She quickly stood to get it.

So did he.

The only thing on the box was an old postmark. Yes, it had been reused. Her name, position, and the address of the publishing company had been written in capital letters with a black marker.

She bumped into him as they both reached for the box. He had it first; she felt his fingers on hers and an intense heat competed with the ice inside her.

She quickly returned to her chair.

Ragnar absently set the box down in front of her. The cardboard was seriously decayed, as if it had been wet. She didn't want it near her computer, so she picked at the packing tape while she talked.

"Ragnar, this is what you believe, but it's not based on anything other than a hunch."

"Just come with me long enough for another interview and see what you think. No, I can't fathom meaning almost magically the way you do, but what he did today seemed rather clear—something anyone could understand without special skills."

"I don't know. I have a dog. I have appointments—"

She broke off.

She'd ripped the cover off the box.

She stared inside.

To her credit—or perhaps just because she was too frozen—she didn't scream.

Fear could be paralyzing.

She just stared.

Ragnar stood and walked forward.

He looked down and swore softly, seeing the one thing in the box.

A skull. A human skull. With bits of flesh and hair and blood still attached.

CHAPTER TWO

Thankfully, Megan had kept her calm. She hadn't screamed and brought all her coworkers running.

Ragnar didn't want this getting out, didn't want the media all over it.

Because whoever had sent the package—through whatever sick, strange fraternity Carver and Ayers had going—obviously wanted the publicity. They wanted it known The Embracer was a hydra, and ugly heads would keep popping up.

Until they reached the heart of the beast.

A media frenzy wouldn't help that.

Megan still hadn't screamed. For that matter, she hadn't said a word.

"I'm going to take it out of here," he told her, replacing the lid on the box. "We can't have a forensic team crawling all over the building. Someone will have to speak with the mail room, but we'll do it quietly. And I'm sorry. I can't leave here without you."

She was still silent, staring at the box.

"Are you all right?" he asked.

She looked at him then and nodded slowly.

"I'm so sorry for the...person. And I... I have a target on my back. They found me at work, a place I love and...yeah. I'm going to say I'll be working from my hotel...that I'm staying close to the case." She winced. "I don't want to put anyone here in danger."

She was rambling. Thoughts racing through her head.

He could only imagine. Megan was a civilian who loved books. She was not accustomed to finding human skulls.

He nodded. They checked that the door to her office was closed and he put through a call to headquarters, aware his words were tense, and Megan watched him as he spoke.

But Jackson Crow agreed with him; he would be making arrangements with the local office to accept the box and begin their forensic investigation. He'd have to be careful transporting it. He hadn't brought a duffel bag with him—he hadn't been expecting to pick up a human head—but he could act the casual part when necessary.

"What do you need to do to leave here with me now?" he asked Megan.

She stared at him blankly for a minute. Then she gave herself a little shake, and said, "I just... I'll stop in and tell Brady Whitfield, our publisher, I'll be working closer to the story. That should be fine. He's the one who wanted the book so very badly. And I'll just ask Nannette to make sure we work out video calls for meetings and... Ragnar!"

"What?"

She shook her head. "This is...human. Decaying. The box should have...smelled. It doesn't smell. How is that possible?"

"It's been treated. Someone knows something about mortuary

work or taxidermy. Or these days, someone is just a great on-line student for the zillions of things you can learn on the web."

She shook her head. "I mean…who could do something like that?"

She was horrified.

Naturally.

But she seemed to understand his way of handling the situation and even appreciated it.

"Are you all right to speak with your boss?" he asked.

"I—yes. I'm fine. I can do it. Honest. But…"

"We'll get this down to the NYC office as soon as possible. When you're ready to leave, we can go there and get this taken care of. All right?"

She nodded and bit her lower lip, then hurried to the door. She headed out.

He stood tensely in her office for a few minutes, staring at the full bookcase behind Megan's desk. When the door opened again, it was her coworker Nannette.

The woman smiled at him. "So, you're bringing Megan back to DC with you and allowing her access to records and witness reports and whatever. That's so wonderful."

"We think it will be helpful, too," Ragnar said. He hoped that books were helpful. He'd read everything written by Roy Hazelwood, John Douglas, and others who had served with the Behavioral Sciences Unit at the Bureau. And across the country, state and local police officers now utilized profiling services.

But they weren't looking for a single person. And maybe, just maybe, they were looking for the same twist in the mind of the strange fraternity they were discovering. Then there was the possibility that Megan observing interrogations could bring some new information to light.

He smiled for Nannette. He wondered if she could sense his concern.

When he'd arrived, he'd been flat-out worried about Megan.

"Well, Megan is a prize, you know?" Nannette said. "I'm going to miss her, so work quickly! She's extraordinary. Even with email! I'll get an email and, well, you know—there's no tone to an email. Someone can say something as simple as 'hallelujah,' and it could be sarcastic like 'Oh, yeah, great, just wonderful—that sucks.' Or it could really mean 'Wow, I'm so happy, thank God, that's truly wonderful.' I can't always tell what someone means, but Megan can read an email and explain exactly what she's getting from it."

"Yes, that's a nice talent," Ragnar muttered.

He really wanted to leave.

There was a box with a head in it in the office, and he wanted to get it out of there.

The woman was looking at him with a broad smile. "I miss her so much when she's out of the office, but this is such an opportunity for her."

Megan walked back in just as Nannette was speaking.

He had no mind-reading talents, but he knew Megan was thinking the "opportunity" was really anything but.

"We should get moving," he said politely.

"Rush hour in New York City," Nannette said. "I think we're heading toward that time."

"But we have to stop by my apartment and pick up my dog, and I have to pack a bag. I really want to get back down to DC before it's too late," Megan said.

She gave Nannette a hug and a smile.

"Hopefully, I'll have this done quickly with everything at my fingertips," she said. "Of course, there will be additions,

changes, and who knows what else by the time we get to pub-
lication. But for the first draft…maybe it'll be quick! And don't
forget, I am available for video conferences. We all got pretty
good at them."

"Megan, do you want me to take anything else? I have the
box. Do you have a computer case or something more?" Ragnar asked.

If he headed out to the reception area, she might get away
more quickly.

"If you just take the box…oh, and my laptop is there. I have
everything in the cloud anyway. Nannette, I just need to make
sure you stay on the Robert Henley book for me, too…"

Ragnar started out. He had the box tucked under his arm.

Luckily, no one had asked about it.

He meant to move on, but he paused. Special Agent Alice
Ainsley had been watching over Megan's office before his arrival. From the NYC field office, she had come undercover, and
the receptionist was telling her she could meet with the head of
the art department shortly.

He nodded at Alice but kept his position in the hall.

He never meant to eavesdrop.

But he could hear Nannette clearly assuring Megan everything was going to be all right.

"I don't want my sister bothered, but I can't help wishing she
and my new brother-in-law were back and taking care of all
this," Megan told Nannette.

"You mean, instead of Ragnar? You have a problem with
him, it seems."

"It's just…a bit complicated," Megan said. She sounded uncomfortable.

"Ooh." Nanette's voice was full of sudden understanding.

"Right, sparks fly. But if you have a problem with Special Agent Ragnar Johansen, you probably shouldn't have slept with him." Nannette laughed.

"I—" Megan began.

He waited. She didn't elaborate.

He knocked on the door to her office. While he'd never meant to eavesdrop, maybe he could give her an out.

"Megan, we really need to get going," he said.

"Yes! Nanette, we'll talk tomorrow," she said quickly.

She didn't linger. She hurried out of her office and was ahead of Ragnar down the hall, pausing only to say goodbye to the receptionist before she was out the door and slamming the little button to summon the building's elevator.

Ragnar decided not to mention what he'd overheard. It was hard, however, to keep from smirking. She was cute when she was flustered. It didn't matter. She didn't glance his way.

As they descended and she followed him to his car, she didn't speak.

Then, settling into the passenger's seat, she groaned softly. "We're traveling with a human head." She shuddered.

"Not far. I'm taking it to the New York offices. We'll just go downtown, drop off the package, and then drive out of the city."

"No, we have to stop and get my dog, Hugo," she said. "And I need to get some things."

"We'll drop off the package, and go pick up Hugo, and be out of the city."

"I still... I think this might be too much."

"You want to be alone after this?" he asked her, indicating the box.

She cast him a long glance. "Well, I wasn't alone, was I? You sent someone to watch the publishing house."

"True."

She shook her head and leaned back. "I hope you can get Carver or Ayers talking! This is ridiculous. How can criminals have such a web? How are they communicating with people outside of the corrections center? How is that even possible? Aren't communications monitored?"

"They are. And we will be studying the tapes from both men."

She let out a sigh again. "How many such horrible freaks can there be?"

"Well, luckily, not the majority of the population."

He made it downtown quickly and found Bureau parking. If they weren't in the position they were in, he would have gone up quickly, leaving Megan in the car.

But he wasn't leaving her anywhere.

"Actually," she said quietly, "we should have stopped at my place first. Midtown. Now we're downtown. Normally, that wouldn't be a big deal. But this is NYC. And we'll be heading into real rush hour. Every hour here is rush hour, but we have real rush hour, too. Rush hours."

"It is what it is," he said. "Come on."

"I need to go in?"

"I'm not leaving you here."

"Even in front of an FBI building?"

"Even in front of an FBI building."

She didn't argue; she got out of the car. At the entry, he flashed his badge. Megan was given a pass and they headed up the elevators.

He did leave her in the reception area, promising he'd be just a minute. There were others milling around. One of the desk clerks told him there was a group of writers who had been given clearance to come in to hear speeches from several different agents.

"Uh," he muttered.

"Oh, it's very normal," he was assured. "We need the public to like us. And we need writers to get it close to right. Even though what's 'right' when it comes to processes and procedures does change over time. Did you know this office's biggest section now is working with cybercrime? Cybercrime—over organized crime!"

"The age of the internet," Ragnar agreed. "Can you direct me? Jackson Crow told me I'm to see Jamie Trent in forensics."

"Down that hall, to the left."

Ragnar headed down. He entered a large lab that almost looked like something from one Megan's science fiction novels. Several people were busy.

But Jamie Trent had been alerted he was coming, and he met Ragnar quickly at the door. Trent was in his early thirties, had a crazy thatch of black hair and intense dark brown eyes that gave him the look of a serious and dedicated man. He offered his hand to Ragnar with a firm shake before accepting the box.

"We met a few years back, during that domestic killing," Trent told him.

"I remember you, sir," Ragnar said. "And that you do phenomenal work."

"Right now, I feel like I'm trying to put together a puzzle with major pieces missing, but we have managed to gather records and data on several victims we suspect are associated with this murderous group. This afternoon, I'll be working with one of our medical examiners and a forensic anthropologist. We'll find out what happened here, I promise you. Whether we can find any evidence to connect different killers…" He shrugged.

"We have two awaiting trial," Ragnar said.

Trent nodded. "We've collected DNA, hair samples, finger-prints…but I'm afraid it's going to take investigation to discover just how far this thing reaches."

"We are investigating," Ragnar promised.

"And don't worry—we keep everything up with our DC of-fices. Anything we have is shared with your separate unit im-mediately as well." Trent was staring at him. He knew many other agents speculated about the Krewe of Hunters, as they were unofficially called. Some referred to them as "ghost bust-ers." Others scoffed, assuming they spent most of their days with so-called psychics.

But many respected them; they had a stellar record when it came to solving cases.

Ragnar handed him the box and smiled grimly.

Trent accepted it. He shook his head. "This was delivered to the young woman who was kidnapped and nearly killed? Megan Law? And her sister is Special Agent Colleen Law? Or should I say Colleen Gallagher now? Or is she changing her name?"

"I don't know."

"Well, it's lucky they're with your unit. They'd probably be split up otherwise. Anyway, I'm so sorry for that poor woman! She must be terrified. I assume she'll be protected night and day."

"Oh, yes, she will be. I guarantee it," Ragnar said. "And thank you."

He hurried out and was surprised to discover Megan was with a group of people in the reception area. She was smiling and ani-mated, her eyes were flashing beautifully, and she looked happy.

He hung back because she was in conversation with the group. But then she saw him. Her smile faded.

Well, he was sorry he was darkening her life. It couldn't be helped.

She excused herself, saying how wonderful it had been to see them, and then she walked back over to him.

The people in the group stared at them both, whispering. Speculating.

"Ready?" she asked, heading for the exit.

"Sure. I hate to draw you away from cocktail hour, though," he said.

She winced. "I know several of the writers who were here today. Novelists tend to be friendly, and it's a big community. Anyway, I was surprised to see them. I think they thought I was part of the group at first, but then the whole thing about the Embracer kidnappings and killings has been in the news, so they made the connection quickly. I just said I was heading back to do some research."

"Ah. Mystery writers. You didn't tell them you'd received a human head in a box?"

She let out an aggravated sigh. "No, of course not. You said to keep it quiet."

"Right. I don't want to feed into any monster's search for fame."

"No," she muttered. "Okay, so let's get Hugo. And I'll be quick, I promise, but I will need to pack a few things."

"You can take your time. It will be better if we start out a little later now anyway. I realize you live here, but I have been to New York before. And I do know about traffic." They got back into his car.

She fell silent, other than directing him to her building. He found street parking about a block from her apartment house. She was on the third floor of a building off the north side of

Central Park, and the entry vestibule was empty when they arrived. They didn't speak in the elevator or as they walked down the hall. But once she had keyed open her door, she seemed to soften.

Of course.

The dog was there and eager to greet her.

"Hugo, he's a friend," she said.

The giant shepherd might not have been trained to the nth degree like Mark Gallagher's Red, but he was obedient. He looked at Ragnar carefully before Ragnar stopped, showed him his hand, and allowed him to sniff it before giving him pats on the head.

"At least you know dogs," she said.

"At least you told him I was a friend," he said dryly.

She didn't reply. "He needs a walk."

"When you're ready, we'll walk him."

"Oh!" she exclaimed. "Right. Right. I'll be quick." It was almost as if she'd forgotten she had received a human skull, and that she did indeed need protection.

She didn't lie about being quick. Megan got a small bag together in about five minutes and returned to her living room with it to tell him they just needed to lock up—she was ready to go.

"Anything else?" he asked her. "Your laptop—"

"In the bag. I keep some things at Colleen's place for when I'm there, so... I should be fine. Because…well, this can't go on forever."

Not forever, he thought. But it had been going on for years before they had even known there was a strange brotherhood of men who liked to bury women alive.

He didn't reply.

"I'll take your bag; you can get Hugo."

"He'll need—"

"Yes, we'll walk him. And we can stop along the way and let him out, too." He paused just a moment and then said, "We will have to let your sister know. I thought we'd be fine leaving her and Mark out of the loop when I was just going on a gut feeling, but now…"

"Now we have a skull."

"I believe, from the autopsies I've been to and the crime scene photos from previous cases, she's been dead awhile," Ragnar said somberly. "But she was dug up and sent to you as a warning—a threat, a tease, or a promise."

"Okay, so… Hugo! Let's go for a walk!" Megan said.

As they walked out he noticed she had a little container of bags to collect Hugo's droppings when necessary.

But Hugo was excited to merely lift his leg here and there as they walked the blocks by the car.

The pooper-scooper bags weren't necessary.

"Is he good in a car?" Ragnar asked as he opened the back door for the shepherd.

"Excellent. He loves a drive," Megan assured him.

Hugo crawled in. Out of habit, Ragnar opened the front passenger's door for Megan.

"I'm really okay," she told him. "Capable."

"And I was taught to be polite. I'm afraid you'll have to get over it," he told her.

She didn't reply. He was sure she was gritting her teeth.

He walked around to the driver's door, but he paused and looked around. Two kids were riding bikes down the sidewalk. A mother was pushing a baby in a stroller. Two college-age boys were discussing something in the sky as they walked along.

Harmless and innocent.

And while night would come soon enough, the sky was a

beautiful shade of deep blue only lightly touched by powder-
puff clouds.

He took a breath.

Whoever was taunting Megan was not there then. He'd wondered if she was being stalked. But maybe they had only been
hanging around outside the publishing office.

Hoping to see the ruckus that might begin when she opened
the box, screamed bloody murder, and the place filled with
police.

They might have been sincerely disappointed.

And come here.

But if so, they weren't here now. And perhaps they hadn't
bothered. Perhaps that person had seen her leave the office with
him.

Seen him holding the box and Megan calmly walking along
beside him.

Maybe the sender thought the box hadn't even been opened yet.

He didn't know. And he didn't believe a place in itself could
be safe—any place.

But come hell or high water, he was going to keep Megan
safe. Wherever they were.

He folded himself into the car and started to drive.

Traffic was already bumper to bumper.

It was going to be a long night.

The safe house was inconspicuous, a colonial-style house next
to other colonial houses. It did have a gate; and while the cameras that showed every angle of the house were not easily vis-
ible, Ragnar assured Megan they were there.

They were greeted by Jackson Crow and Angela Hawkins
Crow.

Colleen had once told Megan her field supervisor—Jackson—

had been the first agent recruited by millionaire philanthropist Adam Harrison to lead their unusual office. Adam wasn't particularly talented or gifted—or cursed—as his agents were, but his son, Josh, had been special, and had died far too young in an accident. But after years had passed, Adam had acquired the ability to see Josh. Maybe his love for his son and his generosity to others had given him what he needed.

Crow was a tall, handsome man with ink-dark hair and eyes a deep shade of blue. Steady as brick. Angela was blonde and lovely. Colleen had also told Megan that Angela was proficient in the office running logistics and their tech team. She was equally able to be a supermom to their adopted son and their toddler daughter.

Both were wonderfully courteous, professional, and welcoming—and they were pleased Hugo was with her. They had dogs themselves, they assured her.

Hugo was on his best behavior and happy to meet them.

"I've informed Colleen and Mark you're here," Angela said. "We felt it would be worse if they found out later, but we've assured them you are in the safe house and under guard."

Jackson picked up the conversation, telling Megan cameras covered all the doors and windows. A state-of-the-art alarm system would go off at any unauthorized attempt to breach the gated wall around the house or the doors. For any entry, they had to enter the code at the gate, then at the house, and use the manual key.

Megan smiled weakly. "It sounds like a very safe house. I know with the Krewe, I'm in the best of hands."

"There will be an agent outside at all times as well. You and Ragnar will be working together; but anytime he needs to leave, there will be another agent assigned."

"Um, perfect, thank you."

"No. Thank you," Jackson told her seriously. "We might be putting a stop to something that has gone on for more than a decade. A very sick fraternity. With your help, the taunts the incarcerated men are throwing out might just turn on them. And while they obviously know about you and know you're Special Agent Colleen Law's sister, they don't know everything we do."

"Right," Megan muttered.

"It's late; you've had a long day..." Angela began.

"Traumatic day. It would be so even for one of us," Jackson finished. "Not even at our offices are we accustomed to receiving skulls in boxes."

"Have we heard anything on that yet?" Ragnar asked.

"They're searching dental records among missing persons. The medical examiner has estimated death at two to three years. They're analyzing the dirt that was clinging to the skull to hopefully give us a place of burial. We know the skull belonged to a female, and we're estimating she was in her midtwenties to thirty," Angela told him. "For now, we're going to get out of here. We have people working through the night seeing what we can find, if anything, in prisoner phone communications. They are all monitored."

"We need to check out their attorneys," Ragnar said.

"We're doing that, of course," Jackson assured him. "Anyway, Megan, try to get some sleep."

"I will try," she promised.

But first, she had to talk to her sister.

She waited until Angela and Jackson had left them. It was late; she was tired. But she knew Colleen would be awake and waiting to hear from her.

Once the door closed, Ragnar said, "We'd better make a call."

She already had her cell out.

Her sister didn't even wait for Megan to speak.

"We're going to get back right away. Oh, Megan, I am so sorry! I never imagined my life could endanger yours. What you've faced already is so horrible, and now to add all this in…I am so, so sorry! Mom and Dad and Patrick—"

"No, no, no! Please, Colleen, tell me you haven't said a word to Mom and Dad!"

"Well, no, but—"

"As far as they know, I'm writing a book. Please. It's important. I mean, I am writing a book, and in all this, I will have access to more information. Please, I'm begging you! Ragnar wanted to keep it on the down low. He believes they want the sensation and the notoriety, and denying them will help in the investigation. Please, Colleen—"

Mark had apparently taken the phone from Colleen because his voice came on deep, calm, and assuring.

"We haven't said a word to your parents. But you have to be with someone night and day, Megan, and I—"

"I'm with Ragnar," she said quickly. He was watching her from the door he had just closed behind Angela and Jackson.

He put his hand out, ready to take the phone.

She passed it to him.

"Mark, Megan is fine. We're at the safe house." He nodded, even though Mark couldn't see it. "Right. So, we have every possible protection, including an undercover agent watching the house at all times along with someone in the offices having an eye on the cameras twenty-four-seven and an alarm that could wake half the city. Not to mention we have Hugo with us, too. I think he'd bite the throat out of anyone who attempted to come at Megan. And I will not be leaving, I swear it. We're going to go in and have interviews with the two men we're holding. At the offices, they're going over every possible communication to find out how those incarcerated are getting messages to whoever isn't. We have no idea how deep this goes; but the point is, we must solve it if Megan is ever to be safe."

Megan couldn't hear Mark's response. But Ragnar was nodding.

Finally, he handed the phone back to her.

Colleen was on.

"You're all right. You're really all right?" Colleen asked.

"Hey, it wasn't a pretty sight, but ask Ragnar. I didn't scream or pass out," she said, trying to sound a bit light.

"I'm not going to tell Mom and Dad, but we do owe it to Patrick to tell him the truth."

"But tomorrow!" Megan said.

"All right, tomorrow. Will you call him?"

"I promise."

"We'll see you by tomorrow night."

"Colleen, I don't want you ruining your honeymoon."

"You're really all right with… Ragnar? You two didn't really seem to hit it off," Colleen said worriedly. "Then again—"

"I'm fine. I swear it," Megan said.

"All right. I love you. See you."

"Colleen! We didn't want you and Mark—"

She grimaced and stopped speaking. The phone had gone dead.

"Okay, well, they're coming back," she told Ragnar.

"Did you expect anything else?"

"I guess not." She let out a long breath. At her feet, Hugo whined softly.

"It's okay, boy, it's okay!" she told the dog.

"I'll let you get some sleep, then," Ragnar told her. He pointed to the right. "The agent's room is the first. It is right next to yours. If anything—"

"Oh, trust me, you'll know if there's anything wrong. As you've probably noted, I am the world's worst coward."

He shook his head. "You're not a coward, Megan. Your grip on your fear helped us take down the two murderers we're holding now. Anyway, I'll, uh, leave you alone. But I'm there. If you need anything at all, let me know."

He turned and went into his room.

She turned and went into her own, calling Hugo to come with her. He would sleep curled up at the foot of her bed.

If she needed anything...

She dug into her overnight bag for a soft cotton T-shirt-style nightgown.

If she needed anything at all...

It had been the night of Mark and Colleen's ultrasmall wedding. And it had started off with an argument and then...and then...

She threw herself on the bed. It was too easy to remember *why* she had fallen into his arms—or they had fallen into one another's arms—in the middle of it all. Too easy to remember the heat and the impulsiveness, and then after...

They'd agreed it was ridiculous to pretend it hadn't happened. It had. But they had their lives, and they still had their differences, and they'd put it in the past. They really didn't need to see each other again, at least not until the trial, and that was in the future. They were adults, intelligent adults, with lives to lead.

And still...

He was closed in his room. She was closed in her room. And

they were only together because she was in in danger, and part of the case he was working on.

And yet, as she curled into bed for the night, she couldn't help but wonder what he was thinking, and if there was too much about that night that haunted him as well.

CHAPTER THREE

She was running. Running because…

She needed to be running. An animal was in danger. But this time, she was running because she was afraid. Running, running, running…

And then she tripped.

Because a monster had seen to it that she did.

She struggled to rise. To fight against the monster.

And it was a monster staring at her, or something that was *monstrous* at the very least.

It was a human skull. And it was horrible. Strands of hair were still attached, bits and pieces of dirt and flesh, and more… worms crawled over it. They crawled from what should have been empty eye sockets, but the eyes were there, dark and plaintive and staring at her with such anguish she could almost see tears falling upon what remained of the cheeks.

And the mouth…

The mouth was opened in a horrible, gaping scream, a silent scream that seemed to go on and on, echoing in her head.

Not real!

Megan forced herself to wake. She was shaking and covered with a fine sheen of perspiration.

Tossing her covers aside, she rose. Hugo raised his head, looking at her curiously.

"It's okay, boy," she told the dog. But her voice was quavering. It wasn't solid. She had to work on that. She'd had a nightmare. Just a nightmare. But she had risen from it terribly thirsty. She should have remembered to bring a glass of water into the bedroom, but she hadn't.

"It's okay," she assured Hugo again, forcing a smile. She had no idea if a dog recognized a smile, or rather if he instinctively knew she was upset.

She opened the door to her room and started; Ragnar was standing in the hall.

"I'm sorry," he said quickly. "I heard you thrashing around and groaning in your sleep, and I wasn't sure if I should wake you, or…"

She might as well tell him the truth. Maybe he would go back to bed.

He slept in his boxers; he had a robe over his shoulders, but it wasn't tied, and she had a good view of his broad, firm chest. He had apparently risen quickly and then hesitated.

Great.

So much for being adults. Things were really awkward between them.

"No, I had a nightmare. It's nothing. I'm just a coward. I'll be fine, and I am truly sorry for disturbing you."

"It's all right," he told her, and he shook his head. "Megan, you keep beating yourself up for being a normal person. Believe me, getting a human skull delivered to you is traumatic.

And don't kid yourself—cops, agents, anyone and everyone in law enforcement, has their share of nightmares."

She looked at him and swallowed weakly.

"Thank you for that. I, um, was just going to the kitchen to get some water."

"Okay, then. I'll see you when you get up."

She glanced at her watch quickly. It was six a.m.

He wasn't going back to sleep. She wondered what he was doing.

He turned back to her, as if he had heard her thoughts.

"I'm going through the files. We're trying to put victims together by vicinity, get names on all of them, and figure out what we have going on. There were three—besides the two girls murdered recently by Carver—but then Angela discovered other bodies with similar causes and methods of deaths. You know that, right? Anyway, so much of this is studying police notes, histories of the victims we know, and trying to separate what might and might not have been done by the same killer. Tedious. And it takes a lot of eyes. Anyway, get your water and go back to sleep. We won't drive out to the corrections center until about nine."

"Okay. Thanks."

"Megan, if you have a nightmare again, it's okay, natural and normal. And you won't bother me in the least." He absently patted Hugo on the head as he spoke.

Then he turned and went back into his room.

The hall felt lonely once he was gone.

She wondered what she would have done if he had touched her.

But he hadn't. There was no use wondering.

She got herself a glass of water and headed back to the room, suddenly aware she should be grateful. Whatever circumstances had brought this all about, she was safer here than she would have been in her Manhattan apartment. Alone.

Well, she wouldn't have been completely alone. She had Hugo. But dogs could be poisoned or hurt. She thought he was a darned good alarm system. But still, neither she nor the dog could be deemed armed and dangerous!

She wanted to sleep. She couldn't. She lay in bed staring at the ceiling.

It was better than dreaming.

Ragnar closed his computer at last, deciding they were going to head to one of the police stations in Northern Virginia when they'd finished talking to Rory Ayers.

Over the last eight years, they'd discovered three bodies buried in the woods. The remnants of boards or planks had been found with them. The bodies had seriously deteriorated, time and the elements having taken their toll.

Local detectives had discovered the identity of one girl: a runaway who had been working the red-light district.

It seemed likely to him the other two victims had fallen prey to the same murderer. Was it possible Rory Ayers had been busy there? Or was it whoever was out on the streets digging up a victim's head to deliver to Megan Law?

Or another person entirely?

One thing was certain—they had to delve further. Somewhere, since there was something that resembled organization, there was a main head on this hydra.

They had to find it.

Showered and dressed, Ragnar walked into the kitchen. Megan was already at the kitchen table, her concentration on her computer. Hugo was sprawled on the floor at her side. She looked up when he came in and told him, "I brewed coffee. This place is...well, very nice and very well equipped. Coffee, tea, eggs, milk, meat, veggies...it's all set."

He went to help himself to coffee. "I believe Angela was the one to make sure it was supplied. But we've had people in here...witnesses against some of the organized crime bosses who couldn't be safe beyond the walls. At least in this case—"

He broke off.

But she was looking at him. She smiled. "In this case, the killers aren't professional hit men. They have to get their hands on someone, and they use subterfuge and they prey on the unwary."

He nodded, carried the coffeepot to the table and hovered it over her cup.

"Refill?"

"Yes, thank you."

"Thank you for brewing the coffee."

"I never mind doing things," she said quietly. "I mean, in a perfect world, we all do things for each other. Cooking, doing dishes, grabbing things from the fridge...and I'm babbling. Sorry."

"That's okay. I like your perfect world." He checked the fridge for cream. "Are you working on your book?"

"I should be." She hesitated, and then shook her head. "There are a lot of conferences in my usual world. And any editor is anxious to pick up new authors who show promise with exciting work. But that means we attend pitch sessions, and when I'm talking to an author, I'm looking for a solid story. Something laid out with a clear beginning, middle, and end."

"You want the same for your book," he said. "And we don't know the ending," he added quietly.

She leaned back. "I've insisted on keeping a few of my authors through all this. I haven't been writing this morning. I've been editing. At the moment, I'm truly enjoying the hero of Syd Braxton's *Moon Fever*, and finding out his protagonist is going to stop the war on Venus from coming to Earth's moon."

"Good writer?"

"Yep. I love his 'voice.'"

He smiled. "I think it's great you're getting to help solve problems on the moon. You will have time to get to your own work." He paused to sip his coffee. "But today may be busy. After I interview Ayers and you listen in, I'd like to meet up with a few detectives in a city not far from here. They were working the cases of three bodies discovered nearby, and I think they may have been close to the truth."

He hesitated and then, leaning forward to speak to her, tried for the right words. "Jim Carver took a woman people were going to search for—a schoolteacher with dozens of people to demand she be found. Ayers made the mistake of kidnapping and attempting to kill his own daughter, ensuring the FBI was brought in on the case. He thought he was smarter than we were. But Deirdre Ayers was still the daughter of a wealthy and—at the time—respected man. With a mother who adored her. The cases would have been pressed hard whether it had been the Krewe or the police or any other agency.

"The problem with some of the other possible connections we're finding is that these women were runaways or just down and out, maybe working the streets. When a homeless woman disappears, she might have just moved on to greener pastures. And there may be no one out there to insist she be found because they may not know she's even missing."

"Everyone deserves justice," Megan said.

"I agree. I'm just telling you the detectives probably came up against too many dead ends. No one could really say when the woman had last been seen. And—with the case of some who were living on the street or finding a bed night by night—no one could say for sure a woman was missing. Sick killers do prey on women in those positions. Unless they're determined like Ayers and Carver that they're smarter than anyone and can taunt law enforcement to no end and think they can still get away with it."

"Do you think Ayers started with some of the victims you're talking about?"

"Possibly."

"Or you think it might be the person who knew where to find a head to dig up and send to me?"

"Possibly."

Megan closed her laptop, glancing at her watch.

"Let's find out," she said softly.

He smiled and nodded and drained his cup of coffee. She stood and he noted she was wearing a tailored pantsuit in navy with a soft blue blouse beneath the darker jacket. It was just a pantsuit.

It fit her exceptionally well.

"What?" she asked, frowning. "I thought I should try for… professional attire. Is something wrong?"

He shook his head. "No. You look…"

"Funny?" she asked worriedly.

"No. I was thinking you look extremely attractive," he said flatly.

"Oh. Um, thank you. I think?"

He found himself laughing. "Yes, it was a compliment."

"I was just afraid that—"

"There is no way in hell I'm letting any of those jerks see you, so not to worry," he said.

"Okay, thanks. I thought I was businesslike. Anyway...you don't have to be..."

"I know. You're perfectly capable. I don't need to open doors for you. Or drive you when you can take a cab or a ride service. You don't need anyone."

She winced. "I didn't mean to be so horrible. I don't want people to feel they need to worry about me. I guess, right now, I do need to be worried about so much, and I very much hope I can be of service in return."

Her words were earnest.

And he wished they weren't. He wished he could believe she was just being obnoxious all the time. That would be far easier than coming to like her.

Not to mention the incredible night they'd spent together.

"Megan, if you help us put away any of these guys—oh, wait, you've already done that. So, let me start over. If you help us get more of them—get to the root of this thing—your contribution will be greater than anything we can do for you."

She smiled. "You saved my life. I see that as pretty big."

"No one will come near you. I swear it."

As if agreeing with him, Hugo let out a woof and wagged his tail.

"Oh! Are we taking him?" Megan asked.

"I don't want to have to leave him in the car. Let's do the interviews; and then if you want, we'll come back for him."

"Then give me a second to give him a last run. Oh! That's one good thing. He's usually an apartment dog and, here, he gets to run."

"There you go. A silver lining everywhere," he said lightly. "Let's let him out, then."

He walked to the back door, remembering he had to key in the code before opening any door there.

"I would have forgotten," Megan muttered.

"No, you would have noted the box and put in the code, too," he said.

"You have a lot of faith in me," she said.

"I do," he said honestly. He quickly turned to watch the dog and look around the yard. He'd worked the house before when he'd been on a protection detail for one of the witnesses against the organized crime bosses he had mentioned to Megan. But it was good to take a look around again. The wall was rigged to the alarm system, which had been tricky at first, he'd been told. They didn't want an alarm going off for every bird or squirrel that made a landing on it. The trees in the yard were small and far from the wall, lest someone try to use them to get over the wall.

It was probably impossible to have a safer place for someone to live in an almost normal atmosphere.

Hugo made a last dash around the yard—he'd made sure to mark every tree—and then ran back to the house.

"Your pup is ready."

"Let's go."

Megan collected the coffee cups and set them in the sink. He went to the front door and waited for her.

"Am I allowed to open it for you?" he asked. He couldn't help himself. She'd been such a stickler when they'd first met about him opening the car door for her; she felt it was wasting time, and she was perfectly capable of opening it herself. At the time she'd been upset because everyone was worried about her and because Colleen didn't want her going to her place alone.

Megan winced. "Look, I'm sorry. Yes, you can open the door for me. I'll say thank you. If I'm ahead of you at some point, I won't wait. I'll open a door for you. I'm not usually rude, honestly. It's just that I came from a home where my dad cooked dinner and did the dishes, and my mom went to work every day, too. It's like I said before, I'm happy when we all do things for each other."

"Great. And so you know, I wash a mean dish."

She smiled.

For a moment, they looked at one another.

He couldn't read minds, but he believed they were thinking the same thing. They really had to stop being so polite to one another.

"To the car," he said.

"I'll get my own door—faster that way."

"Works for me."

In the car, he glanced her way. "What was it like growing up as a triplet? I know you guys are fraternal, and it's you and Colleen and your brother, Patrick. But being the same age at the same time had to have been interesting."

"For my parents?" Megan asked, grinning. "I'm sure it was. Mom said they always had to be careful when we were toddlers because we might take off in three different directions. They're great parents, and they've accepted the fact Colleen and Patrick have taken on dangerous work. That means they focus on me, so I'm trying to be careful what I say to them."

"Sounds like they're wonderful," he said.

"What about you?" she asked.

"My mom passed away a bit after my twenty-fifth birthday.

But she was a lovely woman." He glanced her way. "She was the one who taught me manners. Courtesy was part of one's character in her book. She was sweet and lovable and could also scare the hell out of you with one look. My dad spends a lot of time in Norway now. He has cousins there. But he's a good dad and you would like him. If my mother was going out and asked if he wanted her to fix him anything before she left, he was almost offended. He was far from a gourmet chef, but he knew how to fend for himself."

Megan grinned. "Sounds like they were all cut from the same cloth." Her smile faded. "I'm so sorry Colleen and Mark are coming back. They should have had this time."

"But if someone forced them to stay away, they'd be miserable anyway," Ragnar told her.

"I wish they had more faith in me," Megan muttered.

"Hey, they should have faith in me. It's not that, Megan. Colleen is your sister. She can't help but blame herself for you being in this situation. We can tell her over and over again—and logically she knows—it's not her fault. Anyway, they'll be here later. And that's good. Mark is the best partner I've had since being a cop—and through the agency. Not to mention Red."

"Hey, I'm offended on behalf of Hugo!"

"And I have faith in Hugo, too."

"He can bark, I promise you that."

"And I wouldn't dream of attempting to come at you in any menacing way with that dog around you. He loves you. He'd protect you to the death."

"Let's not say death."

"Okay, we won't. He, uh, would chew anyone to ribbons who threatened you."

"I guess so. He is a big boy; but if you're his friend, he's a loving guy I've had to convince not to be a lapdog."

"He's a beautiful animal," Ragnar said.

They were both silent as he drove the rest of the way to the facility. He parked as directed and was allowed entry with Megan.

Officer Brendan Kent was behind the screen at the desk again. He'd been there before when Megan had come, and Ragnar was glad he wasn't going to have to explain her presence.

"Who are you here for today?" Kent asked him. "Ayers or Jim Carver?"

"I'm going back at Ayers again today. I'll be setting Megan up in the observation room."

Kent nodded at Megan. "You a psychologist? Or a psychic? Either way, these guys seem to have some respect for you."

After Megan's kidnapping and the arrest of Ayers, they'd managed to keep Megan's picture out of the paper. Those who knew her knew. But Ragnar wasn't surprised that while Kent had now met her twice, he didn't realize exactly who she was.

He wondered how she was going to answer.

She smiled. "I'm a speech expert, you might say."

"Well, welcome. And don't let these guys…well, they can do a mind trip on you. Ayers should feel like the belle of the ball today. His attorney, Jeffrey Hindman, just left about thirty minutes ago."

"Hindman, the public defender?" Ragnar asked.

"That's the man."

"Ayers hasn't hired some high-powered firm to work for him?"

"Not that I know about. He has told other prisoners in front of several of the guards he will have the finest representation money can buy, but so far, he's only spoken to the public de-

fender. And if I'm not mistaken, I think Hindman has suggested
Ayers throw himself on the mercy of the court—plead guilty
and give up."

"Thank you for the warning," Megan told him.

"I'll see Ayers is brought to the room," Kent told Ragnar.
"Of course, he can refuse to see you."

"He won't. It's a break from the ordinary in here for him.
And he likes to taunt the police and agents. His favorite hobby,
especially here, I believe," Ragnar said.

The detention center was well-guarded. There was a man
to open the main door and a man ready to greet them in the
observation room. Ayers was being escorted to interrogation
chamber number five.

Ragnar entered the observation room with Megan. He knew
she'd been there before, and understood she could see in the
room but all that anyone in the room could see was a mirror.

"You're all right in here? " he asked.

She smiled. "Yeah, I'm hidden from Ayers. Even if I hadn't
been here before, I've seen enough crime shows."

He nodded. "Right. I meant there is a guard on duty. He'll
be bringing Ayers, and then he'll wait outside. Which means
he'll be right outside this door, too."

"Oddly enough, I'm feeling safe here," she said.

"Good." He frowned. "I'm always watching for anyone following us."

She smiled. "I feel safe with you, too." She shrugged. "They
can't get me when I'm with you."

"Good. Thanks." He looked into the interrogation room,
waiting. He watched as a guard brought Rory Ayers in and
chained him to the bars on the table.

"Not talkative, eh?" Ayers asked the man.

The guard didn't reply. He took up a position by the door, opening it and stepping out to greet Ragnar when he was ready to enter.

"Special Agent Johansen," the guard said. "Let me know when you're ready to leave. I'll be at the door."

"Thank you." Ragnar noted his name tag. Humboldt. He was a young man, maybe in his late twenties.

The guard saw something in Ragnar's face that allowed him to speak. "I only get this duty now and then, thank God. He talks and talks and talks. And, well, I've met lots of scumbags. But most guys…they say they're innocent and try to act the part. This one…"

"He believes himself the first and original 'Embracer,'" Ragnar said briefly. "And he believes the mood of the nation will keep him from the death penalty. I don't think it will, but as long as he's locked up forever and ever, I'll be happy."

"They're worried about these guys at trial. Planning on extra security," Humboldt said.

"Not a bad idea," Ragnar agreed.

The guard suddenly said, "I'm Rick. Rick Humboldt. You need anything, let me know."

"Thank you. I'll be fine. I won't stay too long."

"I don't see how you could take staying too long," Humboldt said, and stepping back, he opened the door for Ragnar to enter. Once he was in, Humboldt quickly shut the door and took up his position just outside.

"You again!" Ayers complained.

"Me again."

"Ah, so you have something new and important to question me about?"

Did that mean he'd expected Megan to have received the skull?

Ragnar shrugged his shoulders. "Nope. Just old stuff."

The man looked concerned and irritated.

"I want Agent Law!" Ayers demanded.

Ragnar eased back in his chair with a smile. "I don't think you're comprehending the circumstances. You're incarcerated. And you're up for kidnapping and attempted murder. We just might find some of the victims you're always bragging about—"

"Deirdre is alive. So is Ms. Special Agent Law's sister."

"But you're the original 'Embracer,'" Ragnar reminded him. "Or so you say. Is that just bragging, trying to impress the guys around you in this place?"

Ayers leaned back. "I can say anything. But I'm innocent until proven guilty."

"Well, you'll get to see Ms. Special Agent Law when you're in the courtroom," Ragnar said.

"Aren't you curious? I could say something to her I wouldn't say to you," Ayers teased.

"That's exactly why you won't see her," Ragnar said.

Ayers shook his head. "But you're supposed to be such an expert lawman. How do you know I won't give her something I wouldn't give you?"

Ragnar leaned forward. "We all know what you want to *give* Special Agent Law. And since we do, she'll just have to be a memory."

"The sister will be in the courtroom, too?"

"Oh, we'll all be there. And I'm here again because you could help keep a needle out of your own arm."

Ayers sat back, smiling. "What makes you think I'd even know the names of women I gave my loving embrace to?"

"I'm shocked," Ragnar said. "When I interviewed Carver… well, I think he was a sophisticated killer. He watched his women. He knew their schedules. And he was discriminating. He didn't pick up just anyone."

"Carver learned...from the best," Ayers said, a slight tic in his jaw. He had gotten under the man's skin. "Thing is, when you're the original, there is learning, there is discovery!"

"So, you did start out by killing women living on the street," Ragnar said.

"I never said such a thing."

"Well, not in so many words; but yes, you did."

Ayers started to laugh. "You'll never know the half of it! I tell you all the time. And I think you're an idiot because you just never really get anything. Come on! I watch crime shows, too. You have organized and unorganized killers. But those behavioral scientists don't know the half of it, either. Do you start out swimming a mile? Were you born an agent? For an agent, you really are an idiot."

"Yeah, but I'm one of the agents who brought you in," Ragnar said.

"Agents, cops, guards, attorneys...attorneys. Those are the men who count."

"Men and women who count," Ragnar corrected.

"No bitch will be defending me. I have plenty of money."

"I heard your wife is divorcing you—and getting her family money back. In fact, I heard she doesn't intend to pay any attorney's fees for you."

Ragnar watched the man's hands knot into fists.

"Stupid Deirdre should have died."

Ragnar shrugged. "But my partners are too good. And we work with some remarkable scientists, too. Just so you know, we have your DNA on record and hair samples."

"That's not legal—"

"Oh, yes, all obtained legally. Your wife was happy to give our forensic people your hairbrush, the glass you used when brushing your teeth…it's all legal. So, if you want to talk…"

"You don't know the half of it," he repeated. "For that matter, you can't even imagine with your little FBI pea-brain the whole of it."

"Ah, well, you see, you put my pea-brain together with other brains, and you just don't know. Your bragging sessions have often been recorded, so…well, okay, I'm off," Ragnar said, standing.

"You don't bring me coffee and you don't offer me a cigarette."

"No smoking in here."

"You should bring me something. I mean, if you weren't an idiot, you would know you should bring me something. Crime scene photos! And coffee. Strong coffee. No watery stuff."

Ragnar leaned on the table, glad of his size and the fact he could be imposing. He brought his face close to Ayers's and said, "You'll never get anything from me. And you won't see Agent Law until the day—"

"The sister would be fine."

"You won't see either of them, I promise you, until the day of the trial. And crime scene photos? You really are certifiably insane."

"I am not insane! I am calculated and extremely bright; and if you weren't so stupid, you'd see that right off. I ran a major business—"

"That's back in your wife's hands. Cool."

Ragnar pushed away from the table.

"Damn you!" Ayers raged. "You don't just walk out like that."

"Well, yes, I do. Because I'm an agent. And you get to sit

there and rot, not able to do a damned thing about it, because you're a psychopath and a killer. Your own words."

"I never said I was a psychopath!" Ayers raged.

The door was opening. Outside, Rick Humboldt had been ready to let him out.

He let the door slam shut once Ragnar had left. Humboldt was smiling.

"That was incredible. He thinks he's so superior! He makes the guards feel like giant apes all the time. You—you can twist him like no one else," Humboldt said.

"Um, thanks. Let him stew a few minutes. I'll be back. A lot, I'm afraid. If they're agreeing to see me, I'll have more sessions with him and Carver."

"Absolutely, Special Agent Johansen." Humboldt nodded.

The door to the observation room opened. Megan knew he was out of the interrogation room.

And she looked as if she were ready to leave.

He collected his weapon and they left, silent until the gates had closed behind them.

"I will never understand how that man lived for years as practically a pillar of the community, stayed married, raised a child, did all kinds of business deals, while going out, tricking people, kidnapping, torturing, and killing them. And no one knew!"

"It's happened before. Monsters don't always look the part. Back with H. H. Holmes—or Herman Mudgett—killers have walked around unstopped for years. Holmes killed somewhere between twenty-seven to a hundred-something people in his torture dungeon, preying on unsuspecting visitors to the Columbian Exposition in Chicago in the 1890s. The man was a pharmacist by trade and walked about seemingly normal. John Wayne Gacy was a shoe salesman who was active in his community and played a clown for local kids. Ted Bundy was supposedly attractive and charming—something that allowed him to play the victim and have unsuspecting victims try to help him."

"That's how Ayers took his own daughter—trying to make her think she'd run over a human being," Megan muttered.

"Right."

"So, if I ever think I've run over someone, just keep going," she muttered.

"And dial 911," Ragnar said flatly. He glanced at her. She was somber, staring straight ahead.

She turned to him. "I don't know how you all do it," she whispered. "It's so cruel and heinous and ugly."

"You said it earlier," he told her.

She arched a brow.

"Justice," he said.

She nodded. "And putting an end to the horror that might come if they're not stopped."

"Exactly."

She was silent and pensive.

"Megan?"

"I'm still trying to figure it out. I mean, from listening today. He emphasizes you don't know the half of it, but he also mentioned a whole. Half—and whole. There's another meaning to what he's saying. He's still feeling powerful, as if he's holding something over everyone, as if he can't be beaten." She twisted in her seat to watch him as she spoke. "Aren't all communications from prisoners monitored and recorded?"

"They are."

"Then there must be a way Rory Ayers is communicating with people out there in the world. And it must be in those communications. Somehow. Because he was anxious to see you.

I could see he was excited, certain you were going to accuse him of having sent the decomposed head of a dead woman to my office."

He nodded. "I thought so, too."

"Is there any way I can listen to those communications?" she asked.

He glanced over at her. "That depends."

"On?"

"We will have to hire you officially as a consultant on the case," he told her. "But, Megan, I worry about you on this. While you have to be in the safe house, I'm concerned about bringing you in at a level that might make someone even more reckless."

"You mean, you worry it might make someone even more determined to kill me," she said flatly.

He shrugged.

"Ragnar, dead is dead. I need to help save myself. Talk to Jackson Crow. And hire me on officially as a consultant." She stared at him hard. "Do it!"

He looked ahead at the road. She was right.

A person couldn't be deader than dead.

"Please," she said softly.

He nodded. "All right. It will be done. Today, if we can, we'll talk to the detectives who worked the cases of a few other possible victims. And if you're still up to it tonight, we'll start on the phone conversations Ayers and Carver have had from jail."

"I will be up to it."

"It may be a hell of a long day and night," he said.

"Live every day to the fullest, right?" Megan said lightly.

He thought she had a far greater courage than she knew. Of

course, her life was in the balance. And yet he thought it was more than that.

She didn't want what had happened to her to happen to anyone else.

"What is it?" she asked, watching him.

He glanced at her and smiled. "Are you reading minds now?"

"I can see yours ticking away."

His smile deepened. "It's just…well, you and Colleen really aren't so different."

"Oh, no. Colleen is so brave!"

He shook his head. "Come on. Courage isn't not being afraid. Courage is doing the right thing even when you are."

"And I am afraid."

"Colleen often has the sense to be afraid."

She smiled and glanced his way. "Thank you for that. And…"

"What?"

"Quit being nice!"

He laughed. She did, too.

And then he winced inwardly. It really was going to be one hell of a long day.

CHAPTER FOUR

Ragnar had promised they'd go back to the safe house for Hugo, and he was true to his word.

There was a gray van down the street, advertising a lawn service company on its sides. Megan wouldn't have thought anything of it, but when they keyed in the code to the gate and brought the car into the curving drive in front of the house, Ragnar said, "We have an agent watching the house even when we're not in it."

"The van out there?" she asked.

He nodded. "Sometimes it will look like a dog grooming facility, sometimes it will be a handyman's van. There are several at our disposal for surveillance."

"Nothing is ever obvious," Megan commented.

"Right. But you are always protected," he said quietly. He turned when they were walking up the path from the car to the house. Megan saw he was reaching into his pocket for his phone. He smiled as he spoke, and she watched him curiously, waiting to walk up to the house.

He ended the call quickly with just a few words.

He looked at her then.

"That was Mark. And you'll be happy to know they'll be at the house by about seven tonight."

"That's…great. And not great. I wish they hadn't come back," Megan said.

"It's your sister. No choice."

Megan nodded, glancing at him, and then hitting the numbers on the code box to gain entry to the house. The door gave way. Hugo was there waiting for them, his great tail swishing in an arc that would have been dangerous to small objects.

"Hey, boy, you're coming for a ride now, okay?" Megan said.

"We have a few minutes," Ragnar told her. "We're meeting with the detectives at two p.m. The drive isn't far, but it is in another county."

"Okay, but I don't need any time. What I'd like to do—" Megan began.

"Is stop by the cemetery and see Sergeant Alfie Parker?" Ragnar finished.

"Now you really are mind reading," she said.

"No. I just know that's something you want to do. You said so back during the end of the last case."

He lowered his head, shaking it.

"What's wrong?" Megan asked. She was startled when she realized she'd walked over to him and set a hand gently on his arm.

He didn't shake her off, but she quickly stepped away.

"I'm sorry. I'm saying last case. We found you; we arrested Ayers. But…it wasn't the 'last' case. But let's do something cheerful—like go and try to see if we can find the ghost of a dead man at a cemetery."

Megan smiled. "Hey! I want to make him cheerful. I'm good

at research. I don't have all the bells and whistles that are available to Angela Hawkins, but I've spent half my life on research. Seriously! If it hadn't been for Sergeant Parker…well, he deserves our help. Which we should give him anyway. Right?"

He nodded, his eyes on hers.

"Right. We do have to find the truth—really end a case—for Alfie. So, ready to go?"

"Yes! Come on, Hugo!"

They drove out again, Hugo happily curled up in the back seat.

"They're not going to have a problem with Hugo, are they? He is registered as a therapy dog—he visits hospitals on occasion, too."

"There's a canine unit attached to the station. I believe anyone there not able to deal with a dog has transferred out," Ragnar assured her. "And he's a well-mannered pup."

"He is that," Megan agreed. She was silent a minute and then said, "Ragnar, yesterday you were interviewing Rory Ayers when he said something that got you scared for me."

"Yes."

"Why were you talking to him?"

"I'm trying to get to the truth. We have several open cases, victims from over the past decade, to the best of what the medical examiners and forensic anthropologists who have studied the remains can determine. I'm trying to discover if Ayers, as the original 'Embracer,' had more victims than we know about. But since the skull arrived in your office… I believe we're dealing with someone else involved, and we have to get all the heads of the hydra."

"But Ayers wants you to visit. He wants to taunt you. Is it… worthwhile? He is trying to talk in circles. Do you think eventually he will realize he might be facing the death penalty? And can anyone really promise he won't get that, if convicted?"

Ragnar took a deep breath, glancing her way.

"It's complicated. We need to know who did what, and sometimes knowing about the past can help with the future. There are times when—as much as some people hate it—it's necessary for the death penalty to be a bargaining chip."

Megan shuddered slightly. "Ayers had a wife and a daughter—he had a family life. And he functioned in the world of high finance! Will he bargain, do you think?"

"You never know. And the fact he kept his life together so well really doesn't mean anything. The Green River killer had a wife when he was incarcerated. He'd been married a few times, but this wife believed he really loved her and that might be the reason that—to the best of anyone's knowledge—his killing rate went down when he was with her. But his interviews are chilling. He just loved killing women. Listening to interviews with the man is an ordeal. In his own words, he loved killing; he wanted to be the best and most infamous serial killer out there. He'd return to have sex with his victims after they were dead because it helped keep him from taking another woman when he was afraid that the police might be looking at him. He had a family. And no one knew. For years. They still don't know how many people he killed—because he doesn't know himself. He lost count."

"That was…just one man," Megan said, shaking her head.

"Gary Ridgway is still alive—he got a plea deal. It's estimated he killed between sixty-eight and seventy-plus women, but no one really knows because he doesn't know. But with the plea deal, he showed police where to find bodies. It brought closure to many families and friends. It's horrible to know a friend or relative—especially a child—was murdered. But it's worse to spend years and years wondering, hoping, and suspecting the worst."

"I can't even imagine," Megan said softly.

"If we can get through to certain killers, we might learn if a case is solved or if we need to keep looking."

"Right," she said. "So… So far, Ayers hasn't said anything. Except he loves telling you that you don't know the half of it."

"Do you think that means we have half the victims?" Ragnar asked her.

She shook her head. "I don't think he knows how many victims there are. Because he wasn't the only one doing the killing. Perhaps we only have half the murderers! There could be many players—recruited as they go along."

"We'll find out if anything these detectives can tell us will help," Ragnar said. He was quiet then. And she was quiet.

They were fine when discussing the case. But otherwise couldn't manage small talk.

"Oh!" she said suddenly. "The cemetery. You didn't forget!"

He glanced over at her and smiled. "And you did, I think."

"Well, seriously, I know you and Colleen and Mark have studied past killers to help with understanding what you're doing, what you're up against, and what…what can make that kind of person tick."

"A complete lack of empathy—they are truly not just sociopaths, but psychopaths," Ragnar said. "And sadly, that old saying is true. You can never judge a book by its cover. Sometimes they look off. Sometimes they are high functioning. Anyway, here we are. You know that while Alfie Parker is buried here he may not be hanging out just waiting for one of us to come by."

"I know. But maybe if he's not, we'll see a friend of his. And we can make an appointment to come back and talk to him."

Ragnar grinned. "He comes to the office sometimes. That's how we knew about Carver, but it's tricky being with the Krewe. Because there is no way to use the testimony of the dead."

He parked the car on the winding path that led through the cemetery near the section that had been dedicated to police officers.

Megan thought a local group must have kept up the cemetery because while some of the graves were relatively new, many went back almost a hundred years. There were stones and plaques, small mausoleums, and a few aboveground tombs. But plants were pruned and there were flowers spread about as well.

The spirit of Alfie Parker was there. He was perched on a tombstone near his grave.

As if he waited for them.

He rose, walking toward them.

Alfie Parker had been tall in life with dark hair just beginning to gray. His eyes had been a green like her own and, even in death, they had a bit of a sparkle when he smiled.

They had met briefly once before, and he had captured something in her heart and mind. Alfie had been on a major bust that had turned into a shoot-out. He didn't resent his death in the line of duty; he had been a cop. But he had wanted to save a young girl, and while his spirit had remained to see the aftermath of everything that happened, the girl had disappeared. The head of the guns, drugs, and trafficking operation had been known as "John Smith." While it seemed that he had escaped, those accomplices who had survived the shoot-out had not been high enough in the hierarchy to know a real name for the puppet master who had been pulling the strings of a criminal empire that had also included murder for hire.

Alfie had died just a few years ago.

"I've been waiting for you to come back," he told Megan, smiling. He glanced at Ragnar and teased, "You, I see you often enough."

"You've been waiting—sitting on this tombstone—all this time?" Ragnar asked him. "Since Megan went back to New York?"

He shook his head. "I was by your offices early this morning. I knew Megan was here and something was going on."

"While speaking with Rory Ayers, I came to believe Megan was in danger," Ragnar told him. "He made a few references to the fact that torturing and killing 'the sister' would have been fine with him."

"Ah," Alfie muttered, looking at Megan. "You've come to help."

"Yes, well, and someone sent a skull to me at my office in New York City," Megan said.

Alfie immediately looked concerned and glanced at Ragnar.

"I was there by the time it arrived. We brought it to the forensic people at the New York office right away without letting anyone know," Ragnar informed him.

"Wise decision. I'm not an expert, but…these guys want the infamy. They want to be feared. And they want to be the best. But how the hell are they managing what they're doing?"

"That's what we're trying to find out," Ragnar said. "We're heading out to see a few of the detectives who were on the cases of some of the other victims—who may or may not have been killed by Rory Ayers. We're trying to piece it all together."

"Did Ayers know about the head?"

"I believe he did. He seemed disappointed I didn't come to see him because of something new that might have happened."

"Did he ask?"

"No, but he couldn't, could he?" Ragnar said.

"Ragnar is right. He knew about it," Megan said.

"Ah, yes, your particular specialty—the subtext!" Alfie said.

Megan nodded.

"I so wish I could help you more," Alfie said. "This being a spirit thing makes it difficult to confront evildoers. Then again, I can get in some places others can't. Maybe I'll sneak myself into that correctional facility and see what I can discover."

"That would be helpful," Ragnar said. "Tonight we're going to listen to all his phone conversations. Everything is recorded and it's all within the law. Full warning is given to anyone who receives a call from a prisoner."

"I know, I was a cop, remember?" Alfie said. "But I can be around when no one thinks they're being watched or recorded. I can't give you proof, but I can give you information you will then have to prove."

"Thank you," Megan said softly. "I mean, that's wonderful. But I told you once I loved history and research. We want to help *you*."

"Jackson Crow has tried. But while he is immensely talented in many ways, he may not see something you do. I don't know why but I believe Susie is out there. And I want to know… I want to know if she's all right." He paused. "Girls were killed that day. Women the organization had kidnapped. She wasn't among the dead. She was just a kid—barely turned sixteen. And I know she went to the home I suggested and then disappeared from there. I don't believe she left on purpose. She ran away from her home because of her mother's boyfriend. She didn't want to be on the streets. She was trying to survive. And I don't know if she was being held somewhere else at the time of the raid or if she escaped, or if…well. That's it. I don't know. And it haunts me. Yeah, haunts. After we raided the Smith compound, some in the group escaped, and I believe they had captives. But they disappeared. The case went cold. Thing is, 'John Smith' is still out there somewhere; and because of that, he's surely started up again. New state, new crew. But men like him don't stop."

"I'll see to it Megan gets all the records on the case," Ragnar told him.

"They'll be at the precinct. How will you explain—" Alfie began.

"I won't. Jackson and Adam have the magic touch. They'll get them," Ragnar assured him. He glanced at his watch. "But we'll be back, and you can tell Megan more from your point of view. We have an appointment we need to get to."

"You go on. And I'll do what I can."

"If you want a ride—" Ragnar asked him.

But Alfie shook his head. "I'll get where I need to be on my own." He grinned at Megan and quoted the Disney Haunted Mansion saying, "'Beware of hitchhiking ghosts!' You two go on."

He gave them a wave. Megan again wished she might have known him when he had been alive. He had been a good man.

"Thank you, Alfie," Ragnar told him.

"Yes, thank you," Megan added.

"Hey, thanks to you guys, too. You still care."

Megan smiled as they turned and went back to the car.

"What do you know about what happened? With the case that killed Alfie, I mean," Megan asked when Ragnar started driving them out the winding road of the cemetery.

"The police were handling it, as Alfie said. One of their undercover officers had gotten a tip and brought it in. We—the FBI—had the man on our radar, but we hadn't been called to investigate. I wouldn't have been here anyway. I've only been with the Krewe about three years," Ragnar told her, his eyes on the road.

Ragnar was apparently deep in thought, even as he spoke. "But their officer learned there were weapons in the compound—illegal weapons—and they staged a raid. Women had disappeared into the place…and they'd picked up two of 'Smith's' people selling heroin. They had enough to go in. But apparently the undercover had set off someone's suspicions. When the cops showed up to the compound, it turned into a horrendous battle. It was amazing most of the officers survived their wounds. Three were killed that day—along with ten of the gun and drug runners and illegal traffickers."

"Compound?" Megan asked.

"A huge place—area, really—consisting of a large office building and a number of apartments. Owned by the same enterprise under dozens of names. I believe the raid was well-planned—the gang just knew they were coming. And the police weren't aware of just how many weapons were being kept there. Most of the weapons were to be sold illegally, but there was an arsenal at their disposal."

"If they knew the raid was coming, why didn't they run?"

"The powerful ones did—leaving the others with promises of greater glory and financial reward, I assume, for fighting the police and escaping."

"And some people escaped?"

"This area of the mid-Atlantic states has tons of forests— as we've discovered looking for the missing. And from what I understand, if someone didn't follow what the head man said, they were shot on the spot for disloyalty. So, I'm sure he was protected, and he had an escape plan in place that he executed before the raid. A way out the back, into the woods…perhaps to a car kept there for just such an occasion. I don't know, of course, but that's what I suppose."

"Alfie must have been a good cop."

"He was. He had several commendations. And he was such a good cop that, well, he still can't let it go."

"He will," Megan said determinedly.

"You think?"

"He needs someone to find Susie," Megan said. "When Susie is found…well, I think he'll be ready to move on."

Ragnar nodded. Then fell silent.

Then they were both awkward.

As if he felt it from the back seat, Hugo whined softly.

Ragnar cleared his throat.

"Laura Nightingale and Harold Elms," he said.

"Pardon?"

"The detectives we're meeting. Their names are Laura Night-ingale and Harold Elms."

"Okay. How are you explaining me to them?" Megan asked him.

He grinned. "An expert witness turned consultant," he said.

"Oh, right."

She was glad when they reached the station. Sitting in the car—even *awkwardly*—she found herself thinking he wasn't a terrible man. But then, she'd never thought he was a *terrible* man. Just autocratic. Maybe even chauvinistic. Then again, maybe he had just learned a steely composure and had an assurance about him—brought on by his job—that made him believe he had to protect and care for others at all times.

Okay, admittedly, she had also been self-assured. Before her ordeal, she would have told anyone that she couldn't fall prey to a predator in the way someone more naive might do.

And...she had tripped. Searching for a puppy. She'd fallen for a simple trick—literally fallen flat—as easily as the most trusting soul in the world.

Now...

She was here. And glad Ragnar was determined to be at her side, because the threat implied by being sent a human skull showed just how vulnerable she could be.

"Ready?"

Ragnar had parked. She smiled grimly and opened the door to get out and then allowed Hugo his freedom from the car as well.

Ragnar arched a brow to her. "There's a little grassy spot at the entrance."

"He's a very well-mannered boy," she assured Ragnar. "But he might enjoy a new bush or two."

Ragnar smiled and hunkered down by the dog, scratching his ears. "Of course, boy, do I have a bush for you!" He shrugged to Megan. "There are lots of places for him to mark."

She smiled and shook her head. They walked to the precinct entry. And as Ragnar had said, the double doors to the reception area were handsomely planted with oaks and grass and bushes.

They gave a Hugo a minute.

Ragnar glanced at his watch and said softly, "Five to two. We're perfect."

He opened the door, allowing her and Hugo in first. He was ready to walk to the reception area, but a woman with jet-black hair securely tied in a bun walked toward them, offering her hand to Ragnar. "Special Agent Johansen? I'm Laura Nightingale and this is my partner, Detective Harold Elms."

The man who had been standing politely behind her stepped forward, shaking Ragnar's hand as well. "Just call me Harry," he said. "And don't let my formal comrade fool you—call her Laura."

Ragnar grinned and nodded. "I'm Ragnar, no nickname, I'm afraid. And this is Megan Law, who is now working with me as a consultant. She has firsthand knowledge of the way these killers work."

"Of course," Laura Nightingale said, nodding gravely. Megan was aware both detectives knew exactly who she was and why she had her firsthand knowledge. "And you have a dog," Laura noted.

"Hugo," Megan said quickly.

"Always helps to have a good canine cop on the team," Harry said.

Megan would have explained Hugo was just her dog, but Ragnar just smiled and said, "We saved a girl with a dog. I'm with you on that; it always helps to have a good canine."

"Come on back; the captain has given us the *good* conference room, though our case has gone cold. Or had been cold, until Special Agent Hawkins called us," Laura said. "We have the screen and I set up my computer. I can show you exactly what we found."

"And if you can help discover who did this, we'll be grateful," Harry said. "We just…we had nothing. Nothing but decomposed bodies and bits and pieces of strange broken wood.

"And the first case went back so far, it wasn't considered high priority. Even the ME and the forensics team were wondering what we'd discovered at first," Harry continued. "In the woods, you have old areas that used to be homesteads; and naturally, people were buried on their property back in the day. Neighbors being so far apart, and also miles away from churches or anything resembling a modern cemetery. The first body…they finally estimated it had been there about ten years. Clothing was completely deteriorated, as was most of the flesh. Obviously, the organs were gone. She was…mainly bones."

"Right," Laura said. "That was the first. And our people were quick to realize the truth. It was just a first impression that the body might have been there forever. But they investigated further. The second body was almost as badly decomposed, and then we found the third. And we knew the truth right away. Dead only about a year." She added dryly, "We knew it was current because there was a designer label on what remained of the clothing, and our medical examiner was quick to inform us the cause of her death was suffocation from being in the earth. She had been in her early twenties."

"Come in, we'll give you the whole lowdown," Harry said, leading the way to a door that opened into a large bullpen with dozens of officers at work. Some paused and nodded; others just kept at their tasks as the group moved through to a hallway and then the conference room. Harry pulled out a chair for Megan and she took it without protest. She considered that progress.

Hugo curled at her feet.

"May I?" Harry asked.

She wasn't sure what he meant at first, but he just wanted to stoop and pet Hugo. She smiled. Hugo politely accepted the invitation.

"Let's get started," Laura said, picking up a remote and flicking a switch that brought a picture up on the large screen in the room. "Here's the first, the northern end of our jurisdiction—off I-95. We really had nothing but bones. A farmer reported that his dog had gotten hold of a human bone. Naturally, we investigated."

Skeletal pieces were shown on a gurney at the morgue.

"Our second, a little more mummified," she said, showing a second corpse in the same position. "This one came to us at Halloween three years ago. There had been some flash flooding; and at first, some kids thought it was a prank, then they went home hysterical, and the parents called us. We had nothing, absolutely nothing, to go on."

"Yes, we investigated the home, the parents, the neighbors... you name it," Harry said. "And now," he added, nodding at Laura, "the time when we knew something was happening, but still didn't have much to go on," Harry said.

Laura flicked the remote.

"She was found just a few miles from here," Laura said. "Our district includes a forested tract due west. We had a report of a domestic disturbance at a popular camping spot along the rural road, and went out to investigate. Someone swore they'd heard shots."

"No shots," Harry said. "It was a car backfiring."

"But when we were out at the site, Harry noted some strange wooden planks. I think a dog had been digging in the area and brought up the bits of wood."

"And the one woman who had called us was certain another camper—a jerk who threw his garbage on the ground and liked to throw rocks at the squirrels—might have killed his wife," Harry said. He shrugged. "So, we started digging, and it wasn't that deep; we found fingers with just bits of flesh on them sticking out of the earth."

As she spoke, Laura worked her remote. She and Harry had carefully documented their search this time. The picture on the screen showed the scene. Scattered trailers were surrounded by woods, little walking paths through them, and at the one where they had dug, something barely discernable sticking out of the earth.

The next picture was a close-up of the fingers, bits of flesh and all.

Megan forced her emotions down and willed herself to sit still, not turning away from the image.

Because, of course, worse followed. The arrival of the medical examiner, the careful digging around the body, and the removal of the remains. It was true the fabric was so deteriorated that, at first glance, the corpse could have been buried there forever. And with bits of dirt-blackened flesh clinging to bone, it was hard to imagine the poor woman had once been a living, breathing human capable of smiles and laughter.

There were more pictures taken at the morgue—what remained of the corpse cleaned up as much as possible.

And then strangely enough, the worst—an image of the woman's face, done by a police artist based on a reconstruction of clay over the bones of the skull, and using remnants of hair and bits of flesh to assume her coloring.

She had been young. A pretty woman with wide eyes and fine features. She didn't smile in the reconstruction, but looked straight ahead, as if listening to someone.

"We found out who she was," Laura said quietly.

"But only one lead, and it led—" Harry began.

"Nowhere," Laura finished.

"We investigated thoroughly, of course," Laura said. "We found out her name was Carole Berlin. Her father died when she was ten, and she left her mother's house in Seattle, Washington, when she was eighteen and wound up on the streets. We had the picture out in the media and another young woman, Grace Menendez, called to say she'd been living rough and making her living on the streets."

"She was an independent sex worker?" Ragnar asked.

Laura nodded. "According to Grace. Carole was also working the streets, and they talked now and then. We interviewed Grace; and I went undercover to speak to every pimp and john I could, and we came up blank."

"And the camper who left his garbage everywhere and tortured squirrels was found with his wife and children in Fredericksburg. Turns out he doesn't throw rocks at squirrels, just bread crumbs. And he swears he doesn't leave trash. We checked him out thoroughly. They had lived in Colorado until he accepted a job in Fredericksburg, and then he and his family moved east. They'd only been out in the area for three months; and every check of every card and bank account showed they were in Colorado when the girl was murdered."

"We investigated every known camper who used the area," Laura said. "But the thing of it is this—someone killed that poor woman. And now we know what the wood was, and that she was buried in a coffin."

Finishing with her slideshow, Laura turned to Ragnar.

"So," she asked anxiously, "do you have our killer?"

Ragnar shook his head regretfully.

"I don't know, but I will do everything in my power to find out. You discovered her burial site just about a year ago?"

"Yes," Harry said, watching Ragnar intently.

Ragnar shook his head. "We have traces on Rory Ayers's movements over the last years. His home, though, is close enough to allow him to have done the deed." He hesitated. "We have two men in custody. Getting the truth from either of them is a rare trick."

Megan knew what he was thinking. She lowered her head. He would speak if he chose to.

"There may be more," he finally said.

"More bodies?" Harry asked.

"More bodies…and more killers," Megan explained.

Both the detectives were silent.

"We'll be on the lookout," Harry vowed. "We'll bring our precinct up to speed—"

"Thank you. We'll put out a warning as well," Ragnar promised him.

"You mean you may have a…like a fraternity of killers?" Laura asked.

"Or a social media group," Harry said dryly.

Ragnar continued. "There's someone at the head of it all. I'm not sure if the original plan was to create murders by various individuals so alike that if any one of them landed in prison, they'd appear innocent when another such murder occurred. But we found one young woman in Jim Carver's basement, another woman rescued from her would-be grave, and then Ayers was caught red-handed, and Gary Boynton was eliminated."

"During your ordeal," Laura said flatly, looking at Megan.

"But you don't think it was just the three men involved?" Harry asked. "I mean, the two being held now are pending trial, so—"

"Oh, my God!" Laura muttered. "None of those men might be…the initiator of all this? Lord help us all if this is a—an organized group of serial killers!"

Hugo whined softly. Laura absently apologized to the dog

for her outburst. "We haven't found any more victims nearby since we discovered Carole's remains. But the killing has gone on in other jurisdictions, although they've been so random. It's since the Bureau became involved we've all been forced to see the scope."

"And what do we do? Dig up every acre of forest? Heading inland from the coast, that could take an eternity," Harry said dolefully.

"We have to find the head of the group," Ragnar pointed out. He grimaced and stood. "I can't thank you both enough; having all teams playing for one goal is everything in this. And we know from your reports you two were thorough and worked the case relentlessly. But we'd appreciate information on how to reach the young lady who identified the dead woman."

"Grace Menendez," Laura said.

"Do you have an address or phone number for her?" Ragnar asked.

"She had no fixed address," Harry said.

"A phone number?" Megan asked hopefully.

But the detectives shook their heads.

"We can give you the corner where she often solicits—though she'll be gone if she senses you're cops. She avoids being arrested with the ease of a slippery eel," Harry said.

"We'll give it a try," Ragnar said. He frowned. "How were you in contact with her?"

"She came to us," Laura said. "She came in every few weeks until...well, I guess she gave up when we didn't get anywhere."

"We talked to her," Harry said. "Tried to get her off the streets even. Really, Carole's death should have been a warning. Everyone knows bad things happen, but thinks it won't happen to them because they're too smart."

Megan set a hand on Hugo's head, glancing downward.

Human instinct? Or failing? She'd certainly thought herself too smart to be taken.

"They've targeted women who weren't street-involved, too. Though she is on a dangerous path," Ragnar said.

Megan stood. "If we can find her, we'll talk to her, too."

"We'll give you a couple of street corners," Harry said. "And a picture, of course."

"And wish you the best of luck," Laura said.

"As Laura said," Harry told them gravely, "we haven't seen her in a while now. Which makes me hope that…"

"That you find her," Laura finished. "And not like we found Carole Berlin."

CHAPTER FIVE

Megan was quiet as they exited the station.

Outside, she said, "Those are good people. Good cops."

"Most cops are good cops. Most agents are good agents. But you'll never change the fact people are people and imperfect. And those who might do bad things slip through," Ragnar said.

"That doesn't make it right," Megan told him.

"No. We're at a period in history where we all recognize that fact; and every officer and agent is equally responsible to try to weed out the bad," he said. He thought about his own situation, turning to her as they neared the car and saying, "We've been lucky as hell at the Krewe. We've never had an agent who was anything other than great at their work—and caring. But then, Adam and Jackson do all the 'weeding' before anyone gets in. Wait—that came out badly. I personally never worked with anyone—cop or agent—who wasn't doing what they were supposed to be doing. I'm lucky and grateful. I'm lucky again in that I have a great partner. Partners," he added quickly. "Mark and Red."

"A dog is always a great partner," Megan assured him.

He laughed. "A dog knows more about loyalty than any person. A dog wants to be loved."

"And fed," Megan put in.

"Well, yeah. But a dog never has a personal agenda, so dogs make great partners. But your brother-in-law is a damned good partner, too."

She nodded thoughtfully. "Must be hard." She pursed her lips. "I think I may need to have you—or Mark or Colleen—take me to a firing range."

They'd reached the car. She had walked around to the passenger's door, and he studied her over the roof of the car.

"You…want to go shooting?" he asked, surprised. Naturally, people had become concerned about excessive force; and just as naturally, it was wrong and against everything those who swore to "protect and serve" should do. But Megan had been through a hell of pure terror; which might make it just as natural that while she'd never want to hurt anyone, she'd want to protect herself from the evil she knew too well was out there.

She shrugged. "I honestly believe I'm mentally stable."

"Hmm. I don't know about that."

"Hey!"

"Just kidding. Yes, I'll take you shooting. And I'll teach you how to properly handle a gun. Unlike other objects, a gun has but one use. So yes, if you want to learn to shoot one, you should learn everything."

"Got ya."

"Your sister never offered?"

"Stop, please! I never wanted a gun," she said. "I also never wanted to need one. I'm not even saying I want to own one.

But I am saying I believe I need to learn if…if I'm capable of shooting."

He inhaled, taking a minute before replying.

"There's shooting—and there's shooting at another human being. When we're really lucky, we never have to do it. And when we do, it should only be when another life is at stake."

"I know," she said softly.

"And I know you know."

"You're afraid I'd hesitate, not wanting to kill someone," Megan said. "But I do value my own life. And I value the lives of others. As in others like the women who have been so brutally taken. So, if I was threatened with death—or watched an innocent threatened with death—I wouldn't hesitate."

He studied her for a minute. Then he smiled grimly and got into the car.

Megan slid into the passenger's seat after allowing Hugo to jump in back.

Ragnar started the car and drove the short distance toward a parking garage near the streets that Laura and Harry had suggested they check.

"Think we'll find her?" Megan asked as they walked toward the busy corner, leading Hugo along.

"Well, it's early still."

"The picture," she said.

"The picture?" he asked. "Oh!" He reached into his pocket and produced the copy of the picture of Grace Menendez the detectives had given him.

Megan studied the photo and handed it back to him, smiling. "Got it. So, we don't just stand there, asking if anyone has seen a certain woman."

"No, we walk the dog and window-shop."

"Okay. We can do that."

They wandered to the corner of an intersection, looking into shop windows as they went. They were staring into the display of a furniture shop when Ragnar noticed a young woman wearing shorts and a flowery halter top, along with very high heels, meandering just outside a neighboring coffee shop. She had short dark brown hair and a pleasant if not beautiful face.

She looked like the girl next door with an attitude.

"It's her," he said. He started off to address the young woman. Megan hung back.

"Grace?" he asked, approaching her.

"I don't know who you're looking for, honey," she said, startled by him.

"Please, wait," he said. Then Megan joined him, walking in front of the young woman with Hugo in a way that made her stop.

"It's about Carole," Megan told her.

The young woman stopped walking; she looked back at Ragnar. "You...you are a cop. Either that or some Norse-god dude come down to right the world."

"I'm not a cop. I'm an FBI agent," Ragnar said.

The woman looked at Megan with curiosity. "And you're his dog walker?" she asked.

"I'm not an anything," Megan said, grimacing. "Well, not with law enforcement. I...was almost a victim. Like Carole," she said quietly. "Are you Grace Menendez?"

"I am. But...does that mean you caught whoever did that to Carole?" she asked hopefully.

"We're afraid he—or someone like him—might still be out there. And we know you tried to help the detectives already, but we'd like to talk to you. May we buy you some coffee? Something to eat?"

"You want my time?" she asked dryly. "A hundred an hour. Of course, that will come with perks. Lots of them, maybe. You're very pretty people."

"I was thinking of the coffee shop," Ragnar said.

"And I was joking. I think," Grace Menendez replied. "I mean, I can joke, right? You said you're not Vice."

"We are not here to harass you," he promised her.

"We need your help," Megan pleaded.

Grace studied Megan and smiled sadly. "I wish I could help! I was devastated to learn about Carole, about what happened to her... Why? Why would someone do something so terrible to people? I mean, I've come across a few quirky guys but...who takes pleasure from killing someone?"

"It's about power. The power of life and death," Ragnar told her. "And the pleasure comes from the power. May we buy you a meal? Would that...help with the time taken?"

"You have to eat, right?" Megan said.

The woman smiled again. "Sure. Believe it or not, the coffee shop serves a lovely filet, and I don't usually spend that much for lunch. So, you can treat me!"

"A pleasure," Ragnar assured her, then turned to Megan, "Hugo?"

"He's cool; he has a support dog vest. I'll just slip it on him."

As Megan pulled Hugo's vest from her bag, Ragnar felt Grace studying him. When he looked at her, she said, "You don't mind being seen in a restaurant with me?"

"We're grateful if you come with us," Megan said.

Grace turned to her, studying her as well and nodding slowly. "Sure."

A few minutes later, they were seated in a corner of the café. Hugo appeared to appreciate the aroma of the place, but he settled half under Megan's chair.

They ordered lunch—all opting for the filet—before Ragnar turned to Grace and asked, "First, you and Carole were friends?"

"We were," Grace said. "There was something about her, even after a year out here. On the streets. She was still so good and sweet and even innocent."

"She sounds wonderful," Megan said.

"Even though she was a prostitute?" Grace asked.

"That wasn't who she was; that's how she was surviving," Megan said.

"You remind me of her," Grace said. "Looking for the good. And that's not bad."

"What did you know about her other friends, her past, any acquaintances?" Ragnar asked her.

"Her past, well. I don't understand some people," Grace said, shaking her head. "I mean, there was Carole, condemned by society for walking the streets, but society doesn't always condemn those that cause a situation. Carole's dad passed away when she was ten, and her mom went a little crazy. I guess she was the type who had to have a man in her life. It's so sad because some people think they can't be complete without a man in their life or a woman or…a partner. So okay, you need someone in your life.

"Carole's mom was so desperate she pretended she didn't see the asshole who lived with them was attacking her daughter! But Carole believed her mother knew damned well what was going on. She just ignored it so the guy would stay. Her teenage daughter's innocence and sanity were worth a guy to fix the plumbing. The very second she could legally get out of there and not be followed or stopped, Carole split. And she told me she'd already endured the worst asshole known to man so working as a pro was going to be a piece of cake because at least she got to choose her johns."

"You never worked with a pimp? She didn't work with a pimp?" Ragnar asked.

Grace shook her head. "I've stayed the hell away. I know a few girls who work with pimps. The jerks beat them up now and then *and* take their money. It never seemed like a good deal to me, and I've avoided the goons who try to sign up the girls by offering protection. Well, let's face it, the entire thing is a horror story. But Carole wasn't about to have anyone else in charge of her life. Good or bad, she was calling the shots."

"Did she fight with any of the pimps? Or the goons?"

"Not that I know about," Grace said.

"And you have no idea of who she went with last, or anyone who might have been a regular john?"

"The last time I talked to her…" Grace mused carefully. "It was here on this corner. Vice comes around—but it's just a good place. Easy for the guys to pull off the road. Most money talk happens before anyone gets in a car, so you need to chat a second, you know? But that night, Carole and I waved goodbye to one another. She was just coming on, and I was just going off. I wish I had been here—I might have seen something, I could have done something!"

"You can do something," Megan said quickly. "You can be careful and save your own life, you know."

"Are you going to make a speech?" Grace asked.

Megan shook her head. "We all do what we need to do to get by. I just think you can do so much more."

"Baristas don't make that much money."

"Baristas can become managers, save up, and start their own businesses. But you don't have to become a barista. There is a lot out there," Megan said.

Grace looked at her curiously. "You work?"

"I'm an editor."

"Oh?"

"I love words and stories and love what I do."

"I don't know enough about words to use the right ones all the time, but maybe I should write a book."

"Maybe you should," Megan told her sincerely. "That's why I love what I do. I help out when a writer has missed something or needs to find a 'right' word."

Grace looked at her, as if trying to determine if Megan was speaking with her honestly.

Ragnar knew Grace would have to make that determination—and any determination regarding her own life—on her own. They still needed information.

They all fell silent as their food arrived. Ragnar was hungry; he was glad for the few minutes where only the scrape of their utensils could be heard.

Finally, he spoke again.

"Here is something interesting," he said. "Baristas make enough to rent apartments. So if you're making more than that, why didn't Carole have an address?"

Grace hesitated. "Are you taping me?" she demanded.

Ragnar shook his head. "We're asking you for help, not trying to trip you up. I am not Vice. I'm trying to find monsters and lock them up."

Grace let out a breath. "She had an address. My address. Jean and Penny live there, too. The apartment is rented under a different name. We don't want people finding us because...well, you don't have to be a serial killer to be a john we don't want to see again."

"Jean and Penny? Do they work with you?" Ragnar asked.

Grace laughed. "Hey, you're funny *and* studly. Work with me! They work at the same vocation, one might say, but they're friends. Yeah, yeah, people would say that we're competition, but we're not. We were like a... I don't know. A company. Supportive of each other. We pooled for the rent. It's a nice apartment."

"They would have recognized Carole's reconstructed image, too, then," Megan said.

"Right. And they did. We talked. I'm the...most abrasive. We thought I should be the one to go in." She winced. "We, uh, we pooled to give her a funeral, too. I couldn't bear the thought of no one caring—her life had been bitter and alone. I didn't want...well, I didn't want her in a potter's field."

"That was wonderful of you," Megan said. "But how did you manage that? Get her released from the morgue and make the arrangements without someone wanting to know your relationship with Carole?"

"Jean went to the morgue." She hesitated and shrugged. "We have talented friends, and I will *not* tell you their names. Jean is the sweetest of us and the best actress, so with a little...advice from those we know, we managed to get her in claiming to be Carole's sister. It wasn't that much of a lie."

"Could we meet the other women?" Ragnar asked. "They might know something that could help."

Grace hesitated. "You're not going to be a pain in the ass and demand to know how Jean pulled it off?"

"We're not here for you," Ragnar reminded her.

"But you are a sworn officer of the law."

"I am. All I know is you have friends. I'd like to speak to

your roommates. I'm not trying to railroad anyone. I am trying to catch heinous killers."

"You may have caught him already."

"True," he said flatly. "But we're not comfortable with what
we have."

"God. An honest cop."

"I'm not a cop, but most cops are honest."

"May I ask my roommates first?"

"Of course!" Megan said. She leaned forward, folding her
hands on the table. "You saw Carole when she was just starting
out for the night. But maybe one of them saw her later. Saw
the car she might have gotten in—if not the man driving it."

"If they knew anything, they would have said so," Grace told
them earnestly.

"I believe you. But you had to have known something was
wrong when she didn't come back to the apartment, right?"
Ragnar asked.

"We called it in. We called her in as a missing person. But
she's an adult. She's apparently allowed to disappear," Grace
said. "Especially when you're not gainfully employed and have
a reputation on the streets. Women like us move on, you know."

They were all silent for a minute.

"I am so sorry," Megan said softly.

"Well, we make choices," Grace said. "Sometimes life forces
circumstances on us, but we're still the ones who make the
choices."

"And I'm still so sorry. Carole deserved so much better from
everyone," Megan said.

Grace looked at her and smiled and arched a brow slowly.
"Do you think I could really write a book?"

"I have a feeling your story is interesting," Megan told her.

Grace smiled. "Well, how do I get back to you?"

Ragnar handed her one of his cards.

Grace accepted it and slid it into a pocket in her shorts.

"Thanks for the steak. And don't follow me around," she said.

Ragnar laughed at that. "Not to worry—we have places to go, people to see."

Grace rose and shrugged, leaving them at last with a smile. They watched her exit the coffee shop.

When she was gone, Megan looked at Ragnar and asked, "Did you get anything out of that?"

"Yeah. They have a friend who makes illegal IDs."

"I mean—"

"I think the situation is damned sad. There's no way not to feel empathy for a murder victim, but Carole's life sounded like pure hell."

"I agree. Oh, and I can say that she was telling the truth. And I'm wondering about Grace now, feeling badly for her too. I can't imagine…"

"What?" he asked her softly.

She let out a soft sigh. "Our parents were great. Growing up was wonderful—camping, traveling, a playset in the yard. My mom or my dad would jump in front of a speeding train to save any one of us. I can't imagine a parent who would…"

"I know. Our human instinct is to protect our young, but sometimes instinct and decency are lost in human desire."

"You're jaded. You've seen too much."

"True. But trust me, I'm not jaded. If any of these things stops hurting, well, it would be time for me to get out. I'm just aware bad things happen, and often, to good people. Anyway, ready?"

"For what?"

"Something more pleasant. We're going to head back to the safe house. Your sister and Mark will be there by now."

"Oh! Right!"

She started to stand up and sat again, shaking her head.

"I know. I didn't want them to cut short a honeymoon either," he said. "But this is just the opposite. You have an amazing family. And there is no way Colleen was not going to come back and get into the situation when you're involved."

"Are you all right with that? Isn't there a rule about people not working on a case when their loved one is involved?"

"I doubt if they're going to check back into work, or at least not officially. And the Krewe works in many ways the main office doesn't."

"Right. They don't check in with the dead."

"We have tons of couple teams in the Krewe," he said. "And that's not normal. Husbands and wives may work for the FBI, but they're usually in different units. Anyway, ready?"

"I guess. Not really. But yes. Just one sec."

She had saved a few scraps of her meal.

She slipped them to the dog.

They paid and left the coffee shop. As they walked back to the car, Megan noted, "Grace isn't on the corner. Do you think she found, um, someone already?"

"Maybe. Or maybe she's decided to try writing a book."

"She probably has a story, too," Megan muttered. "Seriously, her story about Carole is heartbreaking."

He shrugged and said, "You get jaded on the streets. But people do make it. And," he added, "I'm glad you were with me."

"Yeah?"

"I think she was impressed with you, and she listened to me because of you."

"Well. Cool. Glad to be of help. I just don't know if we got anything."

"We'll see. I'm anxious to meet the roommates. Someone who might have seen who Carole went with before she disappeared."

They reached the car and settled in.

Again, they were silent at first.

Then Megan spoke. "Are Colleen and Mark, uh, taking your place at the safe house?" she asked.

"No."

She was silent.

He glanced her way as he drove. "I'm sorry. I know you would far prefer they were there, but they aren't officially on the investigation. If they move into the safe house, they could put Jackson Crow in an awkward position for allowing it. The problem with relatives is that our judgment can be clouded when it comes to the safety of someone we love when—"

"I understand. And…"

"And?"

Megan sighed. "To be truthful, I want them… I want them to be newlyweds. I want them to go back to whichever apartment they kept and sleep there. Alone. I don't want them to be worried every second, every time they hear movement."

"Okay," he said simply.

"You don't mind, do you?" she asked, glancing his way. "I mean, I guess it would be better for you—"

"Not to worry. Red lives with Mark, but visits my place now and then. I don't even have a cat of my own. I heard Colleen has a cat. But I guess you're a dog person?" he asked lightly.

"I like all animals. Hugo is a rescue. And sometimes I really think he rescued me. But he's more than that. You know my brother works with the police in criminal cases. So he encouraged me to have Hugo trained in protection, and even some search. He's not like a police dog, but he did pretty well in the classes. We found them fun, at any rate."

"That's fantastic," he said. "Dogs are so smart."

After a pause, Megan asked him, "What happens now?"

"I want to go back to the correctional facility and talk to Jim Carver." He paused, shrugging. "The boy wonder, Gary Boynton, might have gotten away, instead of shot by Colleen if he hadn't gotten stuck on Ayers's determination to kidnap your sister when they nabbed you instead. That's one thing that bothers me so much. Boynton was young, rich."

"Ayers is rich. Or was rich. I hear his wife is divorcing him, and the money they had was really family money that came from her side," Megan said.

"Right. I guess I mean the young part more than the rich part." He hesitated again. "I think these guys communicate somehow, and old killers are grooming young killers."

"So, young men are apprenticing…as killers," she said. She shook her head, her entire face pinched in a frown of disturbed disbelief. "As an editor, I've come across some frightening stories. I deal with robot aliens, bug aliens who feast on humanity, space warriors out to save the world and even the galaxy. But I haven't come across a bug or any other alien nearly as horrifying as the real monsters we have right here on earth."

"True," Ragnar muttered. He felt his phone vibrating and answered it quickly.

"Ragnar?" a female voice said.

"Yes, this is he." He thought he knew the voice. "Grace?"

"Yes, it's me. I guess you're halfway home or wherever right now, but…feel like turning around? Both the girls would like to meet you."

"Where am I going?"

She gave him an address just on the outskirts of town.

Megan glanced at him.

"I can take you to see your sister—"

"Make a U-turn!" she said sternly. "I'm the one she really likes, remember?"

He smiled without argument.

And made the first available U-turn.

CHAPTER SIX

Working the street corner that was apparently the favorite place of Grace and her friends seemed to be a lucrative business.

Megan was pleased to discover the apartment complex where the girls lived was more of town house arrangement. They had a first and second floor and a little garden area behind a gated entrance to their private quarters.

They kept it pretty, too. Flowers bloomed in the garden. The walkway was swept and clean. And when the door opened and Grace ushered them in, Megan saw the place was incredibly tidy, and the furniture was polished and adorned with pictures and attractive little knickknacks.

"You were expecting a hovel?" Grace whispered from behind her, almost making her jump.

She turned, laughing.

"Actually, I was wishing my place was half so neat! Is, uh, Hugo okay in here?"

Grace smiled. "Hugo is just fine. And I like you!" she said. "Come on, have a seat. Jean and Penny will be right out." She glanced over at Ragnar. "Have a seat, really. I promise, the sofa is safe. This is where we live. We never bring anyone here."

"Never!" another young woman said, coming toward them from a hallway. She was perhaps twenty-five, blonde and pretty—and just a little tired-looking.

"Hi. I'm Penny. Penelope Hamlin. A dog! I love dogs. One day…"

She stooped to pet Hugo, who wagged his tail enthusiastically.

"He's just fine," Grace said dryly.

"Hi!" Megan said to Penny. "Megan Law, Ragnar Johansen—and Hugo."

"Great dog. And wow," Penny said, rising. "Big Swede!"

"Norwegian," Ragnar said, shrugging.

"Whatever!" Penny said, smiling. "Are you…American?"

"I am. My parents immigrated," Ragnar explained. "And you?"

"I haven't the faintest idea," Penny said. "Anyway, Grace said you two were…all right."

"Thank you," Ragnar said to Grace.

Another woman came out the hallway. Where Grace was dark-haired and Penny was light, Jean was right in between the two with red hair and freckles—and pigtails.

"Hi, I'm Jean," she said.

"Would you like coffee? Jean does a killer espresso," Grace told them.

"I don't want to put you to any bother," Ragnar said.

"No bother," Jean said.

"Then I'd love an espresso!" Megan said.

"Coming right up!"

Grace indicated they should take seats. Hugo sat politely at her side.

"Takes two shakes," Jean called from the kitchen.

"I'm the one who saw Carole last," Penny said, taking the armchair across from the sofa.

Ragnar had waited for her and Grace to sit before doing so himself. He leaned forward from his spot on the sofa, facing her closely. "Did you see who she went with?" he asked.

"Here's the thing—we were just starting out that day. I saw her with her first trick, but… I never put much faith in that because…well, we work for hours, and there might have been several more people after?" She had started her words as a statement. They became a question.

"We appreciate anything you can give us. Maybe the man she went with first wasn't her killer, but anytime we can eliminate anyone it's helpful. And anytime you find someone who knows anything, they can sometimes lead you further," Ragnar told her quietly.

Penny nodded gravely. "I didn't get a good look. I mean, I wasn't paying that much attention. When two of us work the same corner, we pick the cross-streets. But I glanced back when I was in position, and I saw her getting into a car."

"Do you remember anything about the vehicle?"

"Yeah. It was an SUV. Blue. I'm not sure about the make, but one of the usual-looking deals. Like an ordinary navy-blue SUV," Penny said.

"And the driver? Young—old? Could you tell anything about him?" Ragnar asked.

"He, uh…" She paused, thinking, "I don't think he was very old. Thirty-five to forty-five—maybe closer to the first. Not that I'm a great judge, and there were people between us…but there was a minute when he leaned toward Carole…that I kind of saw his face?" Again, she made it sound like a question.

"Had you seen him before?" Megan asked.

Penny frowned. "I don't think so and yes! Wait. I think he was maybe about thirty-five because I remember thinking she was lucky. I got a really old dude on my first outing that day. He had to have been close to eighty! And smelled like garlic. But hey."

Megan glanced at Ragnar. And she knew what he was thinking.

Not Jim Carver and not Rory Ayers. Both men were much older.

And Gary Boynton would have probably been too young.

"Do you think you could work with a sketch artist?" Ragnar asked her.

Penny winced. "I, uh, don't go to the police station."

"What if we did a video chat with an artist? That would be like sitting next to an artist."

"Um…"

As Penny gave the matter thought, Jean came from the kitchen, bearing a tray with espresso cups.

Megan took her cue from Ragnar. He didn't push the matter at that moment, but accepted a cup of espresso, turned down sugar, and lifted his cup to taste the brew.

"Okay, this is good espresso!" he said.

Megan tasted her own.

"It's great. And it will help me to stay awake."

"And poor Hugo probably wouldn't like espresso. May I give him a piece of turkey?" Jean asked.

"Sure," Megan said.

"It's good turkey," Jean said. "Grace cooks up one heck of a bird! We just had it yesterday, so it's not bad or anything."

"I trust your turkey implicitly," Megan said, smiling.

Grace laughed and went to the kitchen. Megan told Hugo, "It's okay, boy. Go."

Jean headed back to the kitchen, followed by Hugo.

Ragnar took their conversation back to the point, saying, "Penny, I can set it up so we're with you; we can talk through a tablet. You don't have to go into the station. We have a talented sketch artist. At least we can get an idea and compare him to men in custody, and to others who may show suspicious behavior."

Penny winced again. "I—I—" she stuttered, and then hesitated. "Yes!" she said with sudden determination. "Carole was one of us, and not just that, a good person. Yes, if I can help, I will!"

"Thank you. Thank you so sincerely," Ragnar told her.

"Can we do it now?" Penny asked.

"We have lots of espresso," Jean said. "But it's way after five. Will anyone be working at your headquarters or wherever?"

"Someone is always working, but I have a specific person in mind," Ragnar said. He stood. "Excuse me, I'll make some calls."

He walked a few feet away, pulling out his phone.

Penny looked at Megan nervously. "This is safe, right? I mean, he's not secretly calling Vice—or the IRS?"

Megan shook her head. "I promise you, he's just trying to stop a killer."

"Can he? I've been so nervous...since Carole. I know time has passed, and nothing has happened, but... I... I dropped out of high school. I'm not smart and I can't do anything else. At least when I come here at night, I have friends. I have a nice home during the day, but I'm still terrified, and I—"

"Penny, no one should have to live in that kind of fear," Megan said. "I can't say I know anything about your life, but I was taken by a man who was at least *like* whoever killed Carole. I know the absolute terror of waiting to be shut away in the earth, to die slowly, suffocating. And I can't guarantee anything, but I can promise you, I can look into a way for you to do something else."

She realized Grace had come out of the kitchen and she stood by Jean. The three of them were watching her.

"Okay, I admit it. *I'm* even scared," Grace said. "But I don't know how to get out of this life."

"But you went to college," Jean reminded her.

"Okay, here's what a counselor once told me—think about what you enjoy doing. Then we go from there," Megan said, wishing she had a good suggestion for the women. She smiled. "I had a great counselor in high school. When she asked that question to one of my friends, my friend told her she didn't have any money, but she loved to window-shop. Anyway, the counselor directed her to take some art and design classes; and she turned window-shopping into being a window designer."

"I could design windows!" Grace said. "I stare into them often enough!"

"It's just one thing. It's taking something you love, and putting it toward a way to make a living. Anyway…" Megan paused. Ragnar had finished with his phone call.

"I have my phone, but do you have a tablet in your bag?" he asked Megan.

"Always," she assured him.

"May I?" he asked.

She dug it out and gave it to him. He quickly signed in, and a minute later he had Maisie Nicholson on video.

Maisie was apparently at home—they could see an overflowing bookshelf behind her, a flower vase, and a child's safety gate. She was one of the most stunning women Megan had ever known, a friend of Colleen's from work, with ebony skin, enormous eyes, and beautiful features. She was also an incredibly talented artist, able to take descriptive words and turn them into a likeness so good that it might have been a photo.

"Hey, there!" she said to Megan through the screen.

"Hey, yourself! And thank you."

"My pleasure. Kyle just took the kids for ice cream so the timing is perfect."

"We're here with Grace, Penny, and Jean. Penny is the one who is going to give you a description of a man." Ragnar moved the tablet about so Maisie could see everyone as he introduced them.

"I'm ready to go!" Maisie said, smiling. "Hi there, Penny, Jean, and Grace!"

Each woman responded to her and Megan thought maybe it was a good thing Maisie was at home. It made it easier for them to relate to her than it might have been in an office, any place that could have made them nervous, even from a "video" distance.

Penny began to talk, describing the man. She hadn't known his height, of course. But he'd had clean, sharp features. His hair had been brown, falling over his forehead, but not long enough to hit his neck. His chin, like the angle of his cheekbones, had been sharp. His nose had been round and fat.

There was a bit of trial and error. The cheekbones just a little broader. The nose a little longer.

His eyes had been well-set, his brows had an arch to them, she thought, and one lock of hair had all but covered one eye.

By the end, Maisie created an image that made Penny gasp.

"That's him, yes, that's him!"

But it wasn't anyone that Megan recognized.

"Super, thank you," Ragnar said. "Both of you—thank you!" Megan could tell he was genuinely grateful for their help, but underneath there was a hint of disappointment that the face was of a total stranger.

"Happy to please. I'll shoot this to you, Ragnar," Maisie told him.

"Great."

"Bye, all!" Maisie said, and Ragnar moved the screen around so that everyone could wave.

Then they were done.

"That was painless," Penny said. "She's really cool, really amazing."

"Beyond a doubt, the coolest and the best," Ragnar agreed. "And again, I can't thank you enough, and you know how to reach me. We'd best get going."

"Ah, too bad! You know, you're the only guests we've ever had in here," Grace said.

"Then we're especially grateful and honored," Megan assured her.

"Don't let it go to your head," Grace said, grinning. "Hugo is really our favorite."

"Ah, well!" Megan said. "He thanks you for having him, too. And for the turkey."

A few minutes later, they'd said their goodbyes. "Your sister called. She and Mark were getting worried, even though I said we'd be a little late." He grimaced. "Hey, she's your sister."

"Do you have any siblings?" Megan asked him.

He shook his head. "My folks were older. I think I was a surprise. I've lost them both, but they were cool parents. Mom was forty when I was born, and my dad was in his late fifties. Maybe they'd lived long enough to know anything a kid might pull before I could manage to pull it. I was a decently behaved kid."

Megan laughed. "I would have expected that!"

He shrugged. "My folks never laid a hand on me. They barely raised their voices. I just never wanted to disappoint them."

"They must have been pretty fantastic," she said.

"They were. So. Tell me more about being a triplet. Do you know what each other are thinking, any ESP along with the other strange talents?"

"No real ESP. Not—not usually. But I guess Colleen honed in on me when I was in trouble. I counted on her hearing. I said things aloud and then shouted them in my head."

He nodded. "We're going to need all of it—every single thing everyone has—to put an end to this."

"You don't think Carole was killed by Ayers, Carver, or Boynton."

"I think she was killed by the man Penny described."

"How will you go about finding him? And if you were to find him, how do you accuse him of murder after this much time?"

"There is no statute of limitation on murder," he said flatly.

"But how would you prove it?"

"He might trip himself up. Or…"

"Or?"

"He might try again. And if so, we have to be ready to stop him."

She fell silent and thoughtful.

As they neared the house, she asked, "Could he have been the one to dig up the skull and send it to me?"

"Possibly. Or we could find him; and with your keen ability, when we interview him, you might listen and decide he was just a guy who picked up a prostitute and returned her to the street where she did find her killer. We don't know anything until we follow every lead."

They'd arrived at the house. By the time they entered the gate, Colleen and Mark were coming out the front door along with Mark's dog, Red.

Megan was truly and deeply sorry to have ruined her sister's honeymoon. Colleen was a wonderful person who deserved her moments of happiness. Mark was the perfect match for her sister: strong, and strong enough to accept strength in others.

Megan knew she and Colleen did look a lot alike. They were the same height and approximate shape with the same green eyes and similar facial features. But Colleen had a darker shade of red hair, and her chin was a little sharper. They weren't identical, but they were obviously siblings.

But they had been different through the years in their passions. Literature and books had always meant a great deal to Megan. And from a young age, Colleen had known she wanted to be in law enforcement.

Patrick, their brother, had always known, too. He worked as criminal psychologist with the police in Philadelphia.

Seeing Colleen made Megan realize she needed to talk to Patrick. Make sure he knew she was okay.

And that they didn't tell their parents what was going on!

Hugo ran to greet Red. The two went racing off around the yard, like long-lost friends, though the two dogs had only seen each other a few times before.

Colleen all but flew out, throwing her arms around Megan and hugging her tightly.

"I am so sorry. Oh, Lord, Megan, I never thought I would put you or anyone else in danger. I am so sorry. You've been dragged out of New York again—"

"I did not drag her," Ragnar protested lightly, bringing a smile to Colleen's lips as she disengaged from Megan.

Colleen shook her head. "You didn't do this to her—I did."

"Colleen, stop!" Megan begged. "You didn't do this. Awful, horrible, heinous people did this. And if I make a difference, I'm grateful. You and Patrick have been helping people all your lives. Now, I hope, it's my turn to do something good for others. Speaking of which…"

She looked over at Ragnar.

"Speaking of which," Mark said, stepping forward for a hug. "I get to greet my sister-in-law, too. And speaking of which, let's go in and you two can bring us up to speed."

"You aren't officially on this. You can't be," Ragnar reminded Mark.

"Not officially," Mark protested. "But we're on it. Ragnar, come on, you and I started on this together."

Ragnar nodded. "Oh, I'm not talking you out of doing anything. I'm just reminding you you're not official."

They all trailed into the house, gravitating naturally to the kitchen. Megan went to the coffeepot while her sister went for cups. Mark got half-and-half from the refrigerator and then dug into the cabinets for sugar.

Ragnar noted that they hadn't eaten for a while, so he pulled out deli meat, cheese and condiments, which he set next to a loaf of bread on the counter, indicating that they should all just help themselves.

"How was the island?" Megan asked. She grinned and grabbed a slice of cheese.

"Incredible!" Colleen said. "Pristine beaches, palms that seemed to float in the breeze…it was wonderful."

"I'm so sor—"

"Don't start!" Colleen said. "We'll get back there."

"Bring us up to speed," Mark said, pouring coffee for everyone.

As they fixed themselves some food, Ragnar told them everything, from his conversation with Ayers, to his trip to New York, to the interview that morning, as well as stopping by to see Alfie Parker and then on to the police station and out to find Grace Menendez.

"You must have said all the right things," Mark said. "Grace invited you to her home."

"And Maisie did a sketch. Well, you know Maisie. It's an amazing likeness. I sent it on to Angela immediately. She'll be checking with the local police. Vice may have caught him before if he's been steady soliciting, and we have the likeness going out everywhere."

"I think I'll hit the streets tomorrow," Colleen said gravely. "Unofficially, of course."

"Picking up a new vocation, huh?" Ragnar teased.

"But only unofficially," Colleen assured him.

"Red and I will be near," Mark said. "Unless you want Red with you?"

"We have Hugo," Ragnar said, grinning at Megan.

"Hugo is a pet—" Colleen began.

"Red is your dog and works best with you. Hugo would do anything for Megan. That's what counts if she falls into any danger. Which I'll see she doesn't," Ragnar said.

"We should get going, then," Colleen said. "Megan, I'm so sorry. We can't stay here. If we did—"

"Colleen, I don't want you and Mark here!" Megan said determinedly, setting her sandwich down for emphasis. "I don't want you to do anything whatsoever you shouldn't be doing. I'm fine. This place is a strange techno-fortress and I have a dog!"

"And there's me, too," Ragnar said dryly.

"I'm sorry, I mean…yes, exactly! Ragnar is here, and there's someone in a truck of some kind outside all the time. There are cameras; and quite frankly, these killers may trick someone in the open, but I really don't think they're savvy enough to disconnect this kind of tech and take out two agents."

"No, no," Colleen said. "I just thought that…maybe you'd like my company…" She gave her sister a pointed look.

"Ragnar and I are getting along just fine!" Megan said.

"Oh!" Colleen said, looking at Ragnar apologetically. "I just meant—"

"That we didn't get along before. But we're doing okay now. Honestly. He's a dog guy. By the way, how's the cat?" she asked cheerfully.

Colleen looked at Mark and shook her head. "Jensen is great—he's a cat, jumps and falls on his feet, and he's barely touched his nine lives. Anyway, we'll get on the corner Carole Berlin was working, but you two keep in touch!"

"Absolutely," Megan promised.

"Always in touch," Ragnar said.

"If you see Grace, Jean, or Penny on that corner, you might give them a start, Colleen," Megan said thoughtfully.

"I'm sure other women work that corner. Oh! Because I look like you in weird makeup or something," Colleen said. "Not to worry, I intend to tell them who I am if I run into any of them."

"They're all frightened," Ragnar said.

"I think they'd like to…do something else for a living now," Megan said. "I told Grace she should write a book, but it wouldn't pay their bills immediately even if she could come up with a good story, which I'm kind of betting she could. I told them all to try to think about things they enjoy, or are good at, and maybe think of a different career that way. I just wish there was something I could do to help them."

"Hopefully, they'll be all right," Mark said. "Carole was taken a long time ago, and apparently the killer hasn't struck that corner again."

"That we know about," Ragnar said. "But that is…well, vulnerable women like that can be easy prey."

"That's true," Mark said. "Several of the victims of this murder brotherhood have been working girls. And sad, but true, they come and go from different cities, especially if they believe they've been noted by a vice squad."

"I say we talk to Angela. Maybe she or Jackson will have an idea," Colleen said.

"Good idea," Ragnar agreed. "She's like a magician when it comes to almost any problem."

"We'll talk to her tomorrow," Mark said. "No, wait. You'll talk to her tomorrow."

"Right. Because we're official," Ragnar agreed, grinning.

Colleen and Mark were finally convinced they could go. And no matter how great and obedient a dog might be, it was actually Red who seemed to have a harder time leaving.

But eventually the gate was locked, the door was locked, and all alarms and cameras were on, and she and Ragnar were left standing just inside the doorway.

"That was okay, right?" Ragnar asked.

"Yes, absolutely. I'm happy to see my sister, even if I'm not happy about why," Megan said.

"They're going to be fine, and they'll work off the clock. You

know your sister is a brilliant if young agent and that Mark...
Mark is the best."

"I'm grateful."

"Yeah. I'll be glad to have their help. Unofficially, of course."

"Unofficially." Megan smiled. They stood close together.
Too close. She found herself remembering their bizarre night
together, how they'd sparred from the time they'd met...and
then carried that sparring into his room...and found that passion could lead to...passion.

But it just couldn't be. And she needed to move. Because
he was tall and strong and reassuring, built like granite, and...

"Wow, I'm exhausted," she muttered. It wasn't a lie.

"Long, long day," Ragnar said. "I'm exhausted, too."

"Right. Well, Hugo and I are off to bed," Megan said.

"Yep. Good night." Ragnar turned and disappeared into the
second bedroom.

She watched him go, bizarrely thinking she even liked him
from the back.

Megan called to Hugo, went into her room, and closed her
own door. Long day was right. She turned off the lights and
fell on the bed—clothes and all.

She needed to get up. She could really use a shower since it
had been such a long day. But lying there she realized she really, truly, hadn't lied—she was exhausted.

She could shower in the morning.

She was too tired to care about undressing, too tired to get
up and move or to do anything.

The darkness in the room seemed to encompass her; and it
was a comforting, sweet feeling.

At first.

She felt as if she were walking. No, running. It was as if the darkness slowly changed into something that wasn't quite stygian anymore. There was moonlight, slipping down in vague patterns, dancing on the heavy branches of numerous trees. There was a strange little sign in the middle of a path, shaped like an arrow. She was running too fast to read it, and she just saw letters swimming before her eyes, *M, N, H, S, D*…an arrow on the arrow. She was past it so quickly. There were paths here, but she was weaving through the trees, and she could smell the forest and the earth. And she could hear someone calling. Calling her?

Where was the voice coming from?

She held still, afraid and not sure why.

She didn't know the reason she was in the woods. But she could feel the cool air and the pine cones beneath her feet.

And she suddenly realized she was breathing heavily, because she was running, but she was running because she was trying to escape. Running, running…

Then it was too late.

She slammed into something.

No.

Not a something.

A *someone.*

A dark cloth or hood was slipped over her head. Something that blinded her, closing off the thin wispy moonlight that had come through the trees. The something was a rough material, burlap, perhaps, old and musty. It was something that smelled like…

Death.

She screamed, choking and garbling on the sound.

And she fought. She fought hard. Kicking, screaming, biting…

But she was held in a vise by this person who swore before

slamming her hard so her head seemed to spin. It had been the person calling to her, a person who had known the woods far better than she did.

Her head was ringing, and he quit swearing. He laughed and laughed then.

And as he held her, he spoke in a terrible nightmare whisper.

"You just had to know what happened to Carole? Well, now you will!"

CHAPTER SEVEN

Megan finally began to calm down in Ragnar's gentle hold. He wasn't sure if she wakened naturally or if she heard his soothing tones.

He sat on the bed, having pulled her into his arms as she flailed so violently she almost went off the bed and onto the floor.

He just kept assuring her she was all right; she was with him at the safe house; no one had her.

He thought about the way she had held her own when they had discovered her in one of the hideouts in the woods—having been mistakenly kidnapped in lieu of her sister. She had held her own with remarkable fortitude. Yes, she'd passed out after and fallen into his arms, but even though they'd been a bit at odds at the time, he'd admired her ability to put her thought processes before her fear. For a civilian—someone never trained for any such situation—she had shown amazing courage.

But now...

Something about this was different.

Hugo seemed to know. He was on the bed. Ragnar hadn't had the heart to shove him off, then the dog leaned against Ragnar as well.

Megan's eyes suddenly flew open. She saw him. And the whole of her eased against him; the fight left her. She was trembling and holding him in return.

Hugo whined. Megan set a hand on him, telling him, "It's all right, boy."

"Do you keep remembering the cottage?" he asked gently.

"No, no, this was different."

"Different?" Ragnar asked.

"I am so sorry!" She seemed to regain something of herself; and though she didn't push away from him, she seemed to straighten in his arms. "It was just a nightmare, I guess. But not about the past. I guess I'm too focused on the victims of these guys. I dreamed I was running through the woods. I was trying to escape. Running so hard I slammed into someone, and that someone threw something over my head. It was as if I could breathe in death and decomposition and…oh, I am sorry! I don't mean to keep waking you up!"

"No. I'm sorry," he said quietly. "You shouldn't be in this position. You are remarkably gifted—or cursed, as we can't help but feel at times. But you are not in law enforcement, and you shouldn't have to endure all this. I'd insist you go home and forget all about it, except—"

"Except someone sent me a human skull that had been buried for a long time, and I'm definitely a target. The only way I'm going to survive is if we get to the bottom of all this," she said flatly. "Except there may be no bottom."

"There is," he told her. She looked at him skeptically and he said, "There will always be killers and serial killers out there.

But this is a strange group. They communicate somehow, but they're damned good at their brotherhood or whatever and at keeping those communications secret. They all want to one-up each other, and some started years ago while some—who show just the right tendencies—come in as we go along. We need to find each and every one of these sorry bastards who ever hurt a woman. And when that is done…"

"I can go back to dealing with horrifying bug monsters in space," Megan said, a slight smile on her lips.

"And then you can go back to outer space bug monsters," he agreed. "Or…"

He fell silent. Maybe she didn't want to remember she was writing a book about her experience at the hands of sadistic killers.

"Yeah, yeah, writing my book," she muttered. "Except we don't know the ending." She let out a soft sigh. He released his hold on her, and she straightened, easing from his side apologetically. "Okay, well, I'm truly sorry about passing out on you and waking you again and again…after trying to be so independent and capable! I don't know what's going on. I never used to have these nightmares all the time. I guess it's just these guys take their victims into the woods—different woods in different states. And I have visions of more and more forests and wooded areas dancing around in my mind. And poor Hugo! I must be scaring him."

"This dog is loyal to a fault and loves you, but he's okay. He's resilient," Ragnar assured her. He grinned. "And I'm resilient, too. Stopping these guys is something I'm determined to do. I probably don't have nightmares because…"

"Too much of the real thing?" she asked.

"Yes, it's a lot. But when we are able to do something that saves lives, it's all worth it."

She looked at him and nodded gravely, giving him a weak smile. "I understand," she told him. "You face the horrible, but you do get to save lives. I just wish—"

"Don't start. You probably helped to save several lives."

She cast her head to the side with a shrug. "I wish I could do something more."

He needed to move. He was touching her. It was too easy to remember when he had touched her before and how it had seemed so amazing and right...

And then he remembered how awkward they had been after, determined to walk away, to both accept the fact it had been simple biology that had brought them together when they shouldn't have been together.

He was breathing in the subtle scent of her hair, her skin. Memories came flooding into his mind and his body. She moved with incredible grace and vibrancy; the feel of her against him had been a swiftly building and explosive fire, and then...

The jumping away. The shock at herself for what she had done. The dismay, the agreement they'd forget it because he was Mark's best friend, and she was Colleen's sister.

At the moment, he couldn't forget anything.

And it was all so much worse because now...

He liked her. He understood her. And he could feel her against his flesh. He'd slipped into jeans before rushing into her room when he'd heard her tossing and screaming, but he hadn't grabbed a shirt. And her touching him. And being so close...

He wanted her.

He eased himself away, standing.

There could be no awkwardness here. No regrets. And he

sure as hell couldn't allow Megan to think she needed to be far away from him. He had to be here; they had to work on this until they discovered just how deeply the killer association went, until they rounded up the individuals who wanted in on the bizarre murder clique.

"Are you okay now?" he asked, rubbing Hugo's ears, doing his very best to be both concerned and casual. "The pup is next to you. I'm a shout away at all times."

"Yes, I'm fine, just sorry!"

"Try to get another hour's sleep or rest at least."

She smiled dryly. "And a shower. I fell on the bed and I was out last night."

"I can see that."

She was still wearing the navy dress she'd had on the day before, a soft knit that had been the right combination of not-too-dressy but nice and...

Whatever. It was crawling up her thigh.

He had to get the hell out.

"If you need me," he muttered, pausing in the doorway, looking her way, and then stepping out and closing her door.

He had barely gotten back to his own room when he heard his phone ringing. He frowned; it was barely six in the morning, and he didn't recognize the number.

"Johansen," he said, answering the call.

"Ragnar?" a female voice queried.

"Yes, it's me."

"This is Jean. I... I don't know what to do. And I don't know if I should do anything. But Grace isn't answering her phone. We don't keep phone plans...just buy time on new phones every so often, but we always have each other's numbers. I've been calling Grace, just to make sure she was all right. I mean, there

are times when we're out all night. You know, when a guy is—
never mind. But when we're going to be out with something
good going on, we always let each other know. Grace went
out last night after you left, and she didn't come back. And I'm
scared, so scared!"

"All right, Jean," Ragnar said, his tone as assuring as he could
make it. Coincidence Grace should suddenly disappear? No one
knew they had talked to Grace and the girls…

Not true. Someone might have seen them in the coffee shop.

He continued, telling Jean, "We'll hope she just ran out of
battery or lost her phone, and she's fine and heading home after
what was a…profitable night. But I'll head out now and see if
we can find anyone who knows what happened. Stay calm; I'll
get going. I'll need to know what she was wearing when she
left the apartment."

"A black skirt and a red blouse, kind of puffy, the kind that
ties at the belly button. Her hair was down, and she was carrying her little brown bag."

"Got it, and we'll start a search."

"She could have gone with anyone, in any car, and she went
out at night. I know how early it is, and no one will be there
to ask and…"

"I'm on it. Jean, you and Penny stay in, you understand?"

"You bet!"

He ended the call and walked back into Megan's room. He
heard the shower running.

*Had her strange dream meant anything? They had agents who could
enter the minds of others, see what they saw, experience what they had
experienced. It wasn't something that could be done on command, but
rather something that just happened.*

It was six a.m., but Angela and Jackson would be up getting

their kids ready for the day. And if they weren't, they wouldn't mind the call anyway.

Jackson answered right away; Ragnar told him about Jean's call. He could hear Angela in the background, telling Jackson there was a bank across the street from Grace's corner. They could cull video surveillance from them and perhaps other establishments.

She must have heard him when he mentioned how early it was.

"Oh, Ragnar, I do work in mysterious ways! Besides, security is usually in early," Angela said, taking the phone from Jackson.

"Thank you."

"And I'm not saying this, but call Mark and Colleen. They can search some of the areas we know with Red."

"Right!" Ragnar said.

The shower had stopped. He tapped on the door; now was not the time to see Megan walk out in a towel...or nothing.

"Megan, Grace didn't get home last night. We need to head out right away."

"Oh, no!" she cried.

"We'll find her," he said, and he realized the assurance in his voice was forced. "I'm calling Mark and Colleen. Unofficially."

He returned to his own room for his clothes, weapon, and shoes, calling Mark as he dressed to ask if they'd discovered anything at all the night before.

He could hear Colleen in the background worrying about Megan. Mark told him that they hadn't seen Grace, nor had they managed to gather anything new.

"Thank you. And tell Colleen that moving forward, Megan will be with me. I won't leave her for a second," he promised.

He went out into the hall. Megan was there, Hugo obediently at her side. She was dressed in jeans and a long-sleeved knit shirt, as if she knew they might be heading out to rough terrain.

"Where are we going? What do we do?" she asked anxiously.

He hesitated, wondering just what to say to her.

"I believe you and Grace formed a connection yesterday," he said.

"I like Grace and I'm worried sick about her. And she was totally honest about everything she said to us. She's funny, and sincere. I—"

"Let's get to the car. We're going to go to the corner where she works. Then I need you to use your instincts."

"My instincts?"

"Maybe tell me about your nightmare." He was out the door, punching in the alarm code, even as he spoke. They headed to the car, Hugo following along quickly as if he knew they were on a mission.

"It was brought on by...the power of suggestion, I believe," she told him. "I was in the woods, running to escape. Then I ran into whoever it was I was trying to escape from, I think. I remember something like burlap going over my head."

"Okay, were there a few trees like in a park?"

"Oh, no. The path I was running along was heavily forested. There were paths, yes, but there were trees and undergrowth and..."

She paused.

"What?"

"There was a sign on the road. Not the road, the path."

"What kind of a sign?" he asked.

"White—with just a little arrow."

"What did it say?" he asked.

He was heading toward what he was thinking of in his mind

as "Grace's corner" when his phone rang. He glanced at it, surprised to see it was Angela calling back already.

It couldn't have been more than thirty minutes since he'd
called her.

He put the call on speaker.

"We got something," she told him. "On video—"

"You got video already?"

"I told you—I'm magic. Okay, not really. I called in a favor.
Anyway, one of the bank managers was in already, and I have
the video. It catches that corner perfectly. By the way, I plan
to go back and see if we can get anything on Carole Berlin.
It wasn't pulled when she disappeared because she wasn't an
official missing person until—until she was a murder victim.
Sometimes, the system sucks. Anyway, Grace went with a man
in a dark crimson sports car—we even have a fuzzy image of
his face. We have tech working on it now. If Vice ever brought
him in—or if he was arrested for any reason—we may be able
to discover who her last john was. I'll be back with you."

"Thanks."

He looked at Megan, who was watching him worriedly.

"They've got a lead. That's good," he told her. "But back to
your dream. Do you remember what the sign said?"

"I didn't really have time to read it. But it was white—a little
weathered. It was in the woods, of course."

"Along a path? Pointing to a path?"

She shook her head. "I was running too fast. I think away
from where the sign was."

He suddenly pulled off the road, causing her to stare at him
as if he had entirely lost his mind.

"I'm going to have you close your eyes and try to remember," he told her.

She studied him, her eyes green pools of confusion. "Can it matter? I was having a nightmare, and I think it was brought on by all that I know. Maybe I was seeing the woods by the cabin from before through a sensory memory—"

"Please. Humor me!" he said quietly.

She let out a breath. "Okay. What do you want me to do?"

"Just lean your head back and close your eyes."

"Okay."

"You're running and running. You're afraid."

"I think I've escaped from someone or something. In fact—"

"What?"

"I can hear someone calling me. Or I think they were calling me. The voice was indistinct. I don't know what it was saying. But I knew I was running from the voice."

"Okay, that's good. And then?"

"I noted it wasn't just a park, or anything with just a few trees. I was in the woods—the deep woods. But there were paths through the trees. Not for cars but there were walking paths."

"Good. Deep woods. And the sign?"

"Letters. I remember letters."

"What letters?"

She kept her eyes closed, but she scrunched her face, in deep thought.

"*M... N... H... S... D,*" she muttered. "Oh! The *M* was a capital, and the *N* was a capital, and so was the *H*. There were other letters, lower case. And there was an arrow, so I believe that it was pointing toward something—a point of interest, I guess. For hikers." She opened her eyes, frowning. "Can this mean anything?"

He leaned over and pulled a small notebook from the glove compartment.

"*M… N… H… S… D,*" he repeated, writing the letters down. "*M* and *N* are capitalized?"

"And *H.*"

"How many between them?" he asked.

"The *M* and the *N* were close…a space before the *H.*"

He smiled at her. "See? You remember a lot!"

"But can it mean anything?"

"I think it can," he said. He kept playing with the letters, keeping them in the order she had given him, trying to decide what might come between.

And then he knew.

"McNamara Homestead," he said.

"What?"

He showed her what he had written.

"What is it?" she asked.

"The place is a ruin, but hikers like to make a trip to and from it from any number of starting points. The area is beautiful; a little brook wanders by the back of the shell of the old house. A family named McNamara had a home there years and years ago. It was probably abandoned around 1900. But it's still a place that is popular with hikers. And depending on what trail you take, it's a great hike for beginners. Just west of 'Grace's corner,'" he said.

"Grace's corner?" she asked dryly. "So—"

"We're going to the McNamara Trail," he told her.

"But, Ragnar, wasn't it just a nightmare?"

He turned to her, his arm on the back of the seat, and told her, "Megan, McNamara's Trail is nowhere near the cabin by Harpers Ferry where you were taken. You couldn't possibly remember anything about it."

"Maybe I saw it in a book?"

"You've been reading a lot of picture books about DC hiking trails recently?" he asked.

Megan sighed.

Hugo woofed.

Ragnar got back on the road and turned his attention to driving.

"Ragnar, I'm willing to try anything. I told you, I really liked Grace. I want to see her alive and well. And I want a good life for her. But from what you're telling me, the McNamara Homestead is just a shell and people go there frequently. Or frequently enough for a hike in the woods. How could anyone have used it as a staging ground for murder?"

"There might well be something near it."

She looked ahead as he drove.

"I guess… I know my great-uncle used to have a cabin in the Everglades. They were popular years and years ago, before they became against the park rules, or the state's dictates, or whatever. It used to be a 'guy' thing from what I've heard, and my mom told me it was just because women usually prefer real toilets and running water. I'm just saying anything right now, really, I think. Could it be?" she asked.

"It could."

He had his phone out and he quickly dialed Angela.

"I was about to call you," she told him.

"Oh?"

"First, what do you need?" Angela asked him.

"Please pull up anything you have on the old McNamara Trail. See if you can find hunting cabins or lodges or any kind of structure in the area."

"Got it. You think you have something?"

"Maybe. We're going to give it a try. What do you have?"

"Well, we're still working it, but we think we have the man who was last seen with Grace. He's twenty-five and his name is Joel Letterman. He was picked up three years ago on a date-rape charge, but it fell apart because the woman decided to drop the charges."

"What do we know about him?"

"He works construction, most recently for a company called Treetops Unlimited. Jackson is alerting law enforcement around the area. Of course, unless we make a definitive match, we can't do anything but question him."

"I'm going to hope we find him first," Ragnar said. "I'm calling Mark and Colleen to help. Grace is out here somewhere."

"There are almost seventy-thousand acres of state-run forests in Virginia," Angela warned.

"I think we're close," Ragnar said. "I don't believe this man will go that far from the area. He doesn't need to. What he needs is just west of the cities."

"I'll be back with what I can learn. Keep an eye out. I'll get you visuals as soon as I can."

They ended the call. Megan was looking at him; she'd heard what Angela had said.

"Seventy-thousand acres?"

"It's a big state," Ragnar said. "With a lot of forest, yes, but I know where I'm heading."

He put a call through to Mark and Colleen and discovered they were due south of Manassas. They were going to head toward him.

He found one of the trails off 66, close to the little sign that advertised McNamara Homestead to those hiking the area. If he was right—if Megan had made a strange connection with Grace—getting to the sign might be what she needed.

"Well," Megan muttered as he parked and indicated the walking path, "at least Hugo will be happy. He loves a walk in the woods."

"Stay close to me," he told her.

He watched her as they walked along.

Hugo ran ahead, sniffing, wagging his tail.

Ragnar knew the area well; he and Mark had hiked many of these trails. But they hadn't come across a cabin or shack, nor had Red led them to anything in the vicinity.

But that was a distinction of the strange brotherhood, really. Each kidnapper/killer was responsible for his victims, his "tools," and his place.

"Strange, isn't it? I remember smelling things in the dream. The earth and how rich it can smell in a deep forest," Megan said. "The air and how fresh it can be and cool especially at night."

"Sensory perceptions, perhaps shared," Ragnar said.

"What?" Megan demanded.

He shrugged and was saved from answering her.

They had reached the little white sign that was shaped as an arrow and pointed toward the McNamara Homestead.

Megan stopped dead, staring.

"Is that the sign?" he asked her.

She nodded, slowly turning to him in disbelief.

"That is it. But where do we go now? And this isn't possible!"

"Neither is speaking to the dead," he said softly.

She shook her head. "I didn't want this! I'm an English major, for Pete's sake!"

She stopped and took a breath, tossing her hair back and straightening. "What I want doesn't matter. Grace is out here.

And she desperately tried to escape from a human monster. What do we do now? How do we find her?"

"I don't think we have to. I think Hugo is already on her trail," he said, pointing to the dog. Hugo was sniffing the ground near the sign.

"Which way were you running?" Ragnar asked.

"This way—coming from somewhere in the trees, one of the paths there, away from the sign...but..."

"That one!" Ragnar said.

Hugo had chosen a trail. He was sniffing and moving faster and faster. The dog had always had the right natural instincts, but Patrick's suggestion that Megan have him trained was paying off now.

"Stay close to me! Behind me!" Ragnar told Megan.

The dog could run. And he didn't mind being whipped in the face by the tree branches. But Ragnar had no intention of stopping him, and he could feel Megan right behind him.

The paths here were curving and old, and Ragnar knew some of them had been there long before Virginia had been a colony, originating with the Algonquin.

"Hugo!" he cried to dog, stopping the animal.

They had come upon an area that couldn't quite be described as a clearing. But the thickness of the trees ended, and a broken path led up to a cabin. Ragnar held Megan back from leaving the cover of the trees.

Ragnar estimated the cabin had been erected maybe a hundred years ago. It was simple, a square building covered by the branches of oaks and willows and pines.

Hugo whined, moving around as if he would ignore Ragnar, but Megan stepped around him and said, "Hugo, sit. Wait."

The animal obeyed instantly, but he remained disturbed, whining and pawing the ground.

"Grace gave him turkey," Megan said. "And he has an instinct for people. She's in there, Ragnar, what do we do?"

The sun was hitting the tops of the trees. Grace had now been with her abductor for a long time, since the late hours of the previous evening. But maybe he'd had to move on for the night; maybe she was alone.

Maybe she was already dead and buried, or buried and...

Dying.

He shouldn't have had Megan with him. Except he wouldn't have found this without her.

He turned to her, taking her by the shoulders.

"I'm going to go around. I need you to stay here, with Hugo. He will obey you, right?"

"Of course. But—"

"Stay here, right here. I'm going to look for a window or a back entrance. Hunker down here in the bushes, invisible. Don't move unless I come back for you."

She looked at him, swallowed, and nodded. "Ragnar, do you think she might be in there alive?"

He started to answer that yes, he did. But just as he was about to speak, they saw a man enter the almost-clearing from a different path, one leading more to the northeast. He was young with dark hair. He was the man Jean had described to Ragnar earlier that morning.

He was carrying a shovel and whistling as he walked.

"He just buried her!" Megan whispered. "Oh, my God! She could be—"

"Alive," Ragnar said determinedly. "Stay here, please!"

He stepped out of the brush, smoothly drawing his gun to aim at the young man with the shovel.

"FBI. Stop where you are!"

Stunned, the man—Joel Letterman, if the educated determination at headquarters had been right—dropped the shovel. He looked at Ragnar as if amazed anyone had found him in the density of the forest.

"Hey, uh, sure. What do you want?"

"What were you burying?"

"What? What do you care? Some old trash."

"Show me. Now."

"Hey, come on. I know what I did was illegal. I didn't know the FBI was handing out fines for people burying garbage in the woods. I'll pay the fine. But…" Letterman lifted his shoulders and shrugged. "I don't even know where I was. These paths twist and turn all around."

"You will find the location," Ragnar told him.

"Buddy, I'm telling you, I can't. It weaves around forever out here. I mean, arrest me! Do what you want, but I don't know where I was." He planted his hands on his hips, and Ragnar wondered if he had a gun shoved behind his back in his belt.

"Hands up!" he ordered.

Letterman was going to do it. Go for a gun. And Ragnar could shoot him, but—

"Ragnar!" Megan shouted, bursting out of the brush—behind Hugo.

But Hugo didn't just run. He appeared to fly, landing on the man with ninety pounds of pure muscle, his teeth barred. Letterman screamed as Hugo growled.

Ragnar reached Letterman on the ground with Megan just

behind him. She caught Hugo by his collar, drawing him away as Ragnar rolled the man over to cuff him.

As he'd suspected, there was a small Beretta stuffed into Letterman's waistband.

"Police brutality!" Letterman raged.

"Can't be," Ragnar assured him. "I'm not a cop."

He dragged Letterman to his feet. "Where is she?" he demanded.

"She who?"

"The woman you abducted last night."

"Ah, come on! I paid her, she did her thing, and I dropped her back on the corner."

"No, no, you didn't. Video doesn't lie."

"Video?"

"The bank across the street has a long reach," Ragnar said.

"Well, I don't know what you saw, but I dropped the whore right back where I found her. And there is nothing, absolutely nothing, you can do that can prove otherwise!" Letterman said. "Take me in—I'll call my attorney. I'll be out in thirty minutes, and I may just sue the federal government!"

"Ragnar," Megan said.

He turned to look at her. So did Letterman.

"Wow. At least I'll be dragged into wherever with a damned fine-looking woman!" Letterman said, his confidence complete.

Megan ignored him, not even glancing his way.

"We don't need him. We have Hugo," Megan said.

The dog was already sniffing the ground and heading in the direction from which Letterman had come.

Gripping the man by the arm and dragging him along—grateful for his own size and hours at the gym, since the bastard was fighting him all the way—he dipped down to retrieve the man's shovel and then followed Megan and the dog.

They walked what had to have been the distance of a football field, twisting along forest paths that were barely discernable here.

Then Hugo stopped.

It couldn't even be called an almost-clearing. It was just a spot that was empty of trees and brush. And it was evident the ground had recently been disrupted.

"Grace!" Megan cried, falling to the ground and starting to dig with her hands.

"Watch out," Ragnar said, leaving Letterman cuffed and standing by a tree. He hit the ground with the shovel and began digging as quickly as he could.

Letterman must have decided he was caught. He started to laugh, sounding more crazed than confident.

"I told you I buried the garbage!" he shouted.

They ignored him.

Luckily, he had been lazy, and hadn't dug deep.

Within seconds Ragnar hit raw pine boards.

A rude coffin just a handful of inches under the earth.

Letterman swore, working furiously at his cuffs. He turned, ready to take off into the trees.

It was a bad move. He should have known better, having encountered the dog once already.

Hugo growled and downed him—slamming him into a huge old oak in the process. Megan caught hold of the dog before he could bite down on the man's throat. Megan praised Hugo, telling him he had done a good job, but he was done.

Ragnar barely heard Letterman's groans. He was working desperately at the earth, falling to his knees to work at the pine, using the shovel as a lever. Megan fell to his side, using her hands and working the earth around the coffin to allow him greater access. He nearly broke the shovel, cracking it as he removed the lid of the coffin.

And there lay Grace.

CHAPTER EIGHT

Megan feared the worst. Grace was covered in dirt. Her coffin had not been well made; and though she hadn't been buried long, her face was dusted with earth. Her eyes were closed, her fingertips were bleeding, and her nails were broken. She had clearly fought at first, clawing against the coffin lid.

"No, no, no!" Megan cried. They had found her so quickly.

Ragnar was drawing her from the cheap and poorly constructed box, feeling quickly for a pulse, and laying Grace out on the ground.

"Wow, she went fast!" Letterman cried with delight.

Megan rose and stared at him, knowing Ragnar was doing everything he could.

"Shut the hell up! I'm not the law, and if you speak again, I'll let my dog sink his teeth into your throat."

"She's alive," Ragnar said.

"What? Oh, thank God!"

Megan fell on her knees next to him again, watching as Ragnar adjusted Grace in his arms, allowing her to suck in air on her own.

Then everything seemed to happen at once.

Mark's dog, Red, burst through the trees with Mark and Colleen moments behind him. They were quickly followed by paramedics, weaving their way more cautiously through the brush and trees.

Colleen paused, staring at Megan, making sure her sister was okay. Then she asked, "Are you…?"

"I'm fine. And Grace is breathing!"

Ragnar handed the woman's care over to the paramedics, dusting himself off as he stood. As she was laid out on the gurney, Grace opened her eyes.

She looked around, and then her gaze fell on Megan. Tears welled in her eyes and ran down her cheeks, creating mud on them.

"Oh, my God! You found me. I'm alive!" She was reaching out as she spoke. Megan glanced at the paramedic, who nodded, and she knew Grace was really going to be okay. And it was okay for her to talk to her for a minute while they were setting up portable oxygen.

She took Grace's hand and squeezed it. "We found you," she said, smoothing back the woman's hair from the tangle on her forehead. "Hugo found you—probably because you gave him turkey!" she said, trying to speak lightly.

Grace managed a smile before closing her eyes and leaning back for the paramedic to set up her oxygen. "I'm not sure I need—" she began, but she fell back.

"Take it," Megan commanded.

"And get her into the hospital quickly," Mark said. The paramedics carefully lifted her and walked through the narrow earth path to bring Grace to their waiting ambulance.

Mark looked at Ragnar and grimaced. "We got here as quickly as we could. Looks like you two were doing fine. What can we do now?"

"Take him in," Ragnar said, indicating Joel Letterman.

Letterman was lying silent now where he had fallen.

"Well, we're not officially on this case, but—"

"I can't have him near Megan," Ragnar said.

"Right!" Colleen said, tossing back a lock of red hair. "I don't want these monsters near my sister."

"I think *he's* in more danger from your sister right now," Ragnar said, looking at Megan and smiling.

He was admiring her! she thought. And looking back at him, she felt she had a sudden and deep understanding of why he was able to do this work.

Moments like this.

They had stopped a monster.

They had saved a life. And it felt good.

"We're not official," Mark reminded him.

"But I am."

They looked to the forest trail; Jackson Crow had arrived.

Megan had admired Jackson from the time she had first met him; she'd been grateful her sister worked under the direction of such a man. But while his look was solid and impressive, it was what she had learned about the man that was so impressive. He never asked anyone to do anything he wasn't willing to do himself, down to the most tedious or dangerous detail. He and Angela—despite having two children—answered their phones at any hour of the night.

"In this case," he told Mark and Colleen, "it would have been fine for you to bring this man in. Megan, you know how it goes. Colleen is now too close to the case to work it, but when it comes down to the line, an agent is an agent. But that said… I have a forensic crew on the way to tear apart the cabin. I believe the two of you will want to see your friend is fine at the hospital. By then, we'll have this man waiting for you. I know you'll want to speak with him yourself, Ragnar."

"Oh, I will," Ragnar agreed.

Jackson walked over to Joel Letterman, drawing him to his feet.

"It was a joke," Letterman said then. "It was just play. She's a whore, for God's sake. I was paying her to pretend to be dead. These guys interrupted me thinking it was something real. And I intend to sue! That dog nearly ripped me to shreds!"

"Tell the judge all about it," Jackson said. "You're under arrest for the attempted murder of Grace Menendez."

"I told you—I wasn't trying to kill her. We were just playing a sex game. Oh, I'm sure she'll say something else now—she's trash! She'll make money off anything. She'll glory in the attention she'll receive if she accuses me of trying to kill her."

Ragnar had been looking at his phone. He had probably been about to call Jean and Penny to tell them Grace had been found alive.

But he smiled suddenly and hit a key on his phone.

They heard Letterman's recorded voice distinctly.

"I told you, I took out the garbage!" And then, "Wow, she went fast!"

"Fooling around, just fooling around! And that's out of context. It will never be any good in court. I will get a lawyer. I will sue all your asses and do it so well you'll be sitting in jail! And then you'll get shanked and you—'"

Jackson was already leading him out, but he jerked to turn around and stare at Megan.

"And you—you bitch! You won't get a shank, but you will get all that's special coming your way!"

Ragnar tensed and started to move forward. Megan caught his arm.

"Keep talking," Jackson said flatly to Letterman. "You're now digging your own grave, as they say."

Something about Jackson's warning must have gotten through to Letterman. They heard nothing more but the sound of the branches rustling as the two moved on through them.

"No reason to hang around here," Ragnar said. He looked at Megan. "You want to go to the hospital to make sure Grace is all right?"

"I do, and thank you," Megan said.

"Want to take a look at the cabin first?"

"Absolutely," Meggan said.

"Unofficially," Colleen agreed.

Hugo and Red barked at the same time, as if in total agreement with their humans and themselves.

"Well, I guess that covers it," Mark said.

"Lead the way," Ragnar told him.

They traipsed back through the woods. The first members of the forensic team were just coming through from the back road where they'd had to park their vehicles. The agents and the team members obviously knew each other, and their crew was greeted warmly.

Everyone seemed both serious and up at the same time.

They'd found a woman alive.

And that made for a good day.

Colleen proudly introduced Megan as her sister, and she was greeted warmly as well.

One woman yelled to Mark, Ragnar, and Colleen.

"Don't you go messing up the crime scene!"

"Won't touch a thing!" Mark promised.

"Gloves!" she called.

"Of course," Ragnar said.

Megan followed the others into the cabin. It was small. There was a back door and one window that was open to the elements. No panes of any kind sat in the old frames.

The cabin had one bunk big enough for one person, a broken-down dresser, and little else. But there was a black bag sitting on the dresser. Pulling gloves from his pocket, Ragnar put them on and pried open the bag.

"Something in a bottle—some kind of sedative, maybe," Ragnar said. "Rope—but I don't think he ever bound her. There were no marks on her wrists or ankles. And she only struggled briefly before passing out in the coffin, so… I'm thinking sedative."

"No book or phone?" Colleen asked. "Anything to indicate his buddies?"

"His phone is probably on him," Ragnar said. He looked around.

It was a poor cabin, filthy, with everything broken. There was no sheet on the bunk. The old mattress was stained and ripped.

"He knocked her out before they got here," Megan said. "No one would accept this as a place for a tryst, even a paid-for tryst."

"Girls have worked in alleys," Mark commented.

"I believe he knocked her out," Megan said.

"Did you sense something?" Colleen asked her.

Megan shook her head. "No. I just believe he got her in the

car, knocked her out, and brought her here. He held her here for hours before he buried her. She disappeared last night, and Angela found video that showed him picking Grace up off the street."

"How did you find her?" Colleen asked, curious.

"Ragnar found her," Megan said.

He looked at her and frowned, but he seemed to sense she didn't want to talk about her dreams or nightmares. He was probably surprised, knowing how close she was with her siblings. She was surprised herself. It was just that right now she didn't want Colleen worrying about her.

"The dog, logistics, strange luck," Ragnar muttered. "Very strange luck. Anyway, sadly, he didn't just leave us a book with the names and numbers of his friends and co-killers. Let's leave the place to forensics. There may be prints or something."

They headed out again, saying goodbye to the forensic team. They walked the path together until they reached the cars.

"I wonder if we should still go to that corner," Colleen said to Mark. "As it stands," she said, looking at Ragnar and Mark, "this guy hasn't had a chance to broadcast his achievement to whoever else is out there." She hesitated and shrugged. "And while he might have been the one who took Carole, he is young."

"And for someone supposedly in construction, he built the worst coffin I've ever seen," Ragnar commented. He shook his head. "I am really afraid we have to get to the heart of this quickly. Men like Rory Ayers and Jim Carver groom apprentices."

"How on earth do you advertise for an apprentice to commit murder?" Megan asked, disturbed.

"The dark web," Colleen said. "Cybercrime is huge at the Bureau. They can get a site closed down and another one will pop up. There are ways to route addresses through cities all over the world and make it a nightmare to shut them down."

"Is your team looking into it?" Megan asked.

"Yes. They've shut down some other sites along the way," Ragnar said. "But they don't believe they've found what we're looking for. Anyway, we're going to get to the hospital and check on Grace, and ensure she's guarded. Though I know Jackson is going to have made sure of that. But maybe she can tell us something."

Megan frowned. "We—we caught him. What can she tell us?"

Ragnar glanced over at Colleen and then said, "If he planned on killing her, he might have been trying to contact someone else. To brag or to ask for suggestions…he may have even said something that could lead us to someone else."

"Oh," she muttered. "This guy was an apprentice. She might have been…"

"His first," Colleen said. "Okay, Mark and I will go back to plan A and see if we can glean anything from any of the other girls on the street." She hesitated. "Tonight, we'll take Red and go over to watch Jean and Penny if they want someone there. If the hospital decides to keep Grace overnight, which they probably will considering her ordeal, they'll have protection on her there. But even between agencies, protection may not stretch out to Grace's roommates."

"I know Jean and Penny would be incredibly grateful!" Megan said.

Colleen nodded, smiling grimly. "Okay, so split. Wait. Not yet. Ragnar, you had Megan with you. But she's only here as a consultant. She's not trained, and there was no reason for you to bring her along, and I'm worried—"

"Colleen!" Megan snapped. "I helped on this. And no, I can't shoot like you can, but Ragnar is going to take me to the range. I just might be better at it, considering the fact I got you most of the time with our water pistols when we were kids! I'm an adult, too. Ragnar didn't drag me anywhere. I make my own choices."

Colleen backed up, smiling. "Hey! Tigress showing her claws."

"I didn't choose this; it chose me," Megan said.

"And it was my fault," Colleen whispered.

Megan shook her head. "It's not your fault. And I had a good day—a really good day. I got to help save a woman's life. Don't take that from me!"

"I'm sorry! I just—"

Megan hurried forward and hugged her sister tightly. When she pulled away, she told her, "Colleen, maybe we're right where we're supposed to be when we're supposed to be there. None of this is your fault. You spend your days caring and doing good for the world. Well, I'm in your world right now, but I'm here because I want to be. I understand you all so well now. So! Be happy for me today, and don't worry."

Hugo woofed to accentuate her words.

That made Red let out a woof, too.

"Amazing. Two alpha males, and they don't fight with each other," Mark said.

That made Colleen laugh and look at Megan. "Yeah—" She turned to Mark and Ragnar. "Two alpha males and they don't fight with each other; in fact, they have a great partnership."

Megan laughed, too.

Mark groaned and headed for his car.

"Everyone! Just be careful!" he ordered.

Ragnar turned to his vehicle, opening the door for Hugo. The dog paused, looking at him reproachfully.

"He listens better to you," he told Megan.

"He just wants to know why he doesn't get to race around more with Red," Megan said. "In the car, Hugo. We have to visit a friend."

Hugo jumped into the back seat. Megan shrugged and got into the front passenger's seat. Mark and Colleen were driving out on the dirt and gravel road. Starting the engine of his car, Ragnar turned to Megan before heading out.

"Okay, what was that all about? I thought you and Colleen were incredibly close. Why didn't we tell them about your dream?"

Megan shook her head. "Ragnar, you saw how worried she is, because I'm not trained to do any of this. And I'm probably not good at any of it—"

"Megan, we're different. But I did not save her life. You did. You have something special, and that saved Grace's life. But we should worry. You don't carry a weapon, and you're not trained for dangerous situations. But just because you don't carry a gun doesn't mean you're not just as good at anything the Krewe is known for being good at."

She smiled, lowering her head. "Thanks. That's nice of you to say. Anyway…"

"Yeah, let's go. Hospital and then headquarters."

They drove out. Megan turned to watch the woods as they left.

"You know the woods," she said.

He smiled. "My parents loved to do things as a family. We camped out a lot. Yes, I know these woods. But if you hadn't given me the clue of that arrow sign, we'd have been looking forever. And whatever Grace was given as a sedative, she wouldn't have lasted in that hole another hour, if that."

"We get to feel good," she said.

"We get to feel great," he told her.

When they reached the hospital, Megan put on Hugo's vest so he could join them.

Grace was doing well. She was, in fact, holding court. Penny and Jean had already arrived. Seeing Ragnar, Megan, and Hugo, they both rushed to shower them with hugs, including Hugo.

"We will never, ever be able to thank you enough!" Jean said, drawing back from her.

"Ever!" Penny echoed.

"I think about poor Carole, and how no one thought she was really missing," Jean said.

"It's really not just her," Ragnar told her. "It's any adult. People do often take off, and they're not required to tell others if they choose to leave."

"You're being very political!" Grace called from the bed. "Just admit it. You took Jean seriously when others might not have done so."

"We're just incredibly grateful we did find you," Ragnar said.

"You are a fabulous person, Grace, and it doesn't matter what you do," Megan told her.

"What I do? Hey, I'm going to be a writer. I know an editor. If I'm lucky, she'll help me write a book," Grace said.

"She will, I'm sure," Megan promised.

Ragnar grew serious. "Grace, we need help; we need answers."

Grace looked puzzled. "You—you caught him. Didn't you?"

"We caught him. But we think he might have been working with someone else."

"Oh!" Grace leaned back on her pillow, closing her eyes.

"Do you remember him saying anything, anything at all, that could lead to anyone else?"

She hesitated. "I don't know if I heard him when I was out of it…or if I imagined what I thought he was saying."

"Which was?"

Grace hesitated just a second, wincing, and then she spoke softly. "'I didn't do your friend, that other bitch, but I'm sure as hell going to do you—and better!'"

"So, the man who tried to kill you is an apprentice," Ragnar muttered, glancing at Megan. "Thank you, Grace. That's important to know."

"You think I really heard that right?" Grace asked.

"I do," Ragnar said. "Anyway, we're going to see what we can learn from him, and knowing a direction to go in can always be helpful. You feel better now."

"I don't think they're going to keep me. They're cleaning my system out of the drug he gave me. They x-rayed my lungs, but thankfully, I didn't inhale too much of the dirt. I'm doing good, amazingly. So, when I'm all clear, they're going to let me go home. I'm alive and almost really well. Thanks to the two of you. And Hugo!"

Hugo whined and came up to the bed. Megan had brought him to children's wards several times, and he was good. He knew not to jump on the bed, but he also knew kids loved it when he set his muzzle by them.

Those adults who loved dogs loved it, too. Megan had seen that an animal could be the best therapy in the world.

"I don't know why she wants to go home. It's so safe here!" Penny said.

"You'll all be safe at home. My sister and her husband—I

think Grace got to see them when they arrived in the woods—
are agents. They're going to stay at your place tonight. I don't
see these as people who break in, but safe is always good. Everything we know about these men suggests they look for op-
portunities. They don't want to fight anyone, they don't want
to be where the police may be called or where the police or
agents might even be close. But Colleen and Mark will stay at
the apartment."

"We have an extra room," Jean said. "And that will be great."

"Carole's room," Penny said quietly.

"We will find the man who took Carole," Megan vowed passionately. Then she winced inwardly, glancing over at Ragnar.

We?

She wasn't an agent. She wasn't law enforcement at all.

But she was involved now. Past what had happened to her and
past a human skull having been delivered to her at her office.

These men had to be stopped.

"Okay, we're going to move on. But we'll be seeing you,"
Ragnar promised.

Megan hugged each of the women and then followed Ragnar to the door with Hugo at her heels.

Ragnar turned back.

"Oh, besides Mark and Colleen, you're going to have one of
the best guards I know. His name is Red. Red is great, just like
Hugo. And he's got just about every certificate a dog can have,
and is a valued Krewe agent."

"Cool!" Grace said.

"We'll share our leftover turkey with him, too," Jean vowed.

Megan smiled, waved, and at last they were out the door. She
felt Ragnar watching her as they left.

"What?" she asked.

"You're smiling."

"I'm happy. Those are...good people."

Ragnar nodded but was silent.

"What?" she pressed.

"No. I agree. Those are good women. The streets can be hard. I've seen people who have become jaded from the streets. Those women haven't let the hardness of life or some of the people they might have come across change them from what they are inside."

They didn't speak again as they left the hospital and headed to the car.

Joel Letterman had been taken to Krewe headquarters, and Megan knew they were going there.

"There's a camera in the room where I'll be questioning him," Ragnar said as he drove. "I'll have you in Angela's office with her, and Jackson will be with me. I need you to listen closely to what he has to say, and tell me what he really means by what he says."

"I'm not..."

"Not?"

"Perfect," she said softly. "But I will try, and I'll tell you what I think."

"That's all I ask," he said.

Megan had been to the offices before. They were interesting. There were floors where there were tech teams, floors where there were forensics and science teams, and then floors where the agents had their offices.

"Are you thinking about your last visit?" he asked her.

"I was excited. I was about to meet an author I admire tremendously. I'm glad my instincts were right, and he didn't prove to be anything but a good guy and great author," Megan said.

"I'm glad, too," Ragnar said lightly. "Anyway, this will be different."

Ragnar brought Megan and Hugo straight to Angela's office. Angela was ready for her. She had a chair next to hers behind the desk where they could observe on her computer screen. Her desk was neat and clean, but it was also a desk that belonged to a woman who was dedicated to her family life as well. She and Jackson had an adopted son and a daughter who was now a toddler, and pictures of the little ones sat on both corners. Megan admired the kids when she came in, drawing an instant smile from Angela.

"I don't know about Victoria, but I do believe Corby will grow up to be an agent. He's an incredible kid. Victoria is, too. She hasn't had a chance yet to get into the world. I am, naturally, biased," Angela said. She greeted Hugo as well with an affectionate scratch on the neck.

"How could you and Jackson have anything but wonderful children?" Megan asked, smiling.

"Hmm, I've seen a couple of beautiful celebrities have unusual offspring," Ragnar teased.

Angela hit him in arm.

"But," he said quickly, "I know your children and they are terrific."

They all laughed and then sobered quickly. Angela gestured to the screens. "I'm ready in here. Did you want Jackson in with you or watching from here?"

"Ask him to come in with me," Ragnar said after a moment's thought. "He may come up with something I don't."

He nodded to the two of them and left. Angela made a quick call to Jackson's office. Megan saw Jackson as he passed Angela's office, going to the conference room.

"Okay, Megan. Ready?"

Megan nodded, taking the chair Angela indicated.

Angela's computer screen was already showing the conference room. The camera was directed on Joel Letterman.

He remained handcuffed. When Angela turned up the sound on the computer, she could hear him complaining, shouting angrily. "You wait! You wait until you hear from my attorney. You will be sued so far up the government's ass that you'll all be digging ditches the rest of your lives! This is cruel and inhumane punishment. I have been sitting here—"

"I apologize," Ragnar announced, coming into the room. "I do believe you've been sitting in this room even longer than Grace Menendez was locked in that coffin you buried her in. What, you can't get it up unless it's for a woman who is passed out or dead?"

"I get it up plenty when they're not passed out or dead!" Joel shouted, specks of foam forming at his mouth, his spit landing on the table.

"We'll need a hazmat team in there," Angela muttered dryly.

"But you prefer a woman passed out or dead?" Jackson, standing just to the left of Ragnar, asked.

"Wait, wait, wait! I told you. The bitch was a whore. I paid her. She was fine with drugs. She begged for drugs. She's a junkie, too. She told me it was great to see me because I am young. I had something! And she was willing to play that game. In fact, it was her idea to play the game. She wanted to be buried, and when I dug her up, she'd fall all over me because I was her rescuer. I'm telling you, she was all into it!"

"That's not what she says."

"She's a liar. Who are they going to believe in court?" he asked.

"I think they'll believe her," Ragnar said. "Because there have been women killed in such a manner—several women, including one of her roommates."

"I told you. I didn't do the roommate."

"Right. Because you're lousy at what you were trying to do. I'll bet the real Embracer would be ashamed at how you mangled such a simple thing."

"Bull! I keep telling you—"

Jackson looked at Ragnar. "He's no Embracer," Jackson said.

"Stop! I didn't mangle anything. I did everything just right!"

"I don't think so," Ragnar said, agreeing with Jackson. "I mean, he didn't get away with anything, and he dug the hole so shallow it took just about nothing to get her out. I'm sure you were told to dig the hole to bury the coffin deeper." He stared at Letterman, shaking his head.

"The hole I dug was just fine. The bitch was almost dead!" Letterman cried.

"So, you were trying to kill her," Jackson said.

"No! Wait! I wasn't. I—" He broke off, laughing. "We can deal with all this in court. You'll never know—you'll just never know."

"Well, we do know. Rory Ayers and Jim Carver were two of the teachers—originals. We know that."

"I don't know who you're talking about," Letterman said. "Rory Ayers...bigwig with some company somewhere. The other guy... Carver? Good name, huh?"

"Those are guys who really know how to kidnap, assault, and kill," Jackson said, shaking his head as he looked at Ragnar.

"They had it together. But you—not so much," Ragnar said, hands suddenly down on the table as he stared at Letterman.

"Hey. I am plenty together!" Letterman raged. "And you—

you'll just never know. I am admired. I'm more than you'll ever know. You'll never know because you're stupid, and you're blind. And I'm not saying another word to anyone until I have a lawyer!"

"Fine." Ragnar shrugged. "This guy is penny ante," he told Jackson.

"The hell I am! I am the best ever!"

"Best ever at what?" Ragnar asked, snorting. "You just said you were innocent of anything but hiring a sex worker. No jury is going to buy that. Most men don't bury their dates."

"Most whores don't ask!"

"And this one didn't either," Jackson said, letting out a breath.

"You are idiots, and I will walk! As I should! That whore should be in jail. Soliciting and making a good man look bad."

Ragnar just shook his head and turned to Jackson again. "Is someone coming in to get him for arraignment?"

"Yep, within an hour," Jackson said.

"Okay. See ya," Ragnar told Letterman.

"Wait! You can't just leave me sitting here. I have been in this room forever. You can't—"

"It won't be long," Jackson said, heading to the door.

"We'll make sure you get some water or coffee," Ragnar told him. "Hey, you've got air. That's more than Grace had right from the get-go."

With that, Ragnar followed Jackson out of the room.

Megan and Angela remained behind the desk, still watching the screen, the volume low.

Hugo was staring at the screen with a low growl sounding in his throat.

Because Joel Letterman was unaware of the camera. And he was muttering away, his words angry and barely discernable.

Megan could catch the words "assholes" and "idiots" and then an assurance regarding himself: "I was doing it right, I was good, if it wasn't for the idiots before me. I mean, what were they doing out there in the woods anyway, looking for the cabin, looking for me? The woods are huge! How...how... there are old bits of settlement here and there, and..."

"He's talking to himself," Megan explained to the men as they entered. But she glanced at the screen and saw he had gone quiet. He was just staring at his hands.

"Saying anything useful?" Ragnar asked.

"Well, enough to suggest you've been right about him being new at this. He's muttering about the fact that 'those who came before him' are the reason he's where he is now," Megan said.

"Did you get anything else?" Ragnar asked her.

"Probably what you surmised without me. And he's right about one thing—we're not seeing something. Oh. I suppose you might have gotten this anyway, but he knows exactly who Rory Ayers and Jim Carver are. He repeated their names as if he had no idea—but he does. I think he'll get a lawyer, and he'll really play the part of a poor young man seduced into sadomasochism. But I also believe he'll fall on his sword before giving up his mentor. Unless..."

"Unless?" Jackson asked her.

She shook her head. "In his muttering, I thought he might have been getting angry. Because in his mind, he did do everything right. And he might—he just might—suspect someone gave him away."

"Betrayed him," Ragnar said.

"Carver or Ayers?" Angela mused. "Or someone else still out here?"

"He really believes we are idiots," Megan said. "Thinks he's superior to us all. And he's also laughing inside because we don't see it."

"So. What aren't we seeing?" Ragnar muttered. "We need to question him again. Megan, he may suspect he's been betrayed. He can't know how we found him, so while he'll keep denying his mentors might have given him up, it is there as a thought. We should push the thought," Ragnar said.

Jackson nodded.

Ragnar looked at Megan thoughtfully.

"Maybe this time… Angela and Megan."

"You—you think I should?" Megan was surprised.

"I think the two of you should go in like the 'good' cops after the 'bad' cops. Find out if he does want water or coffee or something. And this time, Jackson and I will watch from here," Ragnar said.

"Could work," Jackson said.

Megan must have shown her concern on her face because Angela quickly reassured her. "You just ask about coffee and anything he might need while he's waiting. I'll mention the fact you found him so quickly—something you couldn't have done without help."

Hugo whined and set his nose in her hand. Megan stroked him, murmuring, "It's all right, Hugo."

She remembered the terror of having been taken.

And she remembered what it felt like to know she had helped save a life.

She smiled grimly.

"I'm ready and willing to get in, listen, and talk," she assured them. She shook her head. "This is all so unbelievable," she said. "A network of sick killers."

Jackson shrugged. "I'm afraid it's happened before. The 'Killer

Clown' and the 'Candyman.' In fact, there's a darned good program on the two of them and others. They had a pedophile network going using pamphlets and their own codes, communicating in a way that appeared entirely harmless." He paused. "What we can't figure out is how two men—Carver and Ayers, since we believe Boynton was new to this, who are incarcerated with their phone calls being recorded—are communicating to their followers."

"It's there somewhere," Megan said. "Their attorneys?"

"Their attorneys are public defenders," Angela said. "Their records show them to be sharp attorneys, but lily white when it comes to corruption. Anyway, let's see what we can do. I won't actually lie; we'll just throw out a few suppositions."

Angela looked at Megan questioningly and then left the office.

"Hugo, mind Ragnar now," she told the dog.

Hugo whined, but sat obediently.

Megan followed Angela out, not looking back.

She had almost died. Other women *had* died.

And this had to be stopped.

CHAPTER NINE

Ragnar sat in the chair Megan had vacated, staring at the screen.

"Hey, Megan is going to do all right," Jackson said.

"She's a civilian."

"And she was with you when you apprehended the man. If he hadn't seen her already, I wouldn't have let her go in. But she is a surprising woman, Ragnar, with more talents than it seems we know."

Jackson probably knew there was more to the story of finding Grace. But he was waiting to hear it from Megan. If Megan wanted to share her strange dream, it was her right to choose when. Since she hadn't wanted him mentioning it to her sister, he thought he should just stay quiet.

"This might be just what we need," Jackson said. "The guy has a problem with women. I think it will be good to see him respond when it's two women in with him."

"Yeah," Ragnar muttered. He shook his head. "I do think any man who wants to knock out a woman and bury her has a problem with women. And here's the thing—anyone who wants to do that is sick in my book. But he was also in training by cold and calculating murderers with the same sickness. So, they all need help. But to protect society, there are few people more deserving of being locked up."

"I'm going on locked up with this group," Jackson said.

"Keys thrown away."

"The DA is going after the death penalty for both Carver and Ayers," Jackson told him.

"Yeah, I keep using that when I try to get them to talk. Jackson, we have no idea how many people are involved in this or how many women have been murdered."

"They're in," Jackson said, indicating the screen.

"Yeah. We'll sit back on this. And watch."

It was ironic. Usually, Megan watched. And listened with her extraordinary ability while he or Mark did the talking. It was going to be interesting to be the watcher—seeing Megan in action.

"Ah, well, hell, at least a better-looking pair!" Letterman drawled as Angela and Megan entered the room.

Ragnar saw the man lean back casually and taunt the two women. Jackson was right. Joel Letterman had a low opinion of women.

"Now what?" he demanded. "Are you two transport?"

That or he had coveted a woman and been hurt by her, perhaps crushed and humiliated by what he saw as a lost love. And now, perhaps, he felt they should all pay.

But had he been directed to that particular corner by someone who knew exactly what had happened to Carole Berlin?

"No, we're not transport. We're the coffee ladies," Megan said. "We came in to see if we could get you anything."

"You!" he said, waving a finger at Megan. "You have that vicious dog."

"My dog isn't vicious. He doesn't like it when people hurt other people. You know, bury them, almost kill them," Megan said. "But I'm not even an agent. I'm just helping on coffee duty."

"How nice! I'd love a large porterhouse steak, a twice-baked potato, and some greens. My mom always told me to eat my greens," Letterman said.

"The man is truly an ass," Jackson muttered, sitting in Angela's chair to keep his eyes on the screen.

"That gives a bad name to an ass," Ragnar told him.

"Despicable excuse for a human being?" Jackson suggested.

"Far kinder to the beast of burden," Ragnar muttered. They both fell silent, listening.

"We don't have a porterhouse. We do have water and coffee or soft drinks," Angela said. "Two officers will be coming; because of the connections to other federal cases, you will be arraigned in federal court."

"Connections?" Letterman said.

Megan stared at Angela. She was doing an excellent job of pretending to worry about what was being said.

"Well, I mean…well—" Angela began awkwardly, playing her part, too. She *was* the agent. The one who should have known better.

"We did find you almost before you finished burying Grace," Megan said.

"Hey!" Angela told her.

"Oh, sorry."

"What?" Letterman demanded. "Yeah, that's right. How?"

"Well, um, we were just lucky," Megan said, looking at Angela again. She gave herself a little shake. "Yeah, we were just lucky. All those woods and we found the derelict cabin where you were. Hey, don't forget we had Hugo—"

"Right! That's it," Angela said. "A dog can find things."

"Even in tens of thousands of acres," Megan said. "So—"

Letterman narrowed his eyes at them. "Liar. How *did* you find me?"

Both women were silent, looking at one another.

"Luck," Megan said at last. "Just…luck."

"You knew where to find me!" Letterman screamed. "They told you, one of those bastards told you!"

"One of those bastards? You mean Rory Ayers?" Angela asked. "Or Jim Carver?"

Letterman waved a hand in the air. "They're afraid. They're so afraid someone will be better than them."

"Better killers?" Angela asked quietly.

"I didn't kill anyone," Letterman said.

"Because Grace survived?"

Letterman was obviously distracted, caught in his own thoughts. "I never killed anyone," he repeated, and he started to laugh. "Yeah, 'cause Grace survived. Wait, no. That's wrong. I wasn't trying to kill Grace. She's kinky. She promised me really hot sex if I would play her crazy foreplay games. Grace wanted what I did to her—"

"Oh, you are like a broken record," Angela said wearily. She walked closer to him and asked softly, "Which one of them gave you away?"

"How the hell would I know which one?" he demanded.

"But one of them did?" Megan asked.

"How?" Angela asked. "How did you tell them what you were going to do?"

He winced.

"They didn't!"

"Ah, come on! You were egged on and then betrayed," Angela said.

Letterman had gone white. His fingers were clutched so tightly into his hands that the knuckles were discolored.

"The notice," he whispered at last.

"The notice? What notice?" Megan prodded, coming to stand on his other side.

"Nothing, I didn't say anything," Letterman said.

"You were just telling us—" Angela began.

"Nothing. I will tell you nothing!" Letterman raged. Then he laughed. "Lost dog! Found, stray cat. House for sale. Garage sale! Notices—the world is full of them! Get me my lawyer!"

"Oh, not to worry. You will get a lawyer," Angela assured him.

"Now. I'm telling you, stop questioning me. I know my rights! I get a lawyer before you bug me with any more of your stupid questions. It's my right to remain silent!"

"Yes, it is," Angela said. "So. For now... Did you want coffee? Or some water? Not too much water. I mean, we wouldn't want you suffocating on it. We want you breathing—freely and clearly!"

Letterman glared at her. She glanced at Megan, shrugged, and walked out.

Megan followed her.

"You're blind! You never see!" he yelled. "Stupid! Idiots. Women, only good for one thing!"

Apparently, the last hit a nerve with Megan.

As Ragnar and Jackson watched, she turned back into the room and walked right up to the man, smiling. "Good at getting to the truth and good at seeing men like you rot in prison!" she snapped. "And women are also good at reading notices."

She smiled sweetly at him.

Then she swirled and left the room, leaving Letterman cursing and shouting names after her.

Ragnar sat back in his chair, watching and feeling a slight smile curve into his lips.

Megan could be good. She could be fierce.

And Hugo—who had been sitting quietly by the desk—stood on all fours and let out a fierce growl. Ragnar didn't know enough about dogs to surmise if Hugo had seen or understood anything they'd witnessed on-screen, but he knew the animal sensed any danger to Megan and he was as loyal to Megan as a dog could be.

"It's okay, Hugo. Megan will be right back," Ragnar assured the dog, patting him on the head. "It's okay, Megan is on her way here."

"She's got something," Jackson said, admiration in his tone. "And she let Letterman know he was an idiot; he'd given himself away. Watch him now; he's truly muttering away to himself as if he wants to kick himself."

Angela and Megan walked back in.

"One of those two—Ayers or Carver—is calling the shots from prison," Megan said.

"Okay, we were figuring that was a possibility. But how?" Jackson asked.

"Notices," Megan said.

"Lost dog? Garage sale?" Jackson asked.

Megan nodded. "They are communicating in ways most people would never notice, and if you did notice, you wouldn't think anything of it. We need to start looking for all the things that are out there posted on lampposts, on trees…wherever people put up their fliers."

"Okay, we can do that," Jackson said, still studying her.

"It will be in what the notice says—and I can only hope the tech people here are good at cyphers—or whatever these guys are using. But what's going on is going to be in the descriptions they're using. 'Brown' dog, or 'Last seen at the juncture of Sycamore and Vine'; of course, those words will mean something else to those who are involved."

"More needles in more haystacks, but we're good at haystacks," Angela muttered. "I'll get the troops on it."

"I need to see both Ayers and Carver again," Ragnar said. "Anytime we have something, we can give them a bit of what we have and hope they'll give away more, just as Letterman did."

"Let's hope," Angela said. "It appears Letterman is a new recruit into this group. Grace was going to be his first kill. And it's a good thing he's new and young. He believes he was betrayed."

"I'll set it up; you can head out to the correctional facility first thing tomorrow," Jackson said. He looked at his watch. "No way to get you in tonight, and you shouldn't go tonight anyway. You need to start fresh."

"It's that late?" Ragnar asked, glancing at his watch.

"The day flies when you're saving a woman and interrogating her would-be killer," Jackson said, smiling grimly. "It's almost eight at night. If you're going after Ayers and Carver again in the morning, you need to get some sleep."

"All right," Ragnar said. Amazing. The day had been full to the brim, but he hadn't been tired, not until he realized just how late it was. He glanced at Megan, who shrugged, looking back at him sheepishly.

"Food, too," she said.

"Food would be good," he agreed.

Yes, it had been one hell of a long day.

"Megan," Jackson said, his tone serious. "You have been such a helpful asset to us in this. Please believe that our depth of appreciation is endless, and you will be protected."

She smiled. "I'm so glad. And thank you."

Angela gave her a quick, impulsive hug and Megan hugged her back.

But before they could start out, Ragnar's phone rang. Mark was calling.

"Hey!" he told his partner. "Are the women all right? Did something happen? I'm in Angela's office with Jackson and Megan. And Hugo. You're on speaker. What's happened?"

"Nothing happened; the women are fine," Mark said quickly. "But I took a walk to the corner the women use. We ran into a friend of Grace who was probably the last person to see Carole alive. She can give us—in her words—a poor description of what the man looked like."

"That's great! When—"

"That's just it; we're with her now. I don't know if we'll find her again. I know it's late, but maybe if you contacted Maisie, she might do a video. I doubt any of the artists are still in the offices, but maybe if not Maisie—"

"I'll call Maisie and get a conference call going," Ragnar told him.

"I'll wait for you to get back to me," Mark said. "Unofficially," he added dryly.

"Unofficially," Jackson agreed. "But I'm officially calling Maisie on my line as we speak."

Ragnar was grateful Maisie was quick to answer Jackson's

call and just as quick to assure him taking a few minutes for an important sketch was no problem at all.

They used Angela's computer and a secure system to put through the conference call right from the office.

Penny's friend said her name was Tia. She appeared to be in her early twenties, an attractive young brunette with just a bit of an edge to her; life on the streets could get to many people quickly. She was frightened—that much was obvious. But Colleen was assuring her no one would ever know she had helped them, and Mark was being gentle and encouraging with the young woman as well.

"I mean, this was the guy I last saw her with. With what we do and the way we work, well, it was a long time ago now, but…"

"We're grateful for any help," Megan said before Ragnar could speak. He smiled inwardly. Though Megan didn't want this world, and she loved what she did for a living, she was here now, and she was going to do her very best. She was also passionately involved, caring for the lives of others. And she had that true talent not just for listening, but for comprehending what lay beneath what was being written or said. There was no choice; they had to exploit that talent.

"Truly grateful. So, Tia, meet Maisie. She is an extraordinary artist."

"Thanks for that!" Maisie said through the computer. "Hi, Tia, and honestly, this is painless. You talk, I'll sketch, you tell me what to fix!"

"Okay, well…he wasn't old, but he wasn't young," Tia said. "I guess he was maybe in his late thirties or early forties."

"That's good, thanks. Round face, skinny face?"

"Not a thin face or a fat face. Maybe a slightly square face.

He had a weird nose—kind of fat, a little round and bulging. Besides his nose, he was good-looking, like a rocker, maybe. And yeah, rockers and good-looking guys pick up prostitutes. They don't always want a bunch of involvement or clinginess from fans."

"Okay...something like this?" Maisie asked.

Maisie had created the bare bones of a face.

"Yeah, I think," Tia said.

"What was his hair like?" Maisie asked.

"It was long, kind of wild, like around his shoulders. I think that he was at least forty, maybe, but like I said, he kind of looked like a hippie musician with that hair. But he was wearing some kind of a button-down shirt. Like a business shirt. He didn't have on any kind of jacket. He looked halfway like an old-time hippie, and halfway like he should be heading to Wall Street."

"Bushy brows? Thin brows?"

"Medium. They didn't meet over his forehead or anything," Tia said. "And his nose was really big."

"Mustache? Beard?"

"No. He was clean-shaven."

"Mouth? Chin? Jaw?" Maisie asked.

"Big lips, maybe. Kind of a pointed chin, with the jawline rounding out a little. I think."

"Can you remember anything else about him? Scar, tattoo?" Maisie asked.

"No, not that I could see. But...hmm, I think he was wearing a ring. I remember I blinked because something glinted on the hand he had on the steering wheel while he leaned over to talk to Carole. And I... I didn't think anything of it when I didn't see Carole. Because...well, I've had other friends, I've known other girls who got tired, or who weren't working well here, who moved on to other places…oh!"

Maisie had lifted her sketch, showing them what she had done via the computer screen.

"That's a—a person!" Tia said.

"Yes, thank you," Maisie said, smiling and gracefully accepting the compliment. "But is it *the* person?"

Tia hesitated. Ragnar could see Colleen gently touch Tia's shoulders, trying to reassure her it would be all right.

"Here's the thing. It was a long time ago. I mean, as I said, I didn't even know Carole was gone until I talked to Grace or Penny days after when they said Carole was missing, and I just can't be sure I've given you all the details right. I think this looks like the guy—but I couldn't swear it. From what I remember, it's good." She paused. Her expression was pained. "I hope I helped. I'm terrified now. These guys are letting me stay here. I… I really liked Carole. You can't believe what a good person she was. You know, she gave to every homeless person she came across. I want… I want her to rest in heaven, okay!"

"Every little thing helps incredibly," Ragnar said.

"Sending the image to your computers now," Maisie said. "And then I'm heading out to read a fairy tale to a toddler. Hey, fairy tales just have ogres and witches. It will be a great break!"

They laughed and thanked her. She said a special good night to Tia and the others and signed off.

"We'll be getting his likeness out to law enforcement all around the area. And, Tia, you just may be the one who helped us find her killer. So, yes, we thank you," Jackson said.

Tia nodded nervously. "Um, great, yeah, thank you. I, uh, I need a drink."

"I'll take care of that," they heard Jean say.

Tia left the area the camera captured for the screen. She was replaced by Mark.

"That's it. Don't worry. Great vacation Colleen and I are having just visiting with friends! Signing off now, too. And again, don't worry, we won't be leaving these friends—we can give you that much."

"Thanks, Mark," Ragnar said, and the others echoed his words before he hung up. Ragnar looked at Jackson and said, "It's bugging the hell out of me. What is it we can't see?"

"At this moment? That you're too tired to see much of anything," Jackson said. "Go home. Or I should say go back to the safe house. Go to sleep."

"We should probably—" Ragnar began.

"Go. There is nothing more to do right now. Remember? Mark and Colleen are back in town and they're seeing those new friends, Grace, Jean, and Penny," Jackson said. "They're still on vacation, you know? Not the usual honeymoon, but I guess they're going to have dinner and watch a few movies. The point is, they'll keep an eye out for the women. We can't stop prostitution. No one has ever managed that, and there would be no way in hell to know if anyone else needed to be protected. And we do have other agents who will watch the corner. You two. Sleep. That's an order," Jackson said.

Ragnar looked over at Megan.

"Yeah. Sleep. Food will be good, but sleep is most important. We can order in and maybe start looking at everything fresh in the morning," Megan said. "Oh! Any news on the skull that was sent to me?" she asked, looking from Angela to Jackson.

"Not yet," Angela said. "They're working DNA from the bits of soft tissue that remained on it, and they're doing a likeness in the New York offices. Hopefully, we'll find out her identity *and* what happened to her or *who* happened to her. Go. Home or away from work. Shake up your minds somehow; and the morning will, at the very least, bring something new. We will get people out there; we will start gathering notices."

Ragnar lifted his hands. "All right. We're out of here. Hugo, let's go!"

Hugo woofed.

Ragnar led the way out. Megan followed him.

"Shake up our minds," he muttered, sliding into the driver's seat and starting the car even as Hugo jumped in the back. Megan took her seat in the passenger's chair.

"Shake up our minds," he repeated. "Any idea of how we can do that?" he asked as he drove out of the parking garage.

She turned to him and smiled. "Actually, I do," she said.

He arched a brow to her, startled. She had sounded almost…

Flirtatious.

"I think you should tell me about yourself," she said. "You know just about everything there is to know about me. My sister is now your partner, too, and you know I'm a triplet and I have weird abilities. I know your parents came from Norway and you're an only child. But…"

"How did I wind up in the Krewe?" he asked.

"Yeah. For starters."

He shrugged. "Like most of us," he said quietly.

"How?" Megan persisted.

He looked ahead as he drove and shrugged. "A Viking," he said dryly.

"What?"

"Yeah, that's the response," he muttered.

"No, no, please!" she said.

"A lot of our agents first saw the ghost of a loved one when they were young, or when something traumatic happened with friends, and the police needed help. I wasn't even in the United States. Well, it did involve danger to my family. Just as they say that imminent danger can bring forth adrenaline and phenomenal strength, I think certain situations tap into what we have."

"Makes sense," Megan said.

"And we know we have areas of the mind we've yet to fathom."

She grinned. "So, your name is Ragnar Johansen, and your 'first' was a Viking. That should really be no surprise. Just, wow, a Viking!"

"I was with my folks visiting family in Greenland. There was an archeological dig going on, and my uncle was involved with it. Anyway, the story goes Erik the Red was banished from Iceland for manslaughter in the late 900s. He formed a settlement on the southwestern coast of Greenland. The group doing the dig included archeologists and scholars from all over, Scandinavia, Great Britain, the States, and more. They seemed to be great. There was a lot of excitement and camaraderie between everyone. My uncle was excited; he was certain Erik was an ancestor. I was ten at the time. Anyway, one of my uncle's friends, a fellow who had a passion for history, had set up the study. And then he just disappeared. He was found at the bottom of a well. While tragic, the group believed at first he had fallen in while trying to decipher some etchings on the old stone well."

"The dig continued?" Megan asked.

"Yes, and I met my first ghost. So, I was just tossing rocks in a stream when this man walked up to me. I believed at first he was an actor someone had paid to do a promo for the dig. One of the educational channels was going to broadcast a special on it. He was angry; he kept slipping into Old Norse. My knowledge of the current language is woeful, but Old Norse is closest to Icelandic. My parents are fluent, and when I pressed them to learn, they'd speak some. But my mom would always ask me, 'And who will you be speaking to if you do become fluent?'

"Anyway, that has nothing to do with it except I had terrible trouble understanding him. But thankfully, through the years of him haunting the place, his English had become better than my Old Norse. Eventually I understood him. He said he was Erik the Red, and that the man had been attacked and murdered by another man on the dig. He described him, and I knew he was talking about Professor Braxton, a man who had argued against the dig, and then joined it.

"I told my father but he was skeptical. But thanks to old Erik the Red, I had planted suspicion in my dad's mind, and when he saw Braxton following my uncle, he went after him and stopped him just before my uncle went off a cliff. Anyway, I saw Erik again when the authorities came, and realized he'd gained some real power. He caused Braxton to slip and almost go off the cliff as he had intended my uncle to do. The man confessed as he begged for help, and I was in awe of Erik." He glanced at Megan. He didn't tell the story often. In his mind, it sounded ridiculous.

"Wow!" Megan said. "Did you see him again? He must have been a fascinating man."

"He was. Born in Norway, his father was banished to Iceland for manslaughter, and later Erik was banished from Iceland himself. Brawls were constant back then. One was over beams with ancient Viking religious symbols written into them. He lived in harsh times. But he is credited with founding the first continuous settlement in Greenland. It's not the chosen vacation spot of the great hordes, but it is beautiful. One of his sons was Leif

Eriksson, who converted to Christianity and sailed to 'Vinland,' four hundred years before Columbus. Some say his brother arrived first and fought with the indigenous people, but…well, I only met Erik and he wasn't there then, so…"

"That's incredible. But there it is again. People are afraid of ghosts, and it seems to me they remain to save lives—"

"Erik almost killed Braxton."

"Ah, but your uncle was saved."

Ragnar smiled. "I'm sure that there are spirits, ghosts, souls that remain—whatever we label them—that are not full of goodness, but in my experience, they remain for some form of justice or to help their loved ones or to protect a place." He paused. "And there are places like Gettysburg where, I believe, even those most skeptical feel the tremendous sense of history and humanity that can fill a building, a field, an area.

"So there you have it. My past. Of course, my parents were truly skeptical regarding what I told them. They were going to get me a shrink. But thankfully, my uncle was more immersed in history, archeology, and legends. He convinced them whatever had happened, it had saved his life. He and I went for a long walk, and he listened to everything I said. He told me I was talented; and with such a talent, I owed it not just to the great unknown God but humanity itself to use it."

He took a breath again. "I served in the Middle East and got some help here and there with everyone thinking I had an unusual tactical mind. And when I came home, I knew I'd be a cop or an agent. My uncle was friends with Adam Harrison. Adam, as you know, is involved with just about every philanthropic organization known to man. They met when Adam pitched in on an expedition in Vinland. Adam sent me to apply to the academy and when I graduated, I started in with the Krewe. I spent two years with our most seasoned agents, and then Mark and I were paired together—along with Red—a year ago, and we made a damned good team."

She smiled at him. "Thank you," she said softly.

"Um, sure."

That drew a laugh from her. "Hey, Colleen told me a few agents met the ghost of Edgar Allan Poe. Oh, I would love to meet him!"

"You never know what can be arranged," he said. Megan didn't seem to be tired—even though it had been a fourteen-hour day and that had begun *after* she'd woken early from her nightmare.

"Well, okay, this is good. We can talk the weird stuff in the Krewe. That should let us 'shake up our minds.' As Angela suggested," Ragnar said.

He glanced her way. She was smiling as she looked down, and then turned to him. "Shake up our minds. I told you, I had an idea on that."

"Okay, right. I told you how I wound up following this path—"

"And that was great. Not what I meant," she said, turning to him.

Her eyes, he thought, were really like emeralds. She was a beautiful woman. Something he had admitted even when he'd found her nothing but resentful and annoying.

And now…

He looked back at the road again. Memory, mental and physical, was shooting through him.

"Okay…"

"You know, I actually almost kind of like you now," she told him.

"I think you just shook up my mind," he said.

CHAPTER TEN

Megan felt her smile deepening. She had surprised him.

She was surprising herself.

Well, she had been so determined to forget the strange night they had spent together after Mark and Colleen's wedding.

But it was true that she admired him tremendously now. And she liked him. Loved his sense of right and wrong, his ability to stand against all odds, and to make her feel...

Valuable.

"I don't believe this, but I'm not tired at all," she said. "I'm still... I'm still riding high, so very amazed and grateful we found Grace. And now, we have another sketch, and something to bring to Ayers or Carver to perhaps trip them up. And we know to look for notices! We can find fliers and other such things and figure out how they're communicating. It's not an ending, but it's a start, Ragnar."

"It is," he agreed.

"I think we get to celebrate, and...we did have amazing hours together once," Megan said.

"Yes, we did." Ragnar nodded, just waiting for her to go on.

"Maybe that's what we get. When we get the chance in life, we need to take the time to have amazing hours." She looked into his eyes, searching them, loving that he was holding back.

Because he was holding back for her.

He smiled slowly. "Maybe you're right. Last time we wound up together—"

"We were passionately angry. Ragnar, right now, I'm passionately happy. I made a difference. And I made a difference because of you." She paused, smiling. "Okay, then again, as one of my colleagues pointed out, you are built like one of those Norse gods in your background and you seem quite adept at utilizing all that you were blessed with."

He laughed. "You do have a way with words. And it is quite profound, what effect words can create on the human body."

"So, do you think—"

"I think we should quit thinking."

Megan wasn't sure how long the drive from Krewe headquarters to the safe house had been before; it seemed quick now.

They had the car parked in seconds and the door opened just as quickly. Megan felt like her whole body was buzzing. Hugo was patted good-night and sent to sleep in Megan's room. Then Ragnar drew Megan with him to his room.

And that was it. They had been here before. She knew the demanding and hot desire of his kiss, tongue tangling with hers, delving. His hands were large, his fingers were long, and he was adept with the buttons on her blouse, while she had to admit she was far more careless with his shirt.

They maintained their kiss, coming closer, moving away, helping one another, shedding their clothing with all the haste they could manage.

They fell on the bed together, as if afraid that if their lips, hands, or bodies weren't touching they'd lose one another. Ragnar rose over her, looking down at her. "You're sure?" he asked.

She felt as if she were on fire. If she didn't have him, she would explode, as if the sky would burst to pieces and take all matter with it.

"I don't think I have ever been so sure of anything in my life," she said.

Their mouths met again, hungrily. His liquid caress then moved down the length of her body, teasing, intimate, until she cried out, rising against him, kissing his shoulders, moving her mouth down his chest, her fingers skimming over his back and down to his buttocks.

Their eyes met again.

Their lips.

And then he was inside her and sheer sensation took over, flying, soaring, the simple and exquisite feel of the ultimate human touch. Then a rocketing pleasure that seemed to surpass all else.

They lay together silently for a few minutes, hearts pumping, lungs easing.

Then Ragnar said lightly, "You do know how to celebrate."

"Thanks."

"I'm so glad you even like me."

"Mmm, I try to please."

"Oh, you do please."

She smiled and rolled toward him. "I spend way too much time thinking about—no worrying about—every possible consequence of any action. But tonight…"

He hiked up to an elbow. "Megan, there is no other consequence here. You needed to be here, and we wanted to be together. The consequence is we're together, and we're going to keep investigating, and keep you alive. Not to mention you being here saved Grace. I have no special talents—well, other than having dead friends and acquaintances—but something told me you could be in danger when I was talking to Ayers. And the head arrived. And then your nightmare led us exactly where we needed to be."

"The arrow with the homestead sign would have meant nothing to me, on my own," she said.

"So, maybe the consequence was we needed to be together to save a life."

"And we have to find all the heads of the monster," she said.

"We're on our way," he assured her. "So, we don't have to regret the past. We don't have to worry about the distant future. We have to live day by day and use everything we have. Remember we have others working with us to find the truth. And guess what?"

"What?"

"I think I kind of like you, too."

"I'm not a complete bi—"

"Nope. Not completely."

"Only halfway?"

He laughed, rolling over her and catching her hands. "Well, if you didn't have that fire within you, I don't know if I'd be quite so impressed."

"What fire?"

"Lots of different fire. Like...hmm. This kind. Steam, volcanic...the kind that slips from you and right into another person."

She started to laugh, and they laughed together and rolled about on the sheets until their lips met again, and she felt it...

The steam. Volcanic...all the heat raging between them, shifting from her body to his and back again; and at last, they lay together again. Close. Simply holding one another.

And it was good. So good that she slept.

Megan didn't dream. She woke late to find Ragnar was out of bed. She collected her things and moved on to her room to shower and change. She saw Ragnar had already taken Hugo out and probably sent him to the yard for his morning ritual.

Coffee was on the table along with two omelets and a plate of toast.

"We never did have dinner last night," he said.

"I—yeah. I forgot."

"I forgot until this morning." He had the coffeepot in his hand and shrugged. "I guess I was simply so extremely, um, exhilarated…"

"We may need to work on your way with words," Megan told him.

"But you know what I mean!" he said.

"I do," she told him, grinning and walking over to rest against him and plant a kiss on his lips.

She sat at the table and took a big bite of the omelet.

"Another gold star," she told him. "You can cook!"

"Four or five things," he said, joining her. "And I fed Hugo. I'm a pro at pouring kibble into a bowl."

He turned serious. "We're back talking to Ayers and Carver today. I made arrangements—I'm having the men pass one another as they come and go from the interview room. I've spoken to the warden, and asked they aren't told they'll see one another. I just want to watch their reactions."

"Because if one of them thinks the other caused the capture of Joel Letterman, they may believe Letterman might betray them. Then he—or they—would be furious."

He nodded. "And I have Angela working on the attorneys again. Letterman kept talking about us being blind. Something is right in front of us. And criminal defense attorneys—by nature of the beast—can be incredibly imaginative. We've also started delving into the lives of the guards. I mean, those guys would be right in front of us."

"We'd be blind, that's true," Megan said.

"But so far, nothing."

"Double lives," she muttered. "Ted Bundy—no one suspected him because he was such a nice guy, worked a volunteer line, and was politically active. Dennis Rader—the BTK—he was active for years, as was Jeffrey Dahmer, who, they suspect, was gaining kill speed when he was caught—with a head in his refrigerator. It's all so…horrible."

"Yeah."

"But we could investigate from here to eternity, and if there is a person communicating for Ayers or Carver, we might never know," Megan said.

"Forensics may find something. And we may find something. And as in the case with Bundy, a traffic officer might pull him over, which happened a couple of times. Tragically he was quite the escape artist, and by that time, he was on the Most Wanted List."

"But they knew who they wanted."

"Megan! What happened to celebrating our wins?"

She glanced his way quickly. "I have nothing against celebrating. I just… I'm frustrated. And wondering again how you do this!"

"A lot of determination," Ragnar told her. "And sometimes patience."

"Okay, so…let's head to the facility and see what we can

get." She picked up her empty plate. She hadn't realized she'd consumed every bite of her food during their conversation. She grabbed his plate as well, setting both in the sink and washing them quickly. When she turned around, she saw Ragnar had poured two coffees for them in to-go cups.

They weren't such a bad partnership.

"Thanks." She accepted her cup, and they headed out together with Ragnar whistling for Hugo to come and join them in the car.

Corrections officer Brendan Kent was the first to greet them again from behind the desk at the entry where—though he knew Ragnar well—Ragnar still produced his credentials and turned in his weapon.

"Hugo is back again!" Kent said, leaning over to see Hugo. "He is really one beautiful animal," he told Megan.

"He's a good boy. A rescue," Megan said. "And thank you."

Kent looked at Ragnar and said, "Same room. I'll open the gates. Megan and the dog can head into observation. Officer Morris—Anson Morris—is on today. The warden told him not to bring Ayers in until Megan was in the observation room. Do you want to go into the interview room and wait, or have him brought in first?"

"I'll head in and be there. Thanks," Ragnar told him. "Oh, by the way. Has either man had any other visitors?"

"Attorneys—both saw their attorneys yesterday," Kent said. "They came in late. I was just getting off. But I guess those guys get the big bucks. Oh, wait. Nope. They both have public defenders. The poor guys are probably working all day and just getting time to see guys with trial dates set when they're done with everything else."

"Possibly. Thanks again," Ragnar said.

The gates were open for them to enter the hallway with the observation and interrogation rooms. The facility offered four such arrangements, but none of the other rooms were currently in use. Officer Morris was waiting behind the bars that opened for them to enter.

Like Brendan Kent, he greeted Hugo with admiration. Then he led them to the observation room.

"You good?" Ragnar asked Megan.

"As good as I can be," she assured him. She knew he worried about her constantly, and not because he considered her to be incapable.

She was just untrained.

"Well, then, here's hoping I say the right things."

He left her, heading into the interrogation room. Megan watched through the two-way mirror as he took the chair across from the prisoner's.

"You're back!" Ayers said with distaste as he was led into the room. He stared at Ragnar as Morris attached his cuffs to the iron bar in front of him.

Ragnar shrugged. "You could have refused to see me."

"I'm so bored in here even seeing your face is worth it for something different," Ayers said.

"Ah, come on. Your attorney was here yesterday," Ragnar said.

"So irritating. You know, I should have had the best that money can buy. But they put me in here, and my stupid almost-ex-wife pulled the plug on the money. You know, I built up that company. The money might have started out with her family, but they didn't have my business ability. That woman, of course she's pissed because I buried her daughter—"

"A girl you raised," Ragnar said, shaking his head.

"But not mine, not my blood!"

Ragnar shook his head and shrugged. "I've had friends through the years who have been adopted. They loved their parents, and their parents loved them. There can be love in knowing you're the parent, biological or not."

"I didn't hate the kid. She was all right. But I didn't bury her. I'm an innocent man. And you just wait, even my wet-behind-the-ears public defender has some smarts. And when we get to trial, things will be all right. I have a defense that is going to blow you away."

"Time will tell. But there may be more damning evidence against you," Ragnar said.

There was something already in what Ayers was saying that bothered Megan. He had just told them something. Not intentionally, but still.

"Evidence? Against me?" Ayers said.

Ragnar grinned and leaned forward at the table, folding his hands as he did so.

"Fliers and notices," Ragnar said. "And a man under arrest caught in the act of burying a woman. It's interesting how a man betrayed might decide to betray others."

"You're crazy," Ayers said.

Megan watched the way Ayers sat back. He was staring at Ragnar as if he hoped he'd suddenly acquire mind radar. He was quiet then, obviously calculating his words.

"Notices?" Ayers said at last. "I don't know what you're talking about."

And then Megan knew what she had heard.

Ayers was planning on having his wife killed. The divorce hadn't gone through yet.

Their money would come to him, and then he could hire "the best" defense out there.

She jumped up, ready to tap on the glass, but caught herself, not knowing if that was the right move. Instead, she stepped out into the hall where Anson Morris stood diligently on duty.

"I need Special Agent Johansen," she said.

"Can I do anything?" Morris asked.

"Yes, please. Get Special Agent Johansen for me," she said.

Morris seemed to be clean as falling snow. But she remembered that she couldn't be sure about anything that was "right in front of her."

"All right. Are you ending the interview? Should I bring Ayers back? And I was just told I was to bring Jim Carver in—"

"Please. Just get Special Agent Johansen for me."

Morris nodded and entered the room, telling Ragnar he was needed. Ragnar stood and came out, looking puzzled.

"We need to go," she said.

He nodded; he wasn't going to ask her questions here. Ragnar was far more intuitive than he realized. "Time to go," he told Hugo.

The dog had followed Megan and was standing by her.

At the desk, Kent was surprised when Ragnar asked for his weapon back and said they'd have to postpone their interviews.

"Something up?" Kent asked.

"Who knows? Powers that be," Ragnar said vaguely. "But I'm sure we'll be back."

They exited the building and headed for the car. They were far out of earshot before he asked her, "Okay, what's going on? What did he say?"

"He's going to kill his wife," Megan said.

They'd reached the car. He got in and she saw he had his

phone out even as he started the car. His call was to Jackson. At the office, Jackson could take it from there. They spoke briefly.

Megan knew they were driving out to the Ayerses' house.

"Has anyone been guarding the house in the time Amelia Ayers has been home?" Megan asked anxiously.

"At first, yes. Now, a patrol car checks on them once a night. Deirdre and her mother have been fine. Well, as fine as people can be when they find out a daughter's fiancé was ready to kill her and was shot and killed himself, and the husband and step-father was a serial killer," Ragnar said. "Jackson has the local police on the way—they'll beat us there. And Deirdre isn't at the house. She needed to get away and so she went with close friends on a trip to Seattle—including the ex-boyfriend who I think is the current boyfriend again, a musician, but a man de-termined to keep her safe after what happened. Anyway, Amelia Ayers is at the house with a housekeeper. Unless…" He paused and shook his head and added, "He's had this plan in action, and we didn't see it. I should have heard that in his words, too. I hope we're in time."

The Ayerses' home was impressive—a beautiful mansion. Megan could see it through the trees as they neared the estate.

But as they arrived, she saw the police cars in the front yard and officers milling about, one who immediately approached Ragnar as he stepped out of the car.

"Special Agent Johansen? I'm Deputy Frank Kenworth. We came as soon as we received the call." He took a deep breath. "Too late, I'm afraid. The house is empty. After Crow's call, we broke in. I'm afraid Amelia Ayers isn't here."

"Any sign of forced entry?" Ragnar asked.

"No. Mrs. Ayers is either out, or she let an abductor in."

"Does she have a cell phone? Has anyone tried calling her?" Megan asked.

"Her cell phone was on the kitchen table," Kenworth said flatly.

"If you don't mind, I'll take a look around," Ragnar said.

"Look anywhere you like; I'm letting my officers return to their patrols."

Ragnar nodded, then he and Megan—with Hugo behind them—walked to the house.

Ragnar stopped and turned back, calling to Deputy Kenworth.

"No sign of the housekeeper, either?"

"The house is empty—completely empty."

"Amelia Ayers has a live-in housekeeper," Ragnar said. "Curious they would both be out. Hold on to your officers for a few minutes. And alert area paramedics; they'll be needed."

Ragnar stood at the door, looking at the entry area. He nodded toward the wood paneling at the side of the entry.

"Scratches," he said quietly.

Hugo began to whine. He ran ahead into the house, and Megan hurried after him.

The dog stood in the kitchen area growling.

"Something happened in here," Ragnar said. He looked at Megan. "Mariana Largo—the housekeeper. She's middle-aged, slim, a little haggard, maybe five-five. She and Amelia were close, and she is adored by Deirdre. That much I know from the last case. Amelia Ayers is about fifty with short platinum hair, and thin. But neither is much in the muscle arena. They were taken in here," he determined.

Kenworth was standing behind him then.

"Get your officers out there, sir. Two women were abducted;

we'll get their pictures to you. We'll need roadblocks. Whoever did this is still in the area. Don't forget the paramedics!"

"What? You want us to stop every van, every car, every vehicle?" Kenworth asked.

"Yes," Ragnar said flatly. "We'll be getting other agents out here as quickly as possible. But we need to find these women now."

Kenworth stared at Ragnar and nodded. "On it," he said, turning to do as directed.

"Let's go upstairs, find clothing or something with a good scent for Hugo, and get out there."

"Ragnar, we may be expecting too much out of Hugo. He isn't Red—"

"He found Grace."

Megan nodded. "I'll find their rooms and pieces of clothing," she said.

She thought Ragnar would follow her, but he was still staring around the kitchen. She started out and realized Hugo wasn't following her either.

He was sniffing around the kitchen.

Time was important, she knew; and she should also just be glad her dog was proving to be an proficient tracker. Maybe Hugo would find something.

She hurried out to the living room and up the stairs. The house was beautiful, well-appointed and well-kept. She tried three doors before deciding she had found the room that belonged to Amelia Ayers. It was the largest bedroom with a balcony overlooking the manicured expanse of the back lawn.

The bed was made; no clothes littered the floor. The closet door was opened to a large walk-in expanse of hanging clothes and small shelves filled with shoes.

Megan noted there was no men's clothing in the closet, and it appeared one side had been cleaned out.

Amelia Ayers had rid herself of everything to do with her husband.

Megan hurried into the bathroom, and as she had hoped, she found a laundry hamper. She pulled out a blouse and went back to the hall.

Maybe the housekeeper's room was up in the attic.

But why? The house was huge. When Deirdre was home, there were just three women living in it now.

She went back through a few of the rooms where all she had done so far was open a door to glance in. One, she quickly realized, was Deirdre's because there were posters on the walls and the room also had a charming balcony overlooking the backyard. She started out of the room and then hesitated, drawn to the balcony. She walked onto it and stared out over the back lawn. Nothing.

But it still bothered her.

Giving herself a mental shake, she moved on. When she opened the next door, she believed she had found the housekeeper's room. There were pictures of children in different places on a dresser and a vase with fresh flowers.

Once again she hurried to the bathroom. There she was grateful Mariana seemed to be a woman with an organized way of doing things. There was a hamper in that bathroom, too.

She found a pink uniform in the basket and decided, whether the women were close or not, the housekeeper also dressed for her role.

With both objects in hand, Megan returned to the hall. But she found herself drawn back to Deirdre's room and the balcony.

She would give it one more quick look and hurry down.

Staring out at the lawn, she saw there was a large oak tree to the far-right side of the back lawn. Beyond it there were trees and bushes. The estates here were several acres each, and she assumed the back brush eventually led to a neighboring property.

But the tree...

The lawn was beautifully manicured. Flowering shrubs were artfully arranged, paths led to little benches.

But by the tree...

The earth was disturbed.

Megan turned from the balcony and went tearing down the stairs and back to the kitchen.

Ragnar and Hugo were heading for the back door.

"What?" Ragnar asked.

"Out back!" she cried.

Ragnar opened the door, and Hugo bounded out before them, running toward the tree.

Ragnar followed him, with Megan close behind.

They reached the tree. This close, it was easy to see the earth had been dug up recently. Ragnar looked around and grabbed a large branch near the tree trunk, digging with it while Hugo woofed and dug with his paws.

"Should I get the cops?" Megan asked quickly.

"Just run to the side of the house and scream for them. She or they will be shallow; we just need to hurry."

Megan ran to the side of the house, shouting for the police. Then she ran back to the hole Ragnar and Hugo were creating.

She fell to her knees, scooping and moving earth the best she could.

There was no wood this time.

Fingers appeared first. Hugo leaped back, as if he was alarmed, and Ragnar stepped in, moving the dirt from the arms of the woman, then grabbing her and drawing her from the loosely packed earth.

She wasn't breathing.

Ragnar started to perform CPR on her, giving Megan instructions on how to help.

Officers had come running, along with, thankfully, the paramedics Ragnar had asked Kenworth to call in.

Politely and quickly they took over.

"Ragnar," Megan said. "Is that…Amelia Ayers or Mariana Largo? Is there another—"

"That's Mariana. He buried the one woman, and he took the other," Ragnar said.

The paramedics were still working. One of the men looked up at them and shook his head.

"She might not have been deep," he said sadly, "but she isn't—"

He broke off.

His partner had tried one more time.

"I got a pulse!" he cried exuberantly. "Faint—but a pulse. Let's get her to the hospital. Oxygen, we need oxygen now!"

"Can she tell us—" Megan began.

"She's barely breathing and unconscious," the paramedic said. "I'm sorry. Hopefully, it will be a few hours. I know… I know there's another woman missing. But she is incapable of helping right now; it's going to be iffy if she survives."

"I'm sorry," Megan said.

"We have to move, now!" the paramedic said.

The yard came to life, officers hurrying to help the paramedics.

"He's taken Amelia. She has a chance if we can find her, but we're talking about minutes not hours," Ragnar said.

Kenworth was there and Ragnar turned to stare at him.

The deputy spoke up quickly. "The roadblocks are up. We have men patrolling the roads."

"Look for a parked vehicle and a trail someone might have taken in from areas where the woods are dense," Ragnar said. He caught Megan's arm.

"The clothes?"

She had dropped them in the yard, she realized. She raced back for them. Ragnar took them from her before she could speak or act.

"Hugo, come on, boy. You are proving to be the best, the very best!"

Hugo sniffed the clothing and started to bark.

Ragnar stood and looked at Deputy Kenworth.

"We'll be out there, too. Keep communication open. If anyone finds anything, get the word out fast!"

He looked at Megan. She nodded and turned, walking back to the car as quickly as she could go.

Ragnar and Hugo followed, but she paused. Ragnar had stopped in front, talking to Hugo.

The dog ran in circles, then headed for the road and started barking.

Ragnar headed for the car then, followed by the dog.

Megan looked at him with a question in her eyes.

"I had to find out which way to go," he told her, shrugging and opening the back for Hugo. "Hugo was born for this. He was going crazy in the kitchen, and made me go to the back door, and, well, I was trying to figure out what that meant when you came running."

"I saw the tree and the disturbed ground from a balcony," Megan explained.

"We have Hugo, and we know what the plan will be. We will find Amelia," Ragnar said.

"Will we, though? Mariana was just buried. No box, no—"

"I don't think the killer expected her. I think Mariana was in the way, and he just had to get rid of her quickly. I'm betting the doctors will find she was hit first with an object that knocked her out. Maybe even the killer-abductor thought she was dead. But she was collateral damage. He's out for Amelia, and I'll bet he's going to make sure Amelia is taken care of using the 'Embracer' method."

"But he'd need a coffin. Shouldn't we be saying they should look for a van or—"

"He could have the coffin ready in the woods. He could be in any kind of a vehicle."

"Ah."

Ragnar looked at her as they drove from the house.

"We will find her," he said. "I just hope that—"

"That we can find her alive," Megan finished quietly.

He was driving down the road that led away from town, deeper into the forest. They came upon a trail that curved off the main, paved road. It was nothing but dirt and gravel, but large enough for cars to maneuver.

And it held tire tracks in the mud that looked fresh.

Ragnar swerved the car, and they drove carefully along the trail.

Until a rusty gray SUV blocked them from going any farther.

CHAPTER ELEVEN

Ragnar didn't like it.

Every time he had Megan with him, he feared he was putting her life in danger.

Yes, he was there. Yes, Hugo would die for her. But they could both die for her, and she could still fall prey to a killer.

But if they didn't stop this, she might be in danger her whole life. If they didn't get to the bottom of it all, she could be thinking about space monsters as she walked down the street in New York and someone could take her by surprise.

"Ragnar?"

He'd parked; Hugo was barking crazily.

"Right, right, let's go. Let's see where he leads us."

They exited the car, and Hugo raced to the SUV barking nonstop. Ragnar hurried over and wrenched open the door, searching the vehicle quickly.

The back seat had been laid flat. The back could have easily accommodated a woman's prone body.

He stood still, staring.

"Ragnar?"

"Blood," he said softly. "Just a smear right there. I believe he used an instrument of some kind and knocked both women out. Then he disposed of Mariana quickly in the backyard and loaded up Amelia to get her out here. Hugo, go on, boy!"

Hugo let out a snort and sniffed around the vehicle, then took off at a run.

"Stay with me!" he told Megan. "Right at my back."

"I'm here!" she assured him.

Hugo was running at a swift rate, drawing them along a trail between the trees. Ragnar didn't know the area. But there had to be something here—a place where someone could have left a crude wooden coffin built especially for Amelia Ayers.

Hugo found exactly what Ragnar expected. The bare bones of a lean-to, something probably used by deer hunters to stash gear out of the rain. It had a back side and a slanted, wooden roof—all built from materials available within feet of it.

Half a box of nails remained on the ground along with a hammer.

He might have carried the hammer with him, ready to have it on hand when he went to the Ayerses' house.

The women had let him in. The lock hadn't been forced. The scratches on the doorframe had happened when he'd carried his burden out to the car.

The dog raced on through the woods. He and Megan followed.

Then Hugo stopped barking.

They were at a point where the trail split.

Ragnar knew he couldn't send Megan one way and himself another.

And he knew Amelia's life was at stake.

"Hugo, show us!" he said.

The dog took off again, down the trail to the left. They followed and Hugo stopped again, digging at the earth.

"This is it," Ragnar said.

Megan was down at his side in an instant.

He dug furiously, angry with himself. He should have known to bring a shovel! He hadn't thought to put one in the car, and this time they hadn't stumbled upon a man carrying a shovel.

He found a hooked branch and used it as he had before. Megan did the same.

Hugo continued to dig furiously, whining as he did so.

Ragnar hit something that sounded hollow with the hard point of the branch.

"Here!" he cried to Megan.

Together, they dug. They reached the wood. He had to use all his strength to wrench and tear at the nailed-down lid. He used the branch again. Thankfully, the wood of the branch was harder than the wood on the coffin. He wasn't able to pull out the nails, but he splintered the wood and was able to wrench the lid off enough to get the woman out.

There was blood on her temple. She was still breathing on her own; the lid of the coffin, though of poor quality, hadn't given in.

He started to tell Megan to call for help; but she was already doing so, allowing her phone to give the authorities their location.

"What can we do?" she asked, kneeling on the ground by his side and looking at him anxiously.

"Wait. She's breathing; she's out because of the injury to her head. There's nothing we can do but hold her and hope she survives the injury."

Megan nodded.

He'd have liked to have cleaned the dirt and blood away from Amelia's forehead. But he wasn't letting Megan out of his sight, so he couldn't send her to look for a brook or a stream, or even head back to his car for water.

"We're going to find out the SUV on the road was stolen, aren't we?" she asked him.

"Most probably," Ragnar told her grimly.

"At the fork in the trail… Hugo didn't know whether to go after the man or try to find Amelia."

Ragnar nodded again. "I believe so," he said. "But—"

"Right now, she's alive," Megan said quietly. "And she knew the man she let into her house."

"Either that or he came in under a guise. Possibly as someone who was there to fix something or from the electric company or…they have an alarm. The alarm company. And they have a camera!"

He pulled his phone out of his pocket, but he imagined Jackson would have gotten to the Ayerses' house by now.

And Jackson would have asked about a camera immediately. Still, there was nothing to do but hold the woman as they waited for help. He called Jackson, who assured him they were accessing the camera as they spoke.

Ragnar watched the woods as well. It was possible the "Embracer" apprentice would come back to watch. Except the man would have heard the dog. And if he came back, Hugo would warn them. The person might not be the brightest or best—following in the footsteps of men like Ayers and Carver did not denote genius-level intelligence—but he'd surely know a dog would be aware of his presence.

But Megan was with him. And so he kept an eye out.

Police and paramedics found them quickly enough. Amelia was put on oxygen before being carefully carried through the trees.

A forensic team arrived to search the lean-to and the burial site, and he and Megan and Hugo left at last.

"Hospital?" she asked.

"Back to the Ayerses' house," he said. "Jackson will have studied the video from the front of the house. We may already know who we're looking for, or at least we may have an idea."

"He's still here somewhere," she said. "But not close—Hugo would know."

"The police are searching," he reminded her.

His phone rang—Jackson was calling.

"So far we know the SUV the kidnapper used was stolen from a parking lot in Richmond, Virginia, two days ago."

"Figured," he told Jackson, nodding to Megan.

"And I'm sending you the footage from the camera at the Ayerses' doorway now," Jackson said. "Naturally, we're running it through facial recognition, but that can fail. And when it doesn't fail, it can take forever. But there's something strange about it."

"What's that?"

"The nose—the rest isn't the same, but the nose could be the exact one on the sketch Maisie did of the fellow who picked up Carole Berlin."

"Stage prosthetics?" Ragnar said.

"That's what it sounds like. It's possible these people are coached to disguise themselves. They know they might be seen. And they want witnesses describing someone unlike them."

"Well, I guess we'll make another trip to the hospital and see what the women remember, if either is able to talk today."

"Give the doctors time," Jackson said.

"Right." He hesitated. "I'll need to get back to talk to Ayers again and then Carver. When Megan sensed what Ayers was up to, we headed straight out. But…"

His voice trailed. He didn't want to say it.

"But we have to hope Amelia's head injury isn't that severe and that she lives," Jackson said flatly.

"I believe the man assumes that if she's dead, all the family money comes to him. But is that true? She has a daughter."

"And the daughter is, by all legal definition, his daughter, too. Even if he did try to kill her. Now, if he's convicted, I'm not sure what the legal ramifications might be. If she dies, he'll claim he couldn't have done it; he was locked up. I think that's why we're having as much activity as we are. Ayers and Carver both want to claim they couldn't possibly be serial killers; the killing has gone on even though they have the most solid of alibis. You can bet they'll try every legal machination in the book."

"Right. But one of these guys could turn on them." Ragnar was hoping that would be the case.

"We'll still need evidence," Jackson reminded him. "And we'll need a jury with sense and intelligence. Or we need to prove something has been going on. That it is a group of killers who would all be the best 'Embracer.'"

"They have to go away for good," Ragnar said.

"We will get what we need, Ragnar. We are closing in, and again, two women are alive today because of you."

"Because of Megan and a dog," he said, glancing her way and smiling. She was watching him so anxiously. "All right. Thank you. We'll study the footage," he told Jackson.

He hung up and looked at his messages. Jackson had already

sent the images the camera set for the front of the Ayerses' house had captured.

"They let that guy in?" Megan muttered, staring at his phone.

The camera caught a man in a courier's uniform ringing the bell. Mariana answered the door, smiling and polite. Amelia came up behind her, greeting the man.

He could have been anywhere between thirty-five and forty-five. He had long blond hair that was tied back neatly. He stood about six feet even, had a medium build, and cradled a box. The camera caught everything that went on visually; there was no sound. It did catch a few features. Brown eyes. Broad cheek-bones. The chin was strangely pointed.

And the nose was bulbous.

"Definitely makeup," Megan said. "And that's the same with the man in the sketch, the man who took Carole and killed her. Is it the same person or a different wig and the same bulbous nose?"

They watched as the man indicated the delivery slip had to be signed; he handed Amelia his pen.

The pen didn't work.

Amelia seemed to say he should step in and wait; she would find a pen.

The trio disappeared into the house.

"Amelia should have been smarter," Ragnar said, wincing. "She and Deirdre were being protected. They still had a patrol car go by every night, and the FBI was notified about Deirdre's trip. After weeks and weeks of protection..."

"She's a kind and decent person. How she wound up with Rory Ayers is a mystery," Megan said. "I'm so hoping she lives. We need to get right to the hospital—"

"No. Police are guarding the place. Jackson said to give the doctors time to work. And police and agents have all been care-ful. Luckily, the Ayerses' place is remote, and the media didn't pick up on something happening at the house. When we see Ayers again, he won't know he failed in having his wife killed."

"Oh? So, we could just wait—"

She fell silent as he reached out and touched her cheek, rub-bing away a smudge of dirt.

"We are going to the safe house."

She looked at him, surprised.

"We need a shower," he said. "No, not because I really do adore you in lather, but because we're going to go to a hospital where they prize cleanliness."

"Ah, are we that dirty?"

"Yes."

"Okay, then. Have you talked to Mark?"

"I will. But I think it's extremely important he and Colleen remain 'unofficial'; and I also think it's important that unoffi-cially they keep an eye on Grace and her friends. I don't know if they—as in this brotherhood or whatever—suspect the women know something. News travels. We were trying to make the men believe one of them gave up Joel Lettermen by reporting the position of his kill to us. They wanted to kill Grace maybe because they know she's the one who followed up on Carole Berlin's death. And maybe now the women are all targets."

Megan nodded. "I'm glad Grace, Penny, and Jean—and Tia now—have Mark and Colleen. And Red. They will be safe."

"Right. So, let's get Hugo and head to the house. Shower—in separate showers, I guess—and then get on to the hospital. That should give them time to..."

"Live or die?" Megan asked, her voice pained.

"To come to, hopefully. Jackson doesn't even have a report

on their conditions. Again, they may come to just fine. We don't know yet."

Megan reached out and touched his face.

"A dirt smudge?" he asked her.

"No. I just wanted to touch your face."

He smiled and set an arm on her shoulders; they made their way back to the car with Hugo following along.

At the house, they let Hugo stay in the yard, but brought him out a big bowl of water and one of dog food.

They did go off to their different rooms to shower. When he was dressed, Ragnar hurried to the kitchen, reheating the coffee that was left from the morning.

Megan appeared. "Power bars!" she said.

"What?"

She opened one of the cabinets and produced three different boxes of protein bars. "We keep forgetting to eat. I'm partial to the crunchy peanut ones."

"You forget to eat often?" he asked her.

"Not as often as you do, I'll bet."

"The crunchy peanut ones will be fine. We can eat in the car."

She collected the bars; he poured to-go cups, and they headed to the door.

"Oh! One sec!" Megan told him, hurrying back to the kitchen.

She returned with a doggie beef stick treat for Hugo.

"He doesn't like crunchy peanut protein bars," she explained.

Ragnar smiled. He suddenly wished he wasn't coming to like her quite so much.

Fantastic moments.

And the case was proving to be a fourteen-hour-a-day situ-

ation, but he also knew that was necessary. They were following lead after lead.

And the crimes seemed to be accelerating. Was that because
of their continued commitment to each lead? Was it making the
killers desperate to get their minions out and working?

No, Ayers had wanted his wife dead. Simple numbers. He
needed her dead to be able to hire the lawyer of his dreams. He
was quiet as they drove, but that was okay. Megan was quiet,
too. He realized their relationship had grown. They could be
quiet and not awkward.

When they arrived at the hospital, they found officers working the hallway making sure information didn't sneak out and
also making sure someone didn't sneak in dressed as a doctor or
nurse to "visit" the patients so recently brought in.

Megan whispered to Ragnar she was thinking they'd have
to be put on payroll soon, since they came so often. Then she
grimaced and added, "Okay, so this is much, much better than
being at the morgue."

"Amen to that," Ragnar agreed.

Some personnel didn't know Hugo yet; and a few nurses and
doctors looked at them warily until Megan showed them his
credentials as a therapy dog, and Ragnar showed them his credentials as a federal agent.

The hospital doctor who had seen both women was Liz
Unger. She had also brought in a neurological specialist because of the blows to the head. "Mrs. Ayers is stable, but we're
keeping a close eye on her," Dr. Clayton told them. "The blow
she received was hard. We still have Ms. Largo on a ventilator;
she inhaled a lot of dirt. Obviously, we've done tests; and the
good thing is, unless there are unexpected complications, both
women should make full recoveries."

Clayton was a medium-size man who appeared to have a wiry strength. He was in his fifties, Ragnar thought, white-haired, somewhat wrinkled, and confident without being aggressive. He gave them a smile and looked at Dr. Unger, who was his junior by a good twenty years, a serious, dark-haired woman, slim with fine features and dark brown eyes.

"Head injuries can be worrisome," she said.

"Lizzie could have handled this fine," Clayton said. "But she's right. We needed scans and we needed to read them, but she was making all the right calls. You can't speak with Ms. Largo yet—not while she's ventilated. But Mrs. Ayers was very lucky. She's not dealing with any lung issues, but due to the pain— the extent of which could cause greater injury—she is sedated. I do believe she can hear you, though, and perhaps say a word or two."

They thanked him and went in. Amelia Ayers looked incredibly tiny and frail against the white sheets of the hospital bed. She was leaning back, but not prone. When they entered, her eyes were closed, but she heard the door and opened her eyes. No sound came from her lips, but she mouthed, *Thank you!*

"You're all the thanks we need," Ragnar assured her. "But we need your help. We weren't able to follow your abductor into the woods."

Tears created a glitter in the woman's eyes. "I was such a fool. A pen! He needed a pen. And we just opened the door, and let him in." Her voice was barely a breath, but she was anxious to talk. "They told me Mariana is going to survive. She shouldn't have to pay for the horrors in my life. I am so grateful, but I don't know... First, my daughter. And then...me. And Mariana caught in it all!"

"Amelia," Ragnar said quietly before hesitating. She wasn't

in great shape. She wasn't at a dangerous age, but she was in her fifties. He didn't want to upset her more, but they needed all the help they could get. "Amelia, we believe that—"

"That heinous creature I lived with—was married to!— brought this about. He's locked up, but that doesn't seem to mean a damned thing. I know he tried to kill me! But he thinks I'm an idiot. Well, I have given Deirdre the business titles and rights; he can't touch it. He thought all along I didn't have the sense to realize my power, but there was a reason I kept my name on all our holdings. Now I understand that he thinks all women are stupid. Well, I was stupid. I thought he loved Deirdre! I thought he loved me. But all he loves is himself and money, and I'm not sure in which order."

Amelia had found her voice, but it was raspy and all but breathless.

"Please," Megan pleaded, stepping up with Hugo. "Don't upset yourself—"

"Red!" Amelia said with pleasure.

"This is my dog, Hugo," Megan said.

"Saved by a dog! Bless those creatures," Amelia said.

"What we need is help," Ragnar told her. "Had you ever seen this man before? Can you tell us more about him?"

She shook her head and laughed, a bitter sound. "I thought, wow, that's an ugly guy at first. And I didn't realize until he picked up the frying pan and creamed Mariana that he wasn't that ugly—he was in makeup. I didn't know he had followed us in until he had the frying pan, and as I watched her fall, I knew. He was in ridiculous makeup! But I knew what a fool I was too late." She closed her eyes, wincing. "He was good, though. The uniform was the customary uniform for the de- livery company. I buy frequently from a specialty food store in the city, and they use Maxwell Delivery Plus. He looked just right, and he was so nice."

"Did you recognize his voice?" Megan asked.

Amelia thought hard. "I—I hadn't thought about that. Maybe? I don't know. He was at the door, and he was so apologetic about his pen we just stepped in and told him he didn't have to wait outside. I keep a drawer with pens and tapes and the like in the kitchen; and we went there, and I guess I knew he was following us, but I didn't think anything of it. Not until he picked up the frying pan, and even then, I was just puzzled and then horrified. Mariana was down, and I tried to run, but he was faster and…" She stopped speaking. Her brow was knit with pain. "And here we are, and I'm praying Mariana doesn't pay for me being a fool. Oh, my God! Do you know how long I was married to that man? And I didn't have a clue!"

"Amelia, these men are good at hiding what they are. Very good. It's happened to people before you, and sadly, I'm sure it will happen to people in the future as well," Megan assured her.

Megan was good with people. She had real empathy, Ragnar thought. She was amazing all the way around, and watching her with Amelia Ayers, he felt something in him tighten.

Maybe he'd been better off when he'd thought her ridiculously independent and rude.

Amelia nodded. "Thanks for that. And… I think there is something familiar about him. It wasn't that I'd seen him. I think I heard his voice before."

"Where, when?" Ragnar asked.

"In town. He was asking a clerk at the big pharmacy if he could put up a flier for something…something he'd lost. Oh, of course! A lost dog! But I definitely don't know him. And I wouldn't have made the connection. I can't be sure, but he was the same height and build. His hair was different, kind of a darkish brown, but—oh, a wig, of course!"

Rory Ayers had counted on his wife being stupid. The whole group believed all women were stupid. And they were proving him wrong.

"Amelia, that is going to help us. It's really going to help," he assured her.

Dr. Clayton came into the room.

He waited just a minute, giving Ragnar a querying look. Ragnar nodded, and the doctor said, "Mrs. Ayers, these people really needed to see you. But now you need to stop talking and rest. Is that all right with everyone here?"

"You can call us for anything," Megan told her.

Amelia smiled. "Deirdre is on her way back to town. Again, thank you. Oh, and besides the people you so kindly provide, we've hired our own security guards. I've discovered what I can do with my own money," she added dryly.

"That's great," Megan said.

"And you're lovely people. I will always try to do anything I can for you," Amelia said.

They were barely in the hallway when Ragnar called Jackson and told him where their team needed to go to look for notices.

"Is there any way you can get me back into the correctional facility?" he asked Jackson. "I want to speak with Ayers today before the media gets hold of any of this."

"I *will* get you in there," Jackson assured him. "There was a shift change at four, and the second crew isn't accustomed to dealing with visitors, but I will get you in. Any visiting hours there usually end at four, but I'll call in some favors."

Megan was staring at Ragnar, and he hesitated.

"Are you all right with this? I can get you to your sister and Mark—"

"Are you kidding? I've got to hear what Ayers has to say now!" she told him.

He nodded, smiling. "And that's great. You hear him better than I do. Come on, Hugo, let's move. Then we can go home and hope the cops and rangers in the woods had some luck looking for the kidnapper."

"You don't want to prowl around the woods at night?" she asked him.

He glanced her way, shaking his head. "Sometimes, there's a gut feeling that maybe I need to be somewhere. But I also know no one works alone. Good people are out there combing the woods. We have to depend on each other."

"Good. Because we probably should have a real dinner and sleep tonight."

"Just sleep?"

She shrugged, smiling. "A little activity always helps sleep."

When they arrived at the correctional facility, the shifts had indeed changed. He didn't know the night crew, but a man named Ned Watson was working the entry cage/desk and a guard named Peter Aubrey was on point at the inner gate to let them in and procure the prisoner for their interview.

Ayers seemed cheerful, almost anxious, to Ragnar.

Ragnar didn't need Megan to tell him the man thought his wife was dead.

"You left so quickly this morning," he said, leaning back comfortably in his chair. "More crime out there? Stuff I couldn't have anything to do with since I'm locked in here."

"No, sorry, I just had to leave because of a personal matter."

"A personal matter?" Ayers demanded, and he laughed. "You don't have a life. You have work."

"Work does take a lot of my time. But I have a big family," he lied. "My aunt was sick. My cousin needed me. And you weren't answering my questions."

"I don't remember your questions."

"They were about the man we caught in the woods trying to kill a woman. He believes *you* were the one who tipped us off. Well, you or Jim Carver."

Ayers stared at him without speaking for a minute. "That's just crazy."

"There's so much that's so crazy! But if you didn't tell us where to go, it had to have been Carver, right?"

Ayers didn't reply. Then he asked, "Is bugging me all you've got to do? I'm sure there was a terrible crime somewhere today. I mean, God knows, there are awful people out there. You know, I may not be speaking with my almost-ex-wife, but I'd hate for anything to happen to her."

"That's magnanimous of you," Ragnar said.

Ayers leaned forward, the concern on his face a pretense. "Nothing has happened to her, right?"

"Should something have happened to her?"

"No, it's just there are bad people out there who know I'm incarcerated, about to face a bunch of bogus charges—"

"Save it for your defense. You forget, I was there when we brought you down."

"It was all Gary Boynton. Thank God that idiot is dead!"

Ragnar laughed. "So he can't tell them about you being his mentor?"

"Wait until you see the lawyer I'm going to get."

"Are you thinking you could borrow the money from Jim

Carver? I don't think so. He doesn't have any. And I don't think your wife intends to give it to you."

"You'll see," Ayers said pleasantly. "I will get the money. And I will walk away from here a free man, and sue the local government, the federal government. You forget. I'm a major league businessman. A man with tons of government contracts—"

"I believe your wife has the government contracts now."

"She will give me the money," Ayers said.

"No, she won't."

"What makes you so sure I won't have that money?"

"Well, I spoke to your wife about an hour ago, and from what she told me, I think she'll be delighted if you get the death penalty."

"You...spoke to Amelia?"

"Yes, why?"

The look on Ayers's face at that moment was worth a dozen fourteen-hour days. He didn't have to say anything.

He had ordered Amelia to be killed. Now, they just had to figure out how.

Ragnar stood. "I think Carver betrayed you, Ayers. It happens. Even in prison, people have an instinct for life. When you cooperate with the law and law enforcement, it might just save that one precious thing—life itself."

He turned and walked out of the room. Ayers started screaming for him to come back.

He walked into the room next door, where Megan and Hugo had been observing. Ayers was still screaming. The guard was standing just outside the door—apparently letting Ayers scream it out a bit before bringing him back to his cell.

"I don't think you need my hearing to know, yes, he ordered Amelia killed. He believed that within days he'd have the company and all its assets back under his control even from here," Megan said.

"Now we have to see if suspicion will fly far enough for Carver to turn on Ayers, or for Ayers to turn on Carver," Ragnar said.

"So what's next?"

"Unless an officer, a ranger, or an agent has managed to find the man who was putting up 'lost dog' fliers at the pharmacy, we'll come in to see Carver tomorrow. He might be willing to talk. And Joel Letterman may wind up interested in giving us some insight, too."

"For now?"

He smiled at her and hunkered down, scratching Hugo's ears.

"Home. Food. And sleep. And whatever might come in between."

At the house, Hugo went bounding off across the yard. Ragnar really had intended to dig into the supplies in the kitchen and come up with an appetizing and sustaining dinner.

They didn't make it.

Their clothing wound up strewn around the living room.

The first time had almost no foreplay, as desperate as they were for each other, but what there was came with lots of searing hot kisses, caresses, touches with fingers and lips and tongues.

The second time was slower, more luxurious, and he found himself fascinated and entranced by the scent of her, the brush of her flesh against his, the green of her eyes. Her smile, her passion, the sensuous vibrancy of her movement, and simply the way she felt in his arms.

It was late when they lay together and he said at last, "Dinner."

"Ah," she teased, running the tip of her tongue over his lips. "You were delicious."

"I'm offering to prove I'm a fabulous cook."

"Your omelets were great."

"I'm not really a fabulous cook," Ragnar admitted. "I'm a capable cook."

"I'm willing to bet there are dinners in the freezer. I'm happy if we microwave a few."

"That might be what I meant by cooking."

Megan leapt out of bed suddenly, reaching for her dress. She slid it over her head without worrying about underwear.

"Hugo!" she said.

"Wait!" He was up just as quickly and into his trousers. "I'll open the door," he told her. He hurried to the door ahead of her, checking the screen above it, which showed whoever an arrival might be should someone make it through the gate.

He opened the door, allowing Hugo—patiently sitting on the steps—into the house.

"I am so sorry, boy! I guess you want your dinner," Megan said, stooping to give the animal pets and affection.

"Right. I'm on it. Dog food and microwave meals," he said, but as he headed for the kitchen, he found his phone in his pocket.

He had a message from Jackson. And it was disturbing.

"They found the man who attacked Mariana and Amelia. His name was Samuel Holden, bricklayer by trade. He's dead. Shot through the heart. He was found at six o'clock by a ranger. The body was still warm, and the medical examiner believes he was killed less than thirty minutes before the body was discovered. His killer was long gone. A dead end. But we have the flier from the pharmacy, and we've collected many others from around town. Come into headquarters after you've seen Jim Carver in the morning; all hands will be needed to determine how the communication is going out."

Megan was staring at him, and he knew his face showed his frustration. He handed her the phone and headed on into the kitchen to feed the dog. When Hugo's dish was full, he walked to the freezer, and as he'd expected, it was stocked with full meals.

Megan followed him and handed back his phone without a word.

"Chicken pot pie for me," she said, and went to refresh Hugo's water bowl.

He put the meals into the microwave. Without their would-be killer, they didn't have the tie to Ayers they needed. Unless they could find the would-be killer's killer.

Megan retrieved iced tea bottles from the refrigerator and set them up along with utensils. He procured their meals from the microwave and sat next to her.

She looked at him and smiled grimly. "We will find the answer. The answer is in the fliers. And I promise you, we will figure them out."

He nodded. "Forensics will help us."

"I meant, I'll know what they're really saying. Forensics can discover where they came from."

He smiled. "Great. And Angela is still searching diligently for anything we can find out about the guards and the defense attorneys. It's just that—"

"A killer can hide beneath the facade of the boy-next-door."

He nodded.

"You really complement me," he said softly. "I mean, we work well together—not a bad partnership."

"Not so bad working with a book editor?"

He shrugged and teased, "In a pinch. After all, my partner was on his honeymoon."

She smiled and took his hand. "We will solve this."

And they would. Her life depended on it.

And that mattered more to him with every passing minute.

CHAPTER TWELVE

Megan should have felt tired. But she woke feeling as if she was imbued with energy. She understood how Ragnar had felt. If they'd only found the abductor/would-be killer alive, he might well have given them what they needed. Then again, Joel Letterman was still alive, and he would only allude to the fact someone was pulling the strings.

He had still given them clues. They knew Rory Ayers had ordered his wife killed. Just how he had done it was what they needed to prove.

And they would, she was determined.

She started to rise but her cell phone was ringing, and she grabbed it quickly. Colleen was on the line.

"Hey. Did something happen?" Megan asked anxiously.

"No, no. Mark and I have been here all night. They're fine. Mark thought someone was watching the house last night, but when he went out, whoever it was had gone. And he has a lock on the gate. Of course, someone determined could scale the gate, but he's also called in some favors and is setting up an alarm system. Seems the gals have all decided to go into another line of business, by the way. Oh! I called to give you a heads-up."

"A heads-up? About what?"

"Patrick."

"Patrick? Our brother?"

"He's on his way."

"What? On his way—where?"

"To the safe house. You should have called him! I've been keeping our folks at bay. They think you're just working re-motely at a safe house for your safety. You need to call them, and you should have called Patrick."

"I thought you—"

"I have been talking to him. I've told him I'd trust Ragnar not just with my life, but with yours and with anyone's life. But he knows about the case—cases—and you know he works with the Philadelphia police, and even if he didn't, so much about arrests is public record, and—"

"No!" Megan said. "Patrick will want to put me in a locked room in a steel bunker!"

"Well, be prepared. He's on his way."

"Thanks!"

Megan ended the call and leapt out of bed. She had known her sister and brother had shared something she didn't—or hadn't. They shared the pursuit of dangerous criminals, or in Patrick's case, the determination of guilt and innocence and the ability to discover the truth.

They had both been protective of her, from the time they'd been little kids. She'd been the smallest. The one with her head in a book all the time, loving fantasy, sci-fi, comic-cons…things to do with the imagination, while they had dealt with harsh reality.

She adored Patrick. He was a terrific brother.

But...

She could hear Ragnar in the kitchen. She fled to her own room.

She showered and dressed in a flash, donning a casual pantsuit with a jacket that allowed it both a leisure as well as a business appearance. She brushed her hair and applied makeup.

She wanted her appearance to reflect someone who *hadn't* spent most of the night making passionate love in a man's bed.

But when she walked into the kitchen, she stopped dead.

Patrick wasn't on his way.

Her brother was already there. He was seated at the table, studying something on his phone. Ragnar was at the stove flipping eggs. He looked her way and shrugged. He knew Patrick, of course. They'd met at Mark and Colleen's wedding. But he hadn't expected him.

Of course he'd let him in.

Patrick turned her way, stood up, and hurried toward her, taking her into his arms for a long hug. Then he pulled away and looked at her anxiously.

"You're all right? Colleen said you were managing beautifully. I had to get down here and see you for myself," Patrick said. His expression changed to one of annoyance and anger. "You might have called, you know."

"Patrick, I didn't want you worrying. And you have your work—"

"I'm independent. I work mostly with the police, yes. But I set my own hours," he reminded her.

"But—"

"Megan! We trust each other, we worry about each other!"

She let out a breath. "You worry more about me. And I'm fine. And…"

She paused, not sure whether or not to tell him just how useful she had been on the case.

And how good it felt.

"I've assured Patrick you've been safe at all times," Ragnar said, calmly moving the eggs from the frying pan to three plates.

"You don't know how to defend yourself!" Patrick said.

"I don't need to defend myself, though I managed just fine when it was necessary," Megan said. "Anyway, I listen. That's what I do, Patrick. I'm good at it. Ask Ragnar. I've been extremely helpful."

Patrick gave her a slow and skeptical grin.

"So much for you just being in a safe house," he said.

Megan drew in a deep breath and mentally straightened. "Patrick, I love you. But I'm an important part of this case, and I intend to follow through with whatever I can do that will help in any way."

"That's what I figured," he said.

"Oh!" Megan said with surprise.

Her brother smiled at her. "That's why I'm here. Another guardian couldn't hurt since I know better than most you are independent and determined—beyond sense sometimes. So, guess what, sis? I'm here. I'd figured a sofa would be just fine, but since the two of you are sleeping together, I can have my own bedroom."

A plate clattered on the table. Ragnar was frowning and staring at Patrick.

Patrick turned to him with a grin and a shrug. "I'm one of the weird triplets, remember? And a criminal psychologist. I can read faces and body language. Sometimes I can even read minds."

Megan had no idea how Ragnar would feel about her brother's announcement.

To his credit, he smiled. "I'll have to speak to Jackson about bringing in another consultant. You don't just move into a safe house. I have to get clearance for you," he told Patrick.

"Do it, please," Patrick said. "Because I also shoot straight, and I've spent years in various forms of the martial arts."

Ragnar nodded. "This morning, we're going back to the correctional facility. There were two men who were incarcerated—with a third one killed—when we, as in Mark and I, became lead from our unit on the Embracer case. They're still pulling strings somehow from prison. They're recruiting—"

"I'm up on the case," Patrick said, interrupting him. "Thanks, but I've been following. There are two things I would like. One, to be a 'listener,' too. I'm good. If you doubt me, you can call the chief of police in Philadelphia. Secondly, I'd like to get Megan to a shooting range."

"Patrick, really—" Megan began.

"Both can be arranged," Ragnar assured him.

"Great. Thank you," Patrick said.

"Then let's eat," Ragnar suggested. "On some days, meals are few and far between, so let's get this one in. You're about to enjoy the culinary results of one of the five things I'm competent at doing in a kitchen. Or outside the kitchen. I grill fantastic fish, steaks, and hot dogs, and whip up some mean honeyed Brussels sprouts—and omelets."

"Brussels sprouts?" Patrick inquired, taking his seat again.

"Mom was old school. Eat your vegetables. They can be good," Ragnar said.

Megan sank into her seat at the table. She studied her brother. In her mind he was an exceptionally good-looking man. He stood at about six-three, and where her hair was light red and Colleen's was a bit deeper and redder, Patrick had a dark auburn color. His eyes were green like hers, his jaw was both classic and rugged; and he kept in shape not because he was a maniac about it, but because he simply loved sports, especially swimming and basketball, and he practiced martial arts regularly. Maybe he did make sure to hit the gym because he spent so much time with hardened criminals.

Ragnar finished setting the table, putting down glasses, orange juice, mugs and coffee, cream and sugar, salt and pepper, and implements. She realized she hadn't helped at all.

She had just sat there, still trying to process the fact her brother had shown up.

"Okay," she muttered at last. "I had actually already asked about heading to the shooting range."

"Things have happened quickly," Ragnar said. "We just hadn't gotten the chance."

"Think we can make the chance today?" Patrick asked.

Ragnar answered carefully. "You know—officially—Colleen and Mark can't work on this case. The Krewe gets away with a lot that isn't usually recognized regarding agents, but when an agent is directly related to an expert witness, they're off the case for dozens of reasons, which I assume you know. But they've been helping."

"I know," Patrick said. "*One* of my sisters talks to me."

"Hey!" Megan protested.

"Anyway, we're heading out to interview Jim Carver. The man we apprehended who was trying to kill a previous victim's friend gave us something—public notices. Megan believes there are messages in some kind of a code in simple fliers people put up—lost dog, house for sale, etcetera. Our agents have been col-

lecting them from around the city, and there is one in particular we know about because yesterday's victim saw the man who
took her putting up one of the fliers in a pharmacy. That flier
has been acquired; and while we have pictures on our phones,
there are more from all over the DC area, Virginia, and West
Virginia. This may go farther, but we've been looking at victims in this general area."

"Right," Patrick said. "So, check in on this Jim Carver, check
in at your headquarters, and go to the shooting range?"

Ragnar looked at Megan.

"Sure," she said. "I…yeah. I don't like guns, but under the
circumstances, I guess I should learn to handle them." She gave
Patrick a grimace. "Like my brother and sister!"

"I really think maybe I can help. And if at any point you want,
I can try talking to this Jim Carver or Rory Ayers," Patrick said.

Ragnar looked at Megan. "Joel Letterman. We can throw
him a curve with your brother."

"Oh! And you need to meet Alfie Parker. Sergeant Alfie
Parker!"

"Is he a cop on the case?" Patrick asked.

"Kind of," Ragnar said. "He's a dead cop. But he was going to
haunt the correctional facility for us and see if he could discover
something. We'd then have to prove whatever he discovered, but
he could point us in the right direction. Angela—Special Agent
Angela Hawkins Crow—is remarkable with her ability to dig up
anything on anyone, but the defense attorneys for Carver and
Ayers have spotless backgrounds. We can't find anything worse
than an old parking ticket on any of the guards at the facility.
I believe someone in there has to be involved. Even if the info
is going out on fliers, someone inside has to be getting the information and instruction that goes out."

Patrick nodded thoughtfully. "Well, many criminals have led double lives."

"Few quite as brilliantly as Rory Ayers," Ragnar said. "And whoever it is who is helping him."

As Ragnar and Patrick continued talking about the case, Megan drew up the photo of the flier from the pharmacy Angela had sent out to them all.

"Lost dog. Friendly. Loves corner fire hydrants. Dark cairn. May bark but will offer up lots of love. If found, please call this number."

"This isn't hard at all!" Megan exclaimed. "This was the call to get Grace. She has black hair—dark cairn. May bark—she may talk! Will offer up love—she's a sex worker. Loves corner fire hydrants—the corner where she was working is the same corner Carole worked. Friendly—a friend of Carole's. And if they didn't understand Carole, whichever man in this strange brotherhood who read it would know she was a friend of *a* victim and might say something to the cops that was damning in some way! Do we know how long ago Amelia Ayers thinks she saw this guy? I'm asking you. I was there talking to her, too. If it was more than a few days ago, the guy who took Amelia had a relationship with whoever is getting the information out of the prison. Letterman read this exact flier before he kidnapped and buried Grace!"

"We can use that on him," Ragnar said. "Give Angela a call and tell her what you've got so far. She can text you more of the fliers. What we need to know is how the information is getting out to the fliers and what's next."

Megan nodded and called Angela, who already knew Patrick Law was now with them.

They'd make sure it was fine for Patrick to stay at the safe house.

"But he's directly related to me, too," Megan said, not sure if she was happy Patrick would be staying.

She loved her brother. But she'd also discovered she loved the time with Ragnar.

"Right. But he's not with the Bureau. He's an independent. Different to the powers that be, even Jackson and Adam."

"Ah, cool," Megan said. "Anyway, send me anything you have, and I'll get on it. Even if it looks like nothing."

"Right," Angela said. "Wait. Jackson is here. Something else has happened. Let me call you back in a few minutes."

Megan stared at the phone. Ragnar and Patrick were both looking at her.

She shook her head and lifted her shoulders. "Angela said something happened; she's going to call me back."

Ragnar suddenly looked at his phone.

"Ah, hell!" he muttered.

"What?"

Ragnar looked at her and then Patrick and back to her.

"We won't be interviewing Jim Carver this morning."

"Why not?" Megan asked.

"He was killed in the cafeteria last night—a shank straight into the back of his neck after a fight broke out. The authorities there are trying to figure out what happened, and who did it."

Angela sent Megan twenty-odd notices; at first glance they all seemed entirely innocuous. She knew she would have to study them a few times.

She also knew Ragnar was more determined than ever to find the connection that proved Rory Ayers was pulling the strings.

It didn't excuse those who followed his directives. But with Ayers shut down, there wouldn't be awed followers thinking he was beyond the law, almost like a god or the devil himself.

Since Megan had the fliers and could study them and think about them—with her brother's strange mind working along with hers—Ragnar had decided they would head straight for the shooting range. They'd go into headquarters later to view the fliers in person, which might amp her ability to read still further.

There was a shooting range close to the safe house that catered to law enforcement and security agencies. Ragnar suggested they go there and come back quickly for Hugo before they went into headquarters.

Megan had figured she'd be thinking about the different fliers while learning to shoot.

She didn't think about them a minute.

She *had* held a gun before, but she'd forgotten how heavy one could feel. And she hadn't known what the recoil felt like.

And just how loud the explosion of the bullet could be.

Of course, Ragnar and Patrick had discussed the best gun for her and come up with a Smith & Wesson M&P Shield 9mm. After she cleared the background check, they purchased one for her right there at the range. It was a small, lightweight—didn't feel like it—weapon with a polymer construction. It was easy for a smaller woman to carry and manage. The weapon had a thumb safety, which they quickly showed her how to use.

But only after they'd argued whether she should have a safety on the gun or not.

But their arguments were kept to facts, points, and discussion, and she was glad. Patrick seemed to like Ragnar. It helped that he noticed Hugo accepted Ragnar.

Patrick was also a dog person. She had asked him about his

pup, an Irish wolfhound named Brian Boru and usually just called Bribo. Dogs, a trainer had told them, usually responded best to a two-syllable name. Bribo was staying with a friend of his. Patrick had seen to it his dog had been trained in several areas; working with the police in so many capacities, Patrick had wanted Bribo to be able to search for drugs and people. With his status as a working dog, Bribo could go with Patrick just about anywhere.

Her brother and Ragnar seemed to get along well. Equally, they seemed all right even when they were discussing the best way to teach her or keep her safe.

Patrick and Ragnar took turns giving her instruction, and then they took turns shooting. Both men had amazingly accurate aim.

Hers was not there yet.

Patrick came over when she had just made a remarkably accurate shot. She smiled at her brother, and then heard a familiar voice. Curious, she turned to look. It was Brendan Kent, the guard from the desk where Ragnar checked his weapon when they went to the facility.

He was talking with someone else. She only caught a few words. "Carver."

"Food fight!" And then, "Go figure."

"The weapon was never found."

"No one has any idea."

Maybe the man figured he might be heard even above the explosive sound of the bullets. Megan quickly turned to Patrick, and she was glad she did.

"Hey!" she heard. She turned back. Brendan Kent was smiling at her. "So, you're just learning? And, wow, hey—you have to be related to her!" he told Patrick.

"Her brother. Patrick Law," Patrick said, extending his hand. The two men shook hands.

"Are you a cop?" Kent asked.

"Shrink," Patrick said good-naturedly. "I'm down from Philly. With two sisters in one city, I had to come."

"That's right! Special Agent Colleen Law."

"Yep."

"Well, nice to meet you."

"And nice to see you when you're not behind a cage," Megan told him. "Is it your day off?"

"It is. And working in that asylum, I like to make sure I can aim," Kent told them. He grinned. He was different today. Out of uniform, wearing a Metallica T-shirt and jeans, he looked like any young man on the street.

The boy next door.

Or was he? She tried to remember every word she heard, and she wished Colleen had been with her because Colleen *would* have heard more.

Ragnar came up to them, greeting the man.

"Officer Kent, I guess you picked a good day to be off."

Kent shrugged. "Well, I didn't pick it—it's one of my days every week. But it did turn out to be a good day off after last night."

"The place must be in uproar."

"You heard? Of course, you heard," Kent said. He shook his head. "There were guards all over. We have cameras, but you can only imagine. There were a hundred-plus men in there. There was an argument at one table, someone sent food flying, and in seconds, there were fights breaking out all over the room. And when they pulled everyone off everyone else, Jim

Carver was dead. I can't say his death upset anyone too much. The man was an asshole. Oh! Sorry for the language."

"I've heard it all before," Megan muttered.

"They don't know who killed him yet?" Ragnar asked.

"No, they didn't get it all dug out until late. It happened at dinner; it was such a confusion of people on people that even though they've gone over the security footage, no one can see who did it."

"Was Rory Ayers in there when it happened?" Ragnar asked.

"I think he was in solitary. He got mad and punched a fellow inmate the day before."

"Interesting. They found the shank that killed Carver?"

"No. It was never found," Kent said, shaking his head.

"So, was it intentional?" Ragnar asked.

Kent shrugged. "Hell if I know. No matter how hard you try, prisoners get their hands on utensils. And once someone with a talent for the deadly gets hold of something like that, well, you know how it goes. Any one of the men in there might have had that weapon—ready to use if necessary. And it might have been the fury of the fight. Strange, though. I always thought Carver had different brotherhoods protecting him in there. He acted like a king, that was for sure. But you get a fight like that going, and a brother might punch his own brother in the mouth. Figuring it all out is above my pay grade, thankfully. I heard the feds have the security footage, so maybe your people will know eventually."

He paused and shrugged. "Anyway, I'm through here. Off to spend some quality time with a young lady. You all take care, and I know I'll see you again. Patrick Law, great to meet you."

"Likewise," Patrick said.

They watched as Brendan Kent left the range. Alone.

"He was talking to someone, but I didn't see who it was behind the range separators," Megan said.

"I just saw him with Dale Barrie, the guy who runs this place," Ragnar said. "The guards from several facilities come in here often. I can't blame them. Some people awaiting trial may prove to be innocent, but in that mix, you also have those who definitely are not. I believe he was speaking to Barrie when you heard him. Kent's probably in here often enough. What did you hear him say?"

"The same thing he said to us. 'Food fight. Go figure—no one has any idea.'"

"But?" Patrick asked her.

"I don't know. We believe it has to be an attorney or a guard who is getting whatever directives these guys have out. But the weapon wasn't found."

"That's convenient," Ragnar said. "Just as it's convenient Ayers was in solitary confinement when it happened."

"Planned," Patrick said.

"You're the psychic. What did you get from him?" Ragnar asked Patrick.

"Well, nothing conclusive."

"Does he know who did it?"

"No," Patrick said slowly. "But I believe he knew it was going to happen."

"It was on his shift," Megan said.

"We will have to watch the man closely, and I'm going to ask Angela to dig deeper," Ragnar said. "And Ayers had Jim Carver killed, I'm sure of it. I wasn't sure whether it was him or Ayers really pulling the puppet strings, but it makes sense. Carver didn't have money. When he was still with his wife, Ayers did. And while a guard or an attorney might now be an acolyte of this Embracer group, they might also simply enjoy the prospect of a lot more money than what is in their paycheck. Still, Ayers must realize that, for him, it's coming close to endgame. As long as Deirdre and Amelia are alive, he can't get his hands on the money he used to throw around. Anyway…" He looked at Megan. "How did you do on the last?"

"She's getting there!" Patrick said. "Hey, she's a Law. Our parents were never cops or agents, but they both knew how to use a firearm. After what happened with Colleen when we were kids—finding a neighbor with a woman in his trunk—they learned all about firearms. Strange. They're cool people. Nice. Like lovable Care Bears. But they're not fools, and while they are usually the eternal optimists, they're grounded in reality, too. Anyway, Megan already showed truer aim than half the cops I know."

"The gun is easy enough to carry?" Ragnar asked her.

She nodded, smiled, and pulled up the leg of her trousers. Patrick had already given her a little holster that held the weapon beneath the pleat of her pants.

"Great. Let's get going and put those notice fliers up on the big screen and see what we can come up with."

"We have to get Hugo first," Megan said.

"Of course," Ragnar agreed.

"You could have brought Bribo!" Megan told her brother. "We have the big yard, and Hugo loves him. It would have been fine."

"Well, if this goes on long, I'll take a day to go and pick him up," Patrick said.

Ragnar drove back to the safe house. Hugo was happy to see them all, and happy just to jump right in the car as well, next to Patrick.

As they left the house, another thought came to Megan's mind. "Ragnar, I was just thinking, we have an inside man in a way... And Patrick should meet Alfie Parker."

"Good idea. As always, I can't guarantee we'll find him, but we will find someone, most probably, and make an appointment." He shrugged. "If Alfie had something by now, though, he'd have hitchhiked to headquarters. But it's not far out of the way."

"Pretty place," Patrick mused as they drove through the winding trails of the cemetery. "A lot of history here with graves going back before the Revolutionary War."

"There was a chapel here once, Church of England," Ragnar said. "So, the place started out as a local graveyard. When Victorian cemeteries—landscaped, etcetera—came into being, it was remote enough and surrounded by enough forest and farmland to continue to grow. I like the area where Alfie is buried—an honor to cops. You get bad cops—just as you can get bad agents—and they have to be weeded out. But for the most part, cops really do protect and serve, and I like they're honored, especially here. Especially when many like Alfie died on duty while protecting and serving."

"Yes. I've worked with some of the best. I also saw the bad once. But luckily, the guy had a captain not about to put up with it and he was gone. Well now, most of the time I work with one precinct in Philadelphia, but I might work with any and with others out in the state. The men and women I've come across are the right kind of people to be the right kind of cops."

"I'm a lucky man, too. Mark is a great partner and so is Red," he added with a smile. "And the Krewe is filled with talented people, agents, and support staff."

They got out of the car, and Hugo barked and ran off immediately. They were the only people in the area; and while Megan wasn't happy her dog had taken off the way he had, at least there was no one around who was going to be upset about it.

"There," Ragnar said. "Hugo went right to Alfie. He's there, leaning against the big obelisk monument."

"Ah," Patrick said.

They strode along the paths between the graves. Megan chuckled to herself. What a strange family they were. When Colleen had first discovered her sense of hearing—and her ability to see the dead—Patrick and Megan had simply accepted it. Soon after, they'd gone to the funeral of a beloved great-aunt, and the kids had all discovered that they could see her. Their dead aunt. Speak with her. They had been surprised, but grateful; she'd assured them that she was fine, that she'd lived a beautiful life, and loved them all very much.

Megan glanced at Ragnar. He was looking at her and smiling. She realized he knew her brother would be as determined to help Alfie as any man could be.

"Ah, the lovely Miss Law, the big brute Viking, and…?" Alfie said. "No, wait! Okay, you are Megan's and Colleen's brother. I mean, you're taller and darker, but yeah. You're the brother."

"I am."

"And you see me clearly."

"I do."

"Alfie?" Ragnar said, searching the man's eyes.

"I'm heading back. I just needed a little break. Okay, right, I'm dead, I know. But my soul is intact and, trust me, a soul can hurt. And that place…yesterday…"

"You were there yesterday? In the evening when Jim Carver was killed?" Ragnar demanded.

Alfie nodded. "It was a free-for-all. A melee. And some of the guards were hurt, as well as several of the inmates."

"Okay, who killed him?" Ragnar asked.

Alfie shook his head. "I'm not sure. I do think the incident was purposely instigated just for that reason. You have a tumble of men in the middle of the cafeteria tables and chairs, and an Olympic athlete couldn't hop the hurdle and see exactly what happened at the bottom."

"But you knew it was planned. How?"

"Ayers is usually kept out of the general population; but after his lawyer went to the judge, he was allowed contact with others at meals. Then he punched someone and nearly throttled him, and he was sent back to solitary confinement. The man is crafty and careful. Although whatever you said to him yesterday, he was in rare form when he was by himself, ranting and raving about his wife being the worst witch in the world.

"He was angry with himself, too. Apparently, he never thought to wrest most of the family money out of her control. Husbands and wives may be fifty-fifty, but that can change in a business. He was muttering to himself about promised payments. He was going to have to assure 'the man' he was getting the money. If the notices didn't keep going out, the reign of The Embracer might end. Ayers really mutters to himself in there. Maybe even a sick murderer gets lonely. He goes on and on, but how can you prove the words of a dead cop? I don't know."

"Knowing where to go, we spend our time investigating in the right direction," Ragnar assured him. "But who was he talking about? The man?"

"All he said was 'the man.' I don't know. But I can tell you this. He has been paying someone to keep it going. He has believed two things all along. He will get off, and he'll get the money he needs to pay for the kind of defense that will free him on a technicality if nothing else. You and Mark—and Red—will have to watch it."

"I'm not worried. Carver was the one who wanted to get us on unlawful entry, and we—and our attorneys—would have been ready. Did he talk about Jim Carver?"

"Oh, yeah. He thought Carver had turned. And he was angry. He went on and on about the amount of women Carver had killed and how Carver considered himself to be the grand emperor of the brotherhood of Embracers. Ayers believed he risked himself to save Carver when he set out to bury Deirdre when Carver was taken in. That way, Carver could claim he was just with a kinky woman. I don't know how Ayers managed a business with government contracts! He really is sick. And I guess he thought so highly of his own expertise at the craft of killing he even had Adam Harrison bring in the Krewe, and still thought you wouldn't catch him."

"Alfie, thank you. We believed Carver and Ayers were the head of this, but we have to stop Ayers now from recruiting every homicidal prospect in the country. It sounds like Ayers was Carver's first apprentice for lack of a better term. And the two of them started their Embracer society." He paused for a minute, shaking his head. "I thought we could get them to turn on one another. I didn't intend for one of them to murder the other."

"I sincerely believe both of them would have gotten the death penalty in court," Alfie told him.

"Right. But that's for a judge and jury to decide."

Alfie studied Ragnar and smiled. "You shoot to kill in order to defend yourself or keep an innocent from imminent death or danger, right? It's what we're trained to do. Is it hard to take a life? Yes. If it's not—we've been in it too long."

"We still don't know how many victims Carver had, do we?" Patrick said.

"We may never know. And we can't change the past. We have to work on the now and the future."

"But you did get to Amelia and her housekeeper in time, from what I gathered from Ayers's rantings," Alfie said.

"We did, thank goodness," Megan said. "I know we will get the answers. Ayers is still there, and I believe eventually Joel Letterman will tell what he knows. He will learn Jim Carver is dead, and that will scare him. He already gave us the information about the notices. And we know now that's how he knew to go after Grace. Oh! Alfie doesn't know about Lettermen and the notices! And there had to have been a notice out there about Amelia and Mariana."

"May I have an update?" Alfie asked. "All I know is what Ayers was ranting."

Ragnar quickly told Alfie what had transpired since they had last seen him.

"Closer. You are getting closer," Alfie said. "I do believe Carver was the first Embracer, but Ayers was active soon after. He was learning from Carver, so their killing spree goes back. And I believe Ayers was responsible for bringing many others in; he had the wherewithal to do it. I wish I could tell you who killed Carver. But not even I could see the bottom of the heap. Many of the men and guards had blood on them. I had to get away for a bit, but I'm going back. I also hoped you would remember what I was doing and stop back by here." He shrugged. "I would have found a way into headquarters today if you hadn't. And may I add, Mr. Law, it is a pleasure to meet you."

"I've heard there's something that keeps you here—your concern for a young woman?" Patrick asked Alfie.

Alfie nodded. "Susie. Yes. The police—and the Krewe—are still trying to find 'John Smith.' So many dead—and yet that bastard managed to escape. He's out there somewhere—maybe in the West, the Northeast, or down in Florida, Georgia, or Texas. He'll have started up again. He has exactly what it takes to continue a criminal empire. He has the knowledge of how to prey on others to make money and a completely antisocial, sociopathic personality. He doesn't care who dies for him. But that's for another day."

"Yeah, we haven't given up on your case," Ragnar said. "First up, though, is trying to make sure that kidnapping and burying women isn't going to be happening on a daily basis. Alfie, thank you."

"I'll get back to the correctional facility," Alfie promised. "I think the officers are speaking with every man who was in the cafeteria at the time, so someone might have some info."

Ragnar nodded.

Patrick reached out as if Alfie could shake hands in the flesh.

Alfie smiled, and took Patrick's hand with his own ghostly hand.

"You deserve justice," Patrick assured him.

"I believe in those who will work on behind me," Alfie assured him.

The ghost gave Hugo a few pats that Megan was sure the dog felt, and then it was time for them to leave. Alfie gave her a smile and told her, "Bye, lovely friend. Stay safe. You guys, you keep her safe!"

"We are on it," Ragnar assured him.

"She's a third of my soul!" Patrick assured him.

As they walked to the car, something occurred to Megan.

"I wonder," she muttered.

"What?" Ragnar asked her.

"The man using the name 'John Smith' disappeared after the raid on the complex. Bodies strewn in his wake. But this guy was into just about everything: drugs, extortion, money laundering, contract killing, human trafficking."

"Right," Ragnar said.

She stopped walking and looked from her brother to Ragnar.

"And his men were completely loyal."

"Right," Ragnar said again.

"Maybe he knew about the men working for him. Maybe he encouraged them in their personal perversions."

"What are you saying?" Patrick asked her.

"I don't know where he is now or much about him. I haven't had time to read all the files, but what if he is still out there, working up his business again? And maybe—while Ayers believed his financial help would come from his wife being dead—there is someone else out there who might be willing to help him now. As in the man who may have been behind it all from the very beginning. John Smith."

CHAPTER THIRTEEN

Megan's words teased at Ragnar as they arrived at headquarters.

It was possible that the former criminal syndicate leader known as John Smith was also linked to the Embracer brotherhood, but they didn't know. They just didn't know.

When they arrived, they went straight to Angela's office. Patrick had only briefly met Angela and Jackson and other members of the Krewe at the wedding, but they were quick to welcome him.

"I understand you're psychic," Angela told him sincerely.

"I don't put a label on anything," Patrick told her. "Sometimes I can hold something, and see what happened to a person who owned the object. It's usually best when it's an item that meant something to them, like a piece of jewelry or the like. I have a wee bit of Megan's ability, with a twist. Sometimes I know exactly what someone is thinking no matter what they say." He shrugged and grimaced. "There is evil in the world; it exists in the human mind. Terrifying, but gratifying when

I am able to use it for something that solves a crime. I admire so much about the Krewe. But I was worried about my sister."

"That's okay. We're glad to have you here," Angela assured him. "So, guys, we head to the conference room. Oh! Just remembered. We have the artist's rendering of the woman whose skull was delivered to Megan in New York. It was sent out this morning to law agencies across the country. We have no idea just how far this might stretch."

"No one has claimed her yet?" Ragnar asked her.

"No," Angela said. "But hopefully someone will match it to a missing persons case. Hugo, hey, come on! Conference room," Angela told the dog.

They filed to the conference room. Ragnar told Angela about their meeting with Alfie as they walked, adding Megan's thoughts on John Smith.

"She could have something there. From what I've seen of the files, John Smith had an extensive criminal empire going. He had 'lieutenants' working under him, several who were killed during the shoot-out that cost Alfie his life. I'm curious if Embracer murders—now or at any point—might have been under his umbrella."

"I would so love it if Alfie's Susie could be found," Megan said.

"A last name would have been really helpful," Patrick said dryly.

"I've been accessing everything I can on that situation," Angela said. "We've been working it ever since Jackson met Alfie. And, Megan, you may just be right. There could be a connection."

They entered the conference room. The screen there was massive. Angela had the computer and screen set to go. The first notice was the one they had figured out already. Ordering or suggesting Grace Menendez be taken.

They went through a few that Megan and the rest of them believed to be honest "lost dog" or "garage sale" notices. Angela verified them by calling the phone numbers left on the notices.

But they came to one notice that was obviously suspicious, perhaps because they knew to be looking for hidden messages in them.

"'Photo album lost at Twenty-Fifth Millennium Café. Pictures of my daughter, priceless to me! Rosy-red cheeks, sun-gold hair, beautiful and charming—to me, of course! If found, please leave with the cashier at the counter. Reward!'"

"That one is easy, but I wonder how new it is, and if we're in time. A woman will be taken outside of this café," Patrick said.

"Sounds easy. But I've checked," Angela said. "There isn't a café anywhere in the surrounding hundred miles with that name. There may not be a café with that name anywhere."

"Have you tried switching the descriptors around? I believe the woman to be kidnapped might be twenty-five years old and a blonde. I believe he's referring to her as a millennial, and the name of the café might be 'Rosy's Café' or something like that," Megan said.

"There's no phone number on that," Angela muttered.

"Give it to the cashier," Patrick muttered. "This doesn't vilify the cashier since even the killers can't put a phone number. That's just a way to make sure the notice isn't seen as a fake."

Angela turned her attention to the computer; Ragnar already had his smartphone out, searching.

"Just on the outskirts of Fredericksburg," Ragnar said. "Rosy's Café, open twenty-four hours. According to this review, it's great food and popular with crews working the three-to-eleven shift at the local hospital plus the weekend theater and cinema crowd. It offers a full bar and a 'happy 'cause it's late but I'm off' special on drinks served from ten p.m. to one a.m." He looked over at Angela. "When was this notice found?"

"Last night. We have Krewe members—especially those from this area—combing everywhere. Special Agent Bruce McFadden found it at the crack of dawn this morning and said he found several along Route 60," Angela said.

"Route 60 heads out west of Richmond, and Richmond is almost sixty miles south of Fredericksburg," Patrick noted.

"But does it matter?" Ragnar said thoughtfully. "There may be a place for posting. And while we're talking a few hours of driving, that may not matter much to men who are called upon to do their leader's bidding, especially since they're all heading to makeshift sites as deep in the woods as they can get to put together their coffins and bury their victims. We need someone out there as fast as possible."

"I'm happy to go. There's nothing like a good café," Patrick said.

"We haven't seen half of the notices yet," Angela pointed out.

"But we need someone out there now," Ragnar agreed. "I'm assuming the man who takes this assignment is going to be young, someone who hopes he's charming enough to lure a woman into believing he has the deepest sympathy for her late hours and is happy to drive her home, no strings attached."

"I'm young," Patrick said. "And charming. And I wonder if more than one person doesn't pick up these assignments? Each would hope to be the one to make the kill and appear to be the best of the best, eventually superseding those who came before them. The psychology in this is strange. On the outside, it looks as if there is nothing to gain by following these directives other than the satisfaction of the kill and the prestige within the group. If someone like Alfie's John Smith is involved, there could be a financial reward out there as well."

"Great. More reason for the evil to be evil!" Megan said, shaking her head.

"For men like Ayers and Carver, I believe it was their sickness. If there is someone over them—this John Smith or someone like him—he changed the game," Patrick said.

"It would be interesting to ask Joel Letterman about money," Angela told them.

"Yes, and we will. But—" Ragnar began.

"Go. But if you don't want to be noted as law enforcement—"

"We'll window-shop. We'll play back and forth," Ragnar said.

Angela nodded. "I'll see who we can send from our unit so we can tag team and make sure no one looks suspicious. I know you're concerned. Get going. For tomorrow, I'll have you set up to talk to Letterman and Ayers. I think it's going to be good you don't rush in right after Carver was killed. It might be best if Ayers assumes we all think good riddance to bad rubbish, and it was just a prison brawl. To the best of our knowledge, we've kept Amelia Ayers's abduction and the attacks on her and Mariana quiet. He knows his wife is alive. But we don't know what else he knows."

"Okay, we're out of here," Ragnar said. He paused, looking at Megan.

"Maybe you should stay here and go through the rest of the notices with Angela. There might be something else," he told her.

She smiled. "Nope. You're just trying to ditch me. I've already been through a few, and I've texted Angela what I believe. Many of them were old and related to past victims. I'll keep working in the car. And then in the café, I'll be having a lovely lunch. Or dinner. Or drinks." She paused. "I don't believe any of this will happen until later, most probably during their late happy hour."

"Why do you think that?" Angela asked.

"The notice says the pictures are of a daughter 'beautiful and caring.' Caring—makes me think the woman is a nurse. And it's not such a wild card. A pretty blonde nurse who is about twenty-five years old. There won't be that many working the three-to-eleven shift who head to the café after work," Megan said.

"I think she's right," Patrick said. "But we're not infallible. I mean, Colleen's hearing is always right on point. But Megan and I are left to read between the lines and go with our instincts that we've got it right."

"Jackson is in the field, but I'll call him and get a few agents out there now. We'll switch off during the day; you can go for right after eleven. Which might not be a bad thing. I have Rory Ayers's court-appointed attorney, Jeffrey Hindman, coming here in an hour. I've gone over every conceivable record regarding the man, and he seems like an upright citizen. But somehow, information is getting from Ayers to others out in the world. I thought a face-to-face would be good, and no one has spoken to Ayers as much as you have, Ragnar. No one officially on the case, that is," Angela said.

Ragnar looked at Megan.

"I really think it will be tonight. I mean, I know no one agent is an island—and I know this kind of case takes a village—but I really think Patrick and I might be best on this. I mean, what do you do? Confront every couple in there?" Megan asked.

Angela smiled. "Even we are more subtle than that. We'll need a few cars in case a few suspicious people leave at the same time. And this is interesting, Carver and Ayers used the Bundy gimmick pretending to be hurt or in trouble and capturing the women who tried to help them. And it was easy enough for men to solicit prostitutes. I wonder who this blonde is and why someone thinks she'd be a good prospect for Embracer burial. In fact…I think I'll make a few calls to that hospital and find out who our caring young beauty might be."

Angela excused herself, packing up her laptop and leaving them in the conference room.

The last "notice" disappeared from the screen.

When she was gone, Megan looked at Ragnar. "If Angela can get a name, shouldn't we warn the woman, and that way she can stay away from the café?"

Patrick and Ragnar looked at one another.

"Angela might have other plans. We won't risk a woman's life, but it might save her and other women in the future if we know who her assailant is," Ragnar said.

"But that risks her life," Megan protested.

Ragnar and Patrick exchanged looks again.

"What they will do is send someone in, an agent or police-woman. Undercover," Patrick said.

"I could go—" Megan began.

"No!" her brother and Ragnar said in unison.

She frowned. "I don't think I like the two of you getting on quite so well."

"You…your hair is too red. And you don't know undercover work."

"And you're a civilian and we have agents and police officers who can do that work," Ragnar said.

"I got it!" Megan told them.

Angela poked her head back into the room. "Jeffrey Hindman just called from the parking lot. He's early. I'd like Megan and Patrick to observe from my office."

Hugo barked.

"With Hugo, of course," Angela said.

The two rose and left the room. Ragnar had no idea what expression might be on his face, but he imagined it must have been concern because Megan paused, smiled back, and assured him, "I'll be fine in Angela's office!"

"Megan—"

"Gotta go!"

She left before he could say more. He waited. A few minutes later, Jeffrey Hindman entered the room. He was a young attorney, probably not long out of law school, tall, lean, dark-haired, with a scholarly demeanor. His youth likely contributed to why Ayers wanted money to hire a top-notch attorney.

Too bad. Ragnar had seen young, determined public defenders do a stellar job in the courtroom.

He stood to shake the man's hand.

They both took seats.

"I think this is off the side of ethical, but since my client may be in line to face further charges, I wanted to come in and assure you the man has not slipped out through any kind of spectral ability or mind control. His phone calls—even with me—have been recorded. Rory Ayers is an upstanding businessman."

"Sure. One who buried his own daughter."

"Not his biological daughter, though he allowed his name to go on the birth certificate," Hindman said.

"He was caught red-handed, attempting to kill another woman."

"That was Carver," Hindman said. He sighed. "And the man's idiot almost-son-in-law—who was killed on-site and in the act."

"Well, Ayers managed to have Carver killed," Ragnar said.

Hindman looked truly distressed. "What? No. Carver was killed in a fight that broke out in the cafeteria. Ayers wasn't even there! I know you don't wish ill on anyone, Special Agent Johansen, but you should be relieved. He was accusing you and your partner and his dog of illegal search and seizure."

"Death never relieves me—unless I'm facing a knife or a bullet and I manage to be the one who lives," Ragnar said. He looked at Hindman and shook his head. "I believe, according to the bar and all codes of ethics, a prisoner can tell you anything and you can't repeat it. But I also know it's against the law for you to fail to report a crime you know is going to occur."

"I don't know of any crimes about to occur."

"To facilitate a crime."

Hindman shook his head and tried to look stern, but Ragnar still thought he was rattled. The young attorney leaned forward suddenly. "I'm telling you I don't know anything about a crime about to be committed. I don't know if you're a religious man, but I'd swear it on a stack of Bibles. I've seen Rory Ayers at the facility three times; we've had phone communication perhaps seven or so times, video three times as well. The video and phone conversations have all been recorded. Listen to the man yourself. He is not committing more crimes. He maintains he's nothing but a businessman."

"His wife is divorcing him. He must be brokenhearted."

Hindman sat back. "I am not at liberty to share his feelings even were I to know what they were."

"But he has told you he intends to hire a high-priced attorney, right?"

"Every man is entitled to the best defense possible. Public

defenders are overworked. You know that. If the man wants to hire a team of criminal defense attorneys, that is his prerogative."

"So, you do know."

"I'm sorry; I had hoped to ease your mind. Your bitterness against my client is too great. I can't talk to you about a man you are determined to crucify. I shouldn't have come in here. It isn't right for me to speak about the case in any way."

"We just wanted to make sure you weren't guilty of abetting murder," Ragnar said.

"There is no murder to abet," Hindman said. He still looked uncomfortable. "And your suggestion my client killed a man when he wasn't present for the riot that caused this death is preposterous."

"Is it?" Ragnar asked.

Hindman stood and collected his briefcase. "I believe we're through."

"As you wish," Ragnar said politely. He rose along with Hindman and smiled pleasantly as he walked the man out of the conference room and the Krewe offices.

Then he quickly headed into Angela's office.

"Well?" he asked the others.

"He really didn't know Ayers arranged for Carver to be killed," Megan said. "And it scared him."

"I thought so, too," Ragnar said. "I guess we're lucky the guy came in. I'm not sure how ethical it was to speak with him."

Patrick laughed. "Hey, come on. Anytime you want to talk to someone about a case, they tell you to call their attorney. Megan is right. He's scared. I don't think he was frightened when he believed Ayers might be guilty. Oh, and we both think he knows his client is guilty of killing women. But the idea he might have killed a man who angered him is frightening to him. I guess he's worried now about what might happen to him when Ayers is convicted."

Angela's phone rang. She answered and her brows shot up. "We'll see what we can do. I'll get back to you."

She ended the call and looked at them all grimly. "I don't know if it exonerates him or not, but that was Jeffrey Hindman. He wants protection while he's on the case and after the trial if he loses."

"Interesting. Well, it means we can follow the man," Ragnar said.

"We'll get an agent on it," Angela affirmed. "I've been trying to reach Carver's attorney, Gerald Atkinson, but I haven't been able. His office keeps taking messages. They may be stalling us or falling on attorney privilege. Of course, Atkinson is also with the public defender's office, and they are extremely busy, so…"

"He really could be busy," Patrick said.

"I say we head out to the café," Ragnar said, looking at Megan and Patrick.

"Window-shopping, walking?" Megan asked.

"Well, Hugo gives us an excuse. But we may spend a lot of time sitting in a car. Do we have someone going in?" Ragnar asked Angela.

She picked up her phone and dialed, lifting a finger for him to wait. Ragnar knew she was checking with Jackson.

She listened and then ended the call, smiling.

"Jackson believes he knows whoever the notice was for will be going after a young woman named Teresa Perry. She's twenty-five, blonde, and according to her supervisor a very attractive and *caring* young woman, and an excellent nurse. Teresa might have had some interaction with Ayers or his family at some point. She was working at the hospital when Amelia had a hip transplant about five years ago. She will be escorted home from work."

"That's good," Ragnar muttered.

"And we have an undercover agent going in. Her name is Jordan Wallace. She's recently out of the academy. Jackson told me Adam had suggested to him he interview her for the Krewe, so you know she's experienced in the unusual. Seems they found the perfect person for the job. She's already at the hospital, dressing the part; and when her shift breaks, she'll head straight to the café. It will be difficult for you but have some faith in her. I hear she excelled during her training," Angela told them.

"Have some faith?" Megan asked, frowning.

"Ragnar knows," Angela said softly. "We need to let this man take her; there will be a tracker on her phone. She'll also be armed. She knows not to drink anything he's touched. Don't follow too closely. But if she is picked up by someone taking orders from Rory Ayers, we need to let her get to wherever he intends to take her and find the coffin in which he intends to bury her." She looked at Ragnar. "You'll have the location on your GPS."

Ragnar nodded. Neither Jackson nor Angela would send an agent out unless that agent was prepared for what was coming. Jordan Wallace would have been briefed. And she wouldn't have accepted the assignment unless she had been willing to do so.

"Faith. Right," Megan muttered.

"Megan, this could be a long night," Ragnar said. "There's no reason for you—"

"There are many reasons. You're not leaving me, remember? You're my guardian in all this. And Hugo has proven himself to be one of the best agents in the world," Megan told him.

"Hugo is great."

Megan glared at him, clearing her throat.

He smiled. "Yes, you've been amazing, too."

Angela laughed softly. "An amazing consultant, indeed."

"Sorry. Not that amazing. I just feel I need to be there," Megan told her.

"Excuse me, but I'm your brother. A pretty good protector, too," Patrick said dryly.

Hugo woofed as if he had to be in on it.

"Let's go!" Ragnar said.

"Right. Go!" Angela said.

They left with Hugo at their heels, almost as if the dog was anxious to get on the job, too. Then again, he had been remarkable, and Ragnar had to wonder if Hugo—and Red—picked up some of the extraordinary abilities of their owners.

"Strange stakeout," Patrick said as they headed to the car.

"Stakeout?" Megan asked.

"Our job is to watch, and if it proves necessary to follow," Ragnar said. His phone rang as they approached the car.

It was Jackson.

"I'm at the café, but I've been here too long. Nothing has happened. No single man has approached a single woman. I'll be down the block in my car. Kat Sokolov and Will Chan are in there now, and I'd say you can go in and replace them. Yes, it will be before eleven, but I'm assuming you haven't been paying attention to the time. If you're just leaving the offices now, you can come, park, take the dog for a walk, and get a feel for the street. Then go inside and order dinner and linger over coffee as the late-off-work crowd arrives. I believe you'll recognize Jordan Wallace; she'll be in nurse's scrubs for one, and while there might be other nurses in there, none quite so young or blonde."

"Great. Dinner sounds good," Ragnar told him.

"Check your phone. It should show Jordan Wallace as still being at the hospital."

Ragnar did as he had been directed. He could see the blip that was Jordan Wallace's current position; he could also see it was the hospital as well as the distance from the hospital to the café.

"Got it," he told Jackson.

"I'll be down the block," Jackson told him.

"Noted. Thanks."

He ended the call.

"You are right about one thing," Patrick told him.

"What's that?"

"You people do forget to eat."

"That's why I learned to excel at omelets," Ragnar assured him.

"Ah," Patrick said.

Ragnar glanced at the man in the rearview mirror. He had leaned back, a hand gently set on Hugo's back. He had the feeling Dr. Patrick Law had worked with some of the worst of the worst; but also, if he was here now, he feared his civilian sister was into the worst. He would worry about Megan because, Ragnar imagined, triplets would be close simply by being triplets. And in the Law family, it sounded as if together activities, as well as love, had flourished.

He was also certain Patrick didn't just spend his days sitting at a desk. He believed Patrick had been out with the police he helped often enough.

"Megan can kind of cook," Patrick offered.

"Hey!" Megan protested.

"She's really good with a few things, so I guess you guys could manage some meals in a kitchen. Of course, drive-through fast-food restaurants and diners are fine, too. But you should think about this eating thing. Megan, this won't be so bad. I mean, half the time in a stakeout situation, you just sit in a car. This time, we get to sit and have food."

"Patrick, I never knew you to be so food obsessed!" Megan told him.

"Just talking. It's a fair drive," Patrick said. "Of course, I could ask you two how long you've been sleeping together."

"Patrick!" Megan snapped.

"I am a protective big brother."

"We're triplets," Megan snapped back.

"I'm a lot taller. It's just interesting. You two avoided each other at the wedding. Well, until it was time for you to do your speeches next to the bride and groom. Then it seemed like little nippy barbs were flying, so—"

"Patrick!" Megan wailed.

Patrick leaned forward.

"Hey, you're my sister," he said softly.

Ragnar glanced at him through the rearview mirror. "I respect both your sisters," Ragnar assured him. "And while this doesn't guarantee her safety, I promise you, I see Megan's life as far more valuable than mine. I also admire her unique and incredibly special abilities, and the fact she has a mind of her own and the right to make choices."

"Good answer!" Patrick said. "Nice choice of words, and she is a word person. You know I can't help it—I need to look out for my sister."

"And I can promise you, I would never hurt her. All decisions on the personal front are hers."

"Guys! I'm sitting right here," Megan implored. "Patrick, why don't you look up the café's menu?" she suggested, glancing at Ragnar. He arched a brow to her.

She smiled, shaking her head.

"I'm sorry," she whispered.

"I heard that!" Patrick said.

"And it's okay. He's your brother," Ragnar said. "And...there. Ahead. We've arrived at our destination."

"I saw Jackson's car but didn't see him in it," Patrick said.

"You won't see him. It's Jackson. Will and Kat Chan are in the café. They're very experienced agents, some of the founding members of the Krewe. They'll hover for a while. When we go in, they'll head out."

"I see a space ahead," Patrick said, leaning forward to point out the on-street parking where Ragnar could pull in.

"Thanks."

Ragnar maneuvered his vehicle into the spot. It was a good one. They weren't directly under a streetlight, and the tint on the SUV's windows would keep them from being seen sitting in the car.

"I'll bet our guy is already in there," Patrick said, staring at the café ahead.

"Quite possibly. But then again, he'd be obvious, sitting in a café for too long even if the café is about to have a happy hour," Ragnar said. He turned to Megan. "You and Patrick take Hugo on out for a walk."

"And what are you going to do?" she asked.

"Study the local street maps. He's going to head for the woods. I want to review the various routes he might take," Ragnar said.

"Right. Except...what if I was wrong about this whole thing?" Megan asked worriedly. "What if I read things that weren't there?"

"Then we'll have a late night but at least we'll have dinner."

"But I'll have made all these people work—"

"Lots of work leads to nowhere. We do the nowhere for the times they lead somewhere," Ragnar assured her. "Go on. Hugo needs his walk. Then we can go in."

She nodded. She and Patrick left the car with the dog.

He smiled, watching them go. He could only imagine what Megan was saying to her brother after his comments in the car.

He pulled up maps on his phone and studied the streets, thinking the killer would head to the southwest. There were acres of wild forested land not far from the outskirts of Fredericksburg.

In a few minutes, they returned to the car with Hugo.

"Do we take him in?" Megan asked. "I have his service dog vest with me. But will we be too obvious with a dog?"

"I think we'll be fine," Ragnar assured her.

The café was a charming place with carved, wooden benches at the many tables that fronted the window on two sides. There was a large wooden bar in the center of the café with two semicircles offering seats in front with certain brands of both alcohol and coffee being advertised in forties-style posters on the walls.

"Back there," Ragnar suggested, pointing to a table across from the entrance. It offered a good view of the semicircles and the patrons sitting at the bar stools.

There was no hostess, so they made their way to the table. They passed an elderly woman dining alone who "Oohed" over Hugo as he passed by, and Megan made sure to backstep and let the woman give him some pats.

Ragnar saw Will and Kat sitting at a table that also offered a good view of the place.

They didn't acknowledge him, and he didn't stop or acknowledge them.

In a few minutes, a waitress came to them with menus and

water. The woman—dressed as if she was in a 1950s diner—pushed the happy-hour specials. She was a little disappointed when they ordered soda water with lime.

Kat and Will paid their check and left the café.

A few minutes later, Ragnar noted the young woman who walked in. She was still wearing scrubs, and as she came in, she pulled off her cap and shook her head, so blond tresses fell around her shoulders.

She looked at the bar and took a seat. They couldn't hear what she ordered, but the bartender placed a glass in front of her that was clear and garnished with a lime.

"Probably soda water," Patrick muttered.

Ragnar nodded.

"There," Megan said in a whisper, and inclined her head toward the bar.

Ragnar looked casually around. She had pointed out a man in a casual cotton shirt and dark jeans who got up from the end of the bar. He was in his twenties or early thirties, about six-feet-even.

"Good-looking?" he asked Megan.

"Decent. Dark hair over the forehead, quick smile for the bartender, but he was at the other end of the bar. Now he's next to the blonde nurse."

Jordan Wallace, Ragnar thought.

He glanced at his phone. Yes, the "blip" that was Jordan Wallace now showed as being in the café.

The undercover agent smiled at the man who had come to sit by her side and talk to her. She played with the straw in her drink and flirted. They chatted awhile. Laughed. Then the man pointed to something out the window and Jordan turned to look. As she did so, he reached toward her drink. He'd had something in his hand; something ready to use with the speed of light.

"Saw it!" Megan said.

Before he could stop her, she was on her feet. He leapt up, but Megan was already on the move.

Patrick caught his arm. "She won't blow it," he said. "Give her a chance."

Ragnar didn't have much choice. Megan was already moving close to where Jordan and the man were sitting, calling to the bartender. "Excuse me, where are the restrooms?"

Her voice sounded slurred, as if she'd been drinking just a bit too much.

And pretending to try to hear the answer more clearly, she moved right between Jordan Wallace. She leaned in with her left arm.

And Ragnar couldn't help but smile.

Megan had no training for this kind of thing, but she brilliantly slipped her own soda and lime into position and turned away with Jordan's spiked drink.

Leaving the dark-haired man with no clue his chosen target would not be in the least bit woozy when he lured her into the woods with dark intent.

CHAPTER FOURTEEN

Megan was amazed at her accomplishment. The man was obviously irritated she'd pushed him aside, but he was also a player.

"To your immediate right," the bartender said, pointing.

"Hey there, are you joining us?" the man asked Megan.

"No, no, I'm so sorry—just a few more of these than I'm accustomed to," she said lightly.

Jordan was looking at her, nodding.

Completely aware of what she had done, aware Megan was part of the Krewe that would be shadowing her every move.

"It's okay, really, not to worry," Jordan said. "Seems like Beau and I are great conversationalists. And we'll get back into it!"

"Teresa is so great and patient," the man said pleasantly. "But you gave me a bit of a jam in the arm there."

"I'm so sorry!" Megan slurred, patting his arm seriously.

"Not at all—it's cool. Hey, it's a bar, right? Going to get a few drunks," the man Jordan had identified as Beau said, smiling.

"But it's not usually me. I am so sorry. I will get out of your way," Megan said, backing out and almost tripping over Hugo. The dog had followed her, to make certain she was all right.

"Aw, beautiful pup!" Jordan said.

"What's he 'service' for?" Beau asked.

"Epilepsy," Megan lied, knowing she had to think of something believable. "And sorry again! I will get out of your way."

She winced as she caught Hugo's collar with her free hand, bringing him back to the table.

"Just keep him here and don't drink that!" she said quickly, putting the glass she had switched with Jordan's on the table. "I made a big deal about the restroom. I think I should head that way."

Megan left Patrick holding on to Hugo's collar after telling the dog to stay and hurried around in the direction the bartender had pointed.

She walked in, waited the appropriate time, and walked back to her table waving to Beau and "Teresa" as she did so.

She noted there were plates on the table, and the aroma arising from them was a delicious one.

"That was brilliant," Ragnar told her.

"Really?" she asked.

"Really," Patrick said seriously. "You are impressive, sis."

"Where's the glass?" Megan asked. The drink she'd brought back to the table—"Teresa's" drink tainted with whatever the man had slipped into it—was gone. "Did the waitress take it away? We may need to know about the contents. I mean, we have no idea—"

"Ah!" Ragnar said. "You're not the only one crafty with sleight of hand! The contents are in a vial, and Patrick managed to be a clumsy fool and break the glass," Ragnar told her.

"Can't be sure whatever would wash away in a dishwasher even using industrial strength."

"You carry vials in your pockets?" Megan asked Ragnar.

"Vials, gloves, and evidence bags," Ragnar said.

"Jackets come in handy," Patrick said.

Megan frowned, looking at her brother. "You have vials, gloves, and evidence bags in *your* pockets?"

Patrick glanced over at Ragnar and then shrugged. "Yeah. I never know when I might be called to a site. I work on negotiations sometimes when hostages are involved."

"We did see him slip something in her drink, right?" Megan asked, looking at Ragnar. He nodded with a slight smile on his lips.

"That was brilliant, Megan," Patrick said. "I thought you might manage to knock the drink over, but to save it in such a way—"

"Brilliant," Ragnar agreed.

She basked a moment in the happiness of being applauded by Ragnar and her brother, too. But then she carefully glanced back to the bar to make sure Beau and "Teresa" were still at the bar.

"Okay, Megan, there's food in front of you now. You should eat it. We ordered their meat loaf special topped with crispy onions when you left the first time, and it arrived while you were in the ladies' room. Try eating a real dinner. Not bad!" Patrick told her.

Megan took a bite. The crispy onions with the gravy made the whole thing delicious. She was too distracted to really enjoy the food, but she ate knowing she needed to.

"She called him 'Beau,'" Megan told the men.

"Doubt if it's his real name," Ragnar said.

"And *'beau.'* 'Beautiful' in French. He thinks he's a beauti-

ful man," Patrick said thoughtfully. "Deserving of whatever
he desires. From what I know, that tracks for Rory Ayers. It's
a stretch for Ayers to think himself beautiful, but he obviously
believes he deserves whatever he wants."

"And he managed it a long time," Ragnar said. "He had the
perfect foil. A loving wife, a lovely daughter. He kept it above-
board with the family until he was just too tempted to take the
'Embracer' title from Carver."

"Hmm. Outwardly, he wanted it to appear he'd only done
it to save Carver," Patrick said.

Her brother held multiple degrees and loved the study of the
human mind. While she had been reading all kinds of fiction
along with history books, Patrick had always been the best student among them, often surprising his teachers with his knowledge and understanding. He'd done his undergrad in psychology
and his full medical degree in psychiatry all before the age of
twenty-six and had been doing his consulting work for about
three years now.

Of course, his special skill of understanding had helped, because he could delve into someone's mind without them having the least idea he was doing so.

She glanced at Ragnar and shrugged. "At least the man is
behind bars."

"And after the Carver incident, they're not going to let him
out. Any transfer will be facilitated with a dozen vehicles and
twice as many guards, cops, and agents," Ragnar said.

"But he's managing to work from behind bars," Megan muttered. "Do you think there is more to what he's doing?"

"We'll work on that tomorrow. Ayers's defense attorney is still
under protection. Someone higher up had to believe he might
be in danger, but I don't know who they will find who doesn't

have the same fear," Ragnar said. "We'll see what his reaction is to that, and if he still believes he's going to have the best defense money can buy with Amelia alive and well and controlling the purse strings."

"I will be listening, too," Patrick promised.

If we get through tonight, Megan thought.

She was surprised when Ragnar, rather than her brother, seemed to read her mind. He set his hand over hers. "We'll stop this tonight," he promised her. "And we will see Ayers in the morning. And we'll take another go at Joel Letterman."

"Oh!" Megan said. "He's asked for the check and her check. She's pretending to fight him. She's letting him pay her tab, and she's still smiling and flirting and…"

"He's made his conquest," Patrick muttered.

"Paying with cash," Ragnar said. "We're going to have to do the same. They're already on the move."

Beau's back was to them. Megan watched as Ragnar pulled out his phone and quickly alerted Jackson that the couple was leaving.

Ragnar left a pile of bills on the table.

"I could have done that," Patrick said.

"We just need to go," Megan said.

"We're going casually," Ragnar reminded her.

She walked ahead with Hugo. The couple had already seen her; and if they were to turn back, she'd just wave and walk Hugo toward the nearest tree.

But the couple didn't turn back. Beau was laughing with Teresa, opening the passenger-side door to a green minivan.

He never looked back but went around and took the driver's seat, then quickly started up the van and pulled out onto the street.

She saw Jackson's car pull out a few seconds after the green van.

As Megan and Hugo hurried for Ragnar's SUV, she knew the two men were right behind her.

Ragnar was back on speakerphone with Jackson as they pulled out, too.

Ragnar had studied the maps. There were two roads the van might take which circled around state forestland with trails. Some of them were vehicle trails, and some that could only be walked. As he spoke with Jackson, the two decided they'd split up on the curves.

Beau had to take one of the roads.

They needed to hang back.

It was about ten or fifteen minutes to the woods. As they drove, even Hugo was silent. Only their breathing could be heard.

"I'm cutting the lights. He's right ahead of us," Ragnar said after a tense ten minutes.

Megan saw Beau had chosen the southernmost of the circular routes.

When Ragnar cut his lights, they were led through an almost stygian darkness by the twin blazes of Beau's taillights. Then suddenly those lights went out.

Ragnar glanced at his phone.

"He's going on foot. Megan, tell Hugo he has to hang back. Agent Wallace will be playing that she's unconscious or barely conscious, letting him guide her along right now. We have to follow to see where he plans to get her into a coffin and into the ground. You never know with these guys. Some hold the women and sexually assault them. Some get off with the act of knowing they've put a woman into the ground and she's screaming, choking, and dying."

"Hugo, stay with me," Megan said, praying the dog would prove himself capable of following commands as well as finding people.

He growled but held close to her side.

Ragnar led them through the darkness. There was only a trickle of moonlight that barely made it through the trees. But Ragnar and her brother seemed capable of maneuvering through the night.

They came to the green van; it was empty. There were two trails leading from the road, on either side of the car.

Ragnar hunkered down by Hugo while drawing out his phone. The GPS was great, but it didn't quite discern all the forest trails.

"Which way?" he asked the dog.

Hugo sniffed the ground eagerly and began down a trail. They moved in that direction, Ragnar quietly calling Jackson and explaining the terrain as he did so.

They came to what appeared to be a well-kept cabin. There were glass-panes in the windows; curtains blocked his view of what was going on within, but it was lit.

Ragnar looked at Patrick. "I'm going around the back."

"We've got the front," Patrick said.

No one argued. No one needed to tell Megan that she should stay where she was hidden in the trees. But Patrick wasn't moving forward; he was waiting for a sign from Ragnar.

It was just a minute before Ragnar came out of the front door. He was wearing a smile and beckoning to them.

Hugo leapt forward with a happy bark.

"He's smiling!" Megan said.

"Because it all came together like clockwork," Patrick told

her, jogging toward the door of the cabin. Megan ran to keep up with the dog and her brother.

Ragnar had turned back into the cabin. When they entered, he was speaking with Beau, who was already handcuffed.

"Beau—or whoever you are—I'm so sorry. This isn't Nurse Teresa, but Special Agent Jordan Wallace," Ragnar was telling the man.

"Yeah, and I'm sorry, I wasn't out of it at all, thanks to the quick work of another agent," Jordan said. "But I had to let you try to stuff me in the coffin. Oh, and be certain that when you were promising me I would get hot sex tonight as soon as you were sure I was going to fit properly, I was recording you. My friend, you are going down."

Beau seemed to be astounded and overwhelmed. At first, he looked at them all, shaking his head. Then he tried the same tactic Letterman had tried, saying, "Don't be ridiculous. I wasn't trying to kill anybody. I like it on the wild side, and you made it sound like it was exactly what you wanted, too." He twisted to look at Ragnar. "I didn't kidnap her. I didn't abduct her! I wasn't going to hurt her—"

Jackson walked into the cabin.

"What was that grave you dug out there for?"

"Rats!" the man said.

"That's one big hole for rats," Ragnar commented.

"I'm afraid we don't believe it for a second," Jackson said. "Beau, or whoever you are, you're coming with me. You are under arrest. You have the right to…"

His voice trailed as he walked the man out of the room.

Jordan Wallace smiled at Ragnar and then their group. To Megan's surprise, she walked over to her and gave her a hug. "You really might have saved my life. I mean, I knew I'd have agents following me, and I had a tracker; but I didn't know what he slipped into my drink. Wasn't sure he'd try that. But if I was knocked out, I wouldn't have been able to pull a gun on him once I was in the coffin. Or it could have been poison. Some of these Embracers have practiced necrophilia. And I am trained to watch, but I will say this for good old Beau, he is quick when he wants to be!" She backed away. "All of you—thank you. The timing was perfect."

"You were doing just fine," Ragnar told her. "Great presence of mind. We got everything on him we needed to get." He looked at the others and said, "Wallace was just drawing on him when I came through the back door. Easy to cuff the man."

"And help me out of the coffin, thank you very much," Wallace said. "So…what's next?"

"A forensics team is on the way. They work all hours of the night. Special Agent Wallace, did he say anything else, about accomplices—"

"I've had my phone recording since he hit on me at the bar," she replied, "And please, just call me Jordan in this group."

Introductions went around and the young woman smiled. "I figured you two were siblings. Oh! I've heard about you!" she said, looking at Megan. "But I thought—"

"Colleen Law is our third," Megan said. "My sister is the agent."

"Oh! Then you're with the police—"

"I'm a book editor," Megan said. "Mostly fiction."

"Oh," she said, her brows knitting.

"It's a complicated case. Megan was the woman taken by Ayers, Carver, and Boynton when they wanted to get their hands on Colleen."

"And Patrick?" she asked warily.

"Criminal psychologist most of the time," Patrick said. "I'm an independent, usually out of Philadelphia."

Hugo rushed forward, not to be left out.

"He's the one who picked the right trail," Ragnar said.

"Then, thank you!" she said, stooping to pet the dog. She stood and stared at Ragnar. "And you really are an agent?"

"I am," he assured her.

"I, uh, I met with Jackson to prepare for the night. I'm grateful. It was my first—my first assignment of this kind. I believe there were people who thought I wasn't ready, but…anyway, I admit to being nervous and so… I'm talking too much."

"We'll head out as soon as the forensic team gets here, and I don't believe it will be long," Ragnar assured her. "Where did he say he was taking you?"

"Home. At the bar, he said he'd just get me home so I didn't have worry about driving. The bartender had been approached by the Bureau as well. He knew not to give me alcohol, but I pretended to swill my soda, and he believed I was drunk. He also believed I was almost passed out in the car. I didn't try to ask him where we were going. When he parked, I just lolled around and smiled, and it was then he promised me the best and most unusual sex I was ever going to have."

She shook her head. "He just…he couldn't be experienced at this kind of thing. He never checked to see if I had any kind of a weapon on me. He fell completely for my bad acting and was stunned when I squirmed in the coffin and reached for my gun. I think he was going to fall back and grab something, but Ragnar burst in at that point and he just wilted. He thought there was no way in the world he was going to be caught." She frowned. "I'm still at a loss as to how you managed to know he would have gone for that nurse, and what he would do!"

"Notices—we discovered through the last man apprehended that whoever is calling the shots is wording notices posted on trees and in stores and on lampposts in ways that convey exactly who he is suggesting be killed," Ragnar told her.

"Oh, wow," she muttered.

Lights were coming through the trees. The forensic team had arrived. One of the women, gray-haired, slim, and wiry, approached Ragnar and said, "Special Agent Johansen, hello. Thank you again—so much better arriving at a scene like this than one with a body."

"Thanks, Maggie," Ragnar said, obviously knowing the woman. "Anything on this cabin?"

"Scheduled for demolition. There were programs taking place out here, but they've moved them to a new place closer to town. This is a little too far for school groups. Angela sent us the information, which makes me think…"

"Go on," Ragnar asked.

"This guy has something to do with the state rangers. He may not be one—I sure hate to think that he might be—but he might do work that's connected. Anyway, we'll be searching, keeping in mind everything that has come before."

"Thanks, Maggie. Any little thing can help."

She nodded, smiled at the others, and walked over to help her team.

"Let's head out," Ragnar said. "Obviously, Jordan, we'll be getting you back."

"Thank you," she said.

"You must be exhausted," Patrick said.

She shook her head. "Adrenaline," she told him. "And gratitude. I'm heading home, and I hadn't told my fiancé about the assignment, just that I was working really late."

"He'll be very proud of you," Patrick said.

She smiled vaguely and said, "I won't wake him. He works early."

"What does he do?" Megan asked her.

She waved a hand in the air. "Politics! Ugh. But we tolerate each other's jobs—vocations, you know. Anyway…you're an editor, and I think that's so interesting," she told Megan. Linking arms, they headed through the woods. "What kind of books?"

Megan knew Jordan didn't want to talk about her personal life. It still seemed bizarre to be leaving the woods—even after a successful operation—and talk about her sci-fi books. But she did. It seemed to be what the young woman needed.

Megan liked her. She was clearly an exceptional agent, but equally casual and friendly. When they reached the car, Jordan was fine to sit in the back with Hugo between her and Patrick.

Of course, Megan liked her more because she was so natural and easy with Hugo.

"What does he usually do? Drugs, cadavers, missing persons?" she asked.

"Treats," Megan said. "He's trained because of my family, but he isn't really a law enforcement dog. He's usually a pet."

"Oh?" Jordan said. "This has certainly been an interesting evening."

"It's an interesting case," Ragnar said, glancing at Megan.

Jordan's address was a home in Georgetown, a nice townhome on a historic block. And though she was an agent who had competently handled a tough task, Megan knew Ragnar would wait until he saw she was inside her home with the door locked behind her.

As she left the car, though, Jordan turned back. "I just want to say again you were wonderful at that bar. You might have saved my life. I knew you were behind me, and I hate to admit it, but I didn't see when he slipped whatever into my drink. You should be an agent."

"Thank you," Megan told her.

"Thank you all again!" Jordan said, lifting a hand and heading for her home.

When she was inside, they started for the safe house.

Patrick leaned forward. "Megan, are you thinking about going to the academy?"

"No."

"You could, you know. It would be convenient for you. Both."

"Patrick!" she wailed.

"Sorry. Anyway, you did give one hell of a performance tonight."

She smiled and remained silent. Ragnar had glanced her way. He was amused.

Celebrate! she thought. Yes, the feeling was there again. An agent had gone in as a duplicate, but as bait she was still in danger. And she had done just what she was supposed to do.

But she had been able to do it because Megan had acted quickly and well.

And once again, it felt good. Really good.

Celebrate...

It would be hard to do so with wild abandon with her brother in the next room!

As they neared the safe house, Ragnar said, "Tonight was good. Megan, we're all grateful for what you managed to read from that notice. But every agent we have can bring in every 'lost dog' and 'garage sale' notice out there, and we might not find them all."

"Can there be that many men who are that sick in one region at the same time?" she asked.

Ragnar winced.

Patrick leaned forward. "Without the notices, without the promise of something more, I don't think all these people would act. For most of us, killing is a painful thing. I've come across contract killers with their own brand of ethics. Killing is their work, but they have standards. They'll kill a man or woman who used a technicality or a lack of hard evidence to get out of a prison sentence, but they draw the line at the innocent. There are killers who dream about the power of life and death over others; but they'd just dream on if they weren't urged, prodded, or promised a reward if they carried through their desires. There are also people who normally wouldn't kill, but they will do so if necessary to further their ends. And then there is the aspect of fame—believe it or not, there are killers who want to be known throughout history for the depth and depravity of their deeds."

"And you lucky people get to deal with them all the time," Megan said.

"Don't your alien spiders kill people?" Patrick asked her.

"Yes, but they're not real!" Megan said. "Anyway..."

"At the moment, you've made yourself an invaluable asset," Ragnar said.

"And that does feel good," she admitted. "But... I don't know." She sighed.

"The whole of it is overwhelming," Ragnar said. She saw him smile. "And still, you want to help our friend, Sergeant Alfie Parker."

"The poor man!" she said. "Haunting that graveyard, working his best even in death. Yes, he deserves our help."

"He does," both men agreed.

She really wished they didn't seem to be quite so in tune with one another.

Megan's phone rang as they reached the safe house, and she answered it as Ragnar put in the code. Hugo leapt around the yard seeking the right place for his last relief, and Patrick stared at her.

No surprise. It was Colleen, anxious and upset, trying to assure herself Megan was all right. Colleen and Mark had heard about what had taken place that night. They were unofficial, but Jackson was still keeping them in the loop.

Patrick took the phone from Megan and began extolling her work that night.

Colleen was calmer when Megan took the phone back.

"At least Patrick is with you now, too."

"Yeah. It's, uh, great," Megan said. "What are you still doing up?"

"Waiting to hear from you. It's a full house here."

Megan started to laugh. "Great honeymoon you're on."

"Yeah, right," Colleen told her. "But it's okay. We'll have time together. It's important that these women feel safe." She hesitated. "And feel as if someone cares."

"Right. And thank you."

"Okay. Get some sleep. I'd tell you that you probably worked better and smarter than many an agent might have..."

"No. I don't want to be an agent."

"I wasn't suggesting it. I know how you love your books."

She did love books. And she hadn't had one in her hand now in days.

Nor had she written a word.

"Okay. Get some sleep," Colleen told her.

"Will do. You do the same."

"Not much else to do in such a full house!" Colleen told her.

They ended the call. She had wandered into the kitchen with Ragnar and Patrick as they'd been speaking, and she saw both men were digging into the refrigerator for water bottles. Ragnar brought one out for her.

"Thanks. So, sleep," she said.

Patrick made a display of yawning. "I sleep really deeply!" he said. "Hugo, you come with me. Now."

Hugo whined and looked at Megan.

"It's okay," she said, and Hugo pattered off after Patrick.

"Bed," Ragnar said, walking toward the bedroom.

She followed him, stripping off her jacket and tossing off her shoes.

"Sleep," she said.

"Yep. I got it. No celebration."

She slipped out of her trousers and remembered the little holster that held the gun Ragnar and Patrick had agreed she needed. She released the catch and set the gun on the nightstand.

"I'll get used to it," she said.

Bed. Sleep. But she wasn't even sure she'd managed to take a nightgown out of the room next door. And looking at Ragnar as he disrobed as well, she decided she was just going to have to crawl in and curl up in the opposite direction.

But her back brushed his flesh. She moved closer.

She turned into his arms, her face wrinkling with dismay.

"My brother is in the next room."

"We could be really quiet."

"Do you think we could?"

"You were brilliant, and I know you like to celebrate."

She smiled. She wasn't too sure they could be *really* quiet. But this time in her life was so unusual. And he was so extraordinary.

She slipped her arms around him, drawing her face to his. In seconds, she was lost in the wet fire of that kiss. They moved together; the length of their bodies giving and receiving the same kind of sweet, searing heat.

They made love, and they curled together.

But that night, Megan couldn't help but wonder how she could just go back to where she had been before. She loved being with Ragnar. She had never felt so incredibly warm, so secure and tenderly held. This time, the closeness they had achieved was important. But by her own words, their relationship was only for this time. And she hadn't even wanted to think it, but she had been lucky. In the midst of all the danger, she'd found something amazing. But she hadn't forgotten about her job, her life in New York City. Which she loved, and had worked hard to build. Nothing she could do about that right now, she thought. They were still far from figuring out how Ayers was pulling the strings, and if there wasn't another shadow puppet master above him. There was too much at stake here.

At last, she slept.

In the morning when Megan woke, Ragnar had already risen. She knew she would find him in the kitchen.

She hoped he and Patrick were discussing the case.

And not her.

Showered and ready, she headed into the kitchen.

"We're going to go at Joel Letterman first," Ragnar told her. As she had expected, he was at the stove. He saw her glance at him, and he shrugged and said, "Yeah, omelets again. But fear not! New ingredients this time. Different cheeses and vegetables."

"And bacon! Because I requested it," Patrick said. "Hey. We've been talking. I'm going to go in with Ragnar. We're letting both men think the government has decided they need a psychiatric evaluation."

"Wait! If they see you as a psychiatrist, it won't be ethical to share anything they tell you."

"No, they won't be seeing me as their counselor. I'll just be introduced as one in case they want to go that route to claim not guilty by reason of insanity."

"You think Rory Ayers will claim insanity?" she asked skeptically.

"No," Ragnar said. "But I am interested in his reaction if it's suggested he's less than together, mentally. And that is a route he can take if he doesn't get the high-priced attorney he thinks is coming his way."

"Okay," Megan said.

"And I'm listening…for everything he isn't saying out loud," Patrick added. "I find it more effective in person."

Ragnar nodded gravely. "It will be more important than ever. Also, Angela is still trying to arrange to talk with the man who was Carver's attorney. She still hasn't been able to reach him."

"Carver is dead. He can't be getting any messages from him anymore," Megan said.

"He's a public defender. He has other men in those facilities he is still defending," Ragnar said.

"But there's nothing in his background that would suggest he is a killer," Megan said.

"The man who called himself 'Beau' from last night proved not to have so much as a parking ticket," Ragnar said. "His real name is Ned Bentley, and he works for a paper production company—one that buys some of their raw materials from the forestry service when trees or bracken need to be cleared out. That was how he knew about the cabin."

"How did he know to read the notice?" Megan asked.

"We don't have an answer to that yet," Ragnar said.

"Something has to give somewhere." Patrick sounded confident.

"Angela and the tech team are still working on Carver's and Ayers's computers," Ragnar told them. "What we can't figure out is how they communicate from the beginning, how the apprentices get drafted into this strange murder ring in the first place. There has to be a site on the dark web that goes up and then gets taken down. But we have to catch it when it's up."

"Seems like a needle in a haystack…" Megan muttered.

"And we must find out who is pulling the strings at the facility," Ragnar said. "We can hope Letterman can give us more. He may be fearful for his own safety since the attack on Carver."

Megan was silent, thinking it all over. She was surprised to look up and discover both Ragnar and her brother were looking at her with concern.

"Megan, if you—"

"Let's eat these omelets and get going," she said. "They had better be good!"

"Demanding, isn't she?" Ragnar asked Patrick.

Patrick laughed. "You haven't seen the half of it yet!"

"Hey!" she protested.

"Well, it's true," Patrick teased. He turned to Ragnar. "Very independent. And careful. We learned to be suspicious as kids after the episode with Colleen and the neighbor, and the three of us talking, finding out all of us could see the dead. I can tell you it has kept her close to the family, but she has been extremely guarded—even in friendships—and remained closed off. Demanding, independent, but wary of others, and careful she not be hurt or hurt someone else."

"Argh! Patrick! No shrink stuff on your sister," Megan protested.

Patrick grinned. "That's okay. Because I just nailed Ragnar, too. His close friends are all in the Krewe. His relationships have been casual because he knows his work will sometimes draw out that which is unusual in him, his gift or curse."

"Being in the Krewe is like being sane," Ragnar said, smiling at Megan. "Hmm, and I think the shrink just evaluated himself, too."

It was Patrick's turn to groan. "Let's go use our gifts. We'll see today if I can peer into any minds. But I have a feeling we need Megan's talents today. When it's suggested he might be insane, I think Ayers is going to have a lot to say." He was reflective a minute. "You haven't seen the half of it. Something that Rory Ayers said, too. And while that's a good threat and a leading comment, I'm annoyed at myself—no 'talents' have kicked in yet to let us know just what the 'half' is that we haven't seen yet."

CHAPTER FIFTEEN

Before setting out they learned Joel Letterman *was* being held at the same federal facility as Rory Ayers.

Ragnar wasn't sure why, but he wished Megan wasn't coming with them, even though he needed her. They still hadn't seen one of the attorneys, and he couldn't help thinking about Sir Arthur Conan Doyle's Sherlock Holmes and the iconic line the author had given readers: "When you have eliminated the impossible, whatever remains, no matter how improbable, must be the truth."

The only possible way for communications to be getting out of the correctional facility was if someone was helping Ayers. No matter how squeaky-clean people seemed to be, there had to be a leak.

But Ragnar now knew Megan. She wasn't staying behind. She would be with him and Patrick and Hugo the entire time. Plus the facility had many guards, and it was unlikely they were all compromised.

Still, he'd be happy when they left.

They were coming to know Brendan Kent, and he greeted them with a grim smile.

"You're filling the place up for us," Kent said dryly. "We were informed you were coming. They're going to have to put you on payroll here soon."

"Just about," Ragnar said.

"And you're working with Ragnar?" he asked Patrick. "Is Mark coming back on? You two seemed to be the dream team. With the dog. Oh, well, you've got a new dog."

"Hugo is just working this case," Ragnar said.

"Is Mark still on his honeymoon?"

"Still on his honeymoon," Ragnar said, setting his weapon down. Patrick did the same. Megan didn't move; he reminded her she had a gun strapped to her ankle.

"Oh! Right!" she muttered, and she added her newly acquired gun to the group.

"So, Letterman is eager to see you. Ayers has agreed once again. He seems to think it's funny you keep coming back. There's no reason, but what the heck, he's bored."

"We'll start with Ayers," Ragnar said.

Kent grimaced. "Morris is on again. He hates that detail. I don't see how, but he seems to think Ayers might have killed Carver, too. Sorry, shouldn't be giving you any opinions. He just doesn't like dealing with the guy. To be honest, I'm glad I'm out here on the desk."

"Can't say Rory Ayers is my favorite person," Ragnar said.

"You'll be speaking with him, too?" Kent asked, looking at Patrick.

"We're going to offer him Patrick's professional expertise," Ragnar said.

"And you and Hugo will be in the observation room," he said, looking at Megan.

She gave him a smile. "Yes," she said.

Kent smiled at that. "Well, see you on the way out."

Anson Morris greeted them as the gates were opened. He was wearing a bleak expression.

"You wish to be seated or have me bring him in first?" he asked Ragnar, then gave Patrick a curious look. Then he glanced at Megan.

She smiled.

"This is my brother, yes. He's consulting on this case as a professional psychiatrist and criminal psychologist. Patrick, Anson Morris. He's been helpful to us in bringing Ayers out—"

"Too many times," Morris interrupted. "I can't wait for the trial. He will wind up at a prison facility once he's convicted. With any luck, he'll get the death penalty. Sorry if that sounds harsh. I've worked among these guys too long."

As Megan went into the observation room, Morris escorted the prisoner in and appeared to be vexed at the task. He barely nodded to Ragnar as he held on to Ayers's arm until he was seated at the table—letting go only to connect the man's handcuffs to the metal bar on the table.

Ayers stared at Patrick, obviously seeing something familiar in him, and not at all sure why.

"Who is this?" he demanded, his tone harsh, his brows almost a single line as he frowned.

"A psychiatrist," Ragnar said flatly. "Dr. Law."

"Psychiatrist?" Ayers repeated. "Why?"

"I don't think you're getting your high-priced attorney. I thought you might want to talk to a psychiatrist and...well, maybe you can plead not guilty by reason of insanity," Ragnar said.

Ayers leaned back, shaking his head. "Like you would be happy to see me let me off because I was crazy."

"Oh, you wouldn't be let off. You'd be at a facility for the criminally insane," Ragnar said. "But it would save you from the death penalty."

Ayers leaned forward, still studying Patrick.

"I'm not getting the death penalty. I didn't do anything. And the thing is, you can't prove I did anything. It's going to be one person's word against another, and that doesn't allow for reasonable doubt. And," he added, staring hard at Patrick, "I'm not crazy."

"Oh, well, we don't use the term *crazy*," Patrick said. "But you are mentally impaired. Any man who thinks he can arrange a murder in a facility like this and believe someone isn't eventually going to talk is lacking rational sense. Of course, your confidence that your Embracer operation is going to continue through the use of coded fliers is unhinged as well."

"I don't know what you're talking about," Ayers said.

"We all know you do. We're curious as to why you wanted Teresa Perry killed. Except she was your wife's nurse at one time. Did your hatred for your wife extend to anyone and everyone who ever helped her?"

Ayers looked as if he was about to explode. He remained silent.

He hadn't known Teresa's would-be killer had failed. He probably would figure out the would-be killer was now in custody. And he didn't know the "Teresa" who had been attacked had been Special Agent Jordan Wallace.

"I am stone-cold sane. And I have no desire to see a shrink

even if you are related to Colleen Law and her sister. You want something from me? Let me see one of *them* again!"

"Not going to happen," Ragnar said.

"Here's the thing," Patrick told Ayers. "Do I really think Special Agent Johansen here cares if you get the death penalty or not? No. But it's my job to separate those with genuine mental health challenges from the simply mean, greedy, and lethal. You are a businessman. And you could do something for us and save your own life in the exchange. No one is giving you anything. Life is compromise."

Ayers started to laugh. "Not my life!" He leaned closer to the two of them. "I don't compromise. I don't have to compromise. I'm not crazy—just way smarter than you. I will not get the death penalty. Doesn't matter who my attorney might be. The world is full of bleeding hearts. All against the death penalty. I promise you. I will not get the death penalty. And I will get off."

"You do know your wife is alive and well, and she's just about to receive her divorce?" Ragnar said. "The judge has been very sympathetic with her. You've received all your papers."

Ayers leaned back, smiling.

"Do you fools really think I depend on a bitch for anything?"

He started to stand up; his chains clanked on the table.

He sat again. "Get out of here. I do not have to talk to you. And right now, I do not want to talk to you!"

"That's okay. We have other people to talk to," Ragnar said with a shrug.

Ayers's eyes narrowed and he forced a mean smile to his lips.

"Well, now, won't that be interesting for you." He stared at Ragnar and Patrick a second. Then he screamed, "Guard!"

Morris, looking startled and scared, stepped into the room.

"We're done here," Ayers said politely.

Morris looked at Ragnar, and Ragnar shrugged. "We're done, I guess. But we'll wait here."

Morris nodded gravely, aware he was to bring Letterman in next.

He unshackled Ayers, and they left the room.

A minute after the men were gone, Megan burst into the interrogation room.

"They need to get Letterman in here quickly and then out of this facility!"

"Interesting—but even I picked up on that threat," Ragnar said.

"Morris should be going for Letterman now—" Patrick began.

"No, no—*right* now," Megan said.

Ragnar had his phone out; she wasn't sure who he dialed but he voiced his fears for Letterman—wherever he might be at the moment—and was assured a guard would go check on him immediately.

"He's been here at the same facility. If Ayers is so afraid of him, it's surprising he hasn't found a way to strike already," Ragnar said, frowning.

"Ayers has to be careful. The struggle in the cafeteria was staged so Carver could be killed without raising too much suspicion. He can't have someone just walk up and kill Letterman—that would be too obvious. But I am afraid for Letterman. We don't know what Ayers might have manipulated this time, and we need to get Letterman out of here before he can devise something," Megan said.

They heard a whining sound.

"Oh, I don't want Hugo panicking. I'm back in observation," Megan said.

When she was gone, Ragnar looked at Patrick.

"Did you get anything?" he asked.

"Severe personality disorder, certainly. Usually, a sociopath has disregard for most people, rules, and laws, though they are capable of forming bonds with certain individuals. In the field, it's believed the psychopath has something that is a physiological defect. Studies have shown psychopaths don't have the connections between the ventromedial prefrontal cortex and the amygdala as a 'normal' person does. The first might be caused by childhood trauma—either slight or major. Sociopaths may improve in the right circumstances, and they may show remorse," Patrick said.

"So, Ayers is—"

"In my estimation he's both. He truly has no regret. And in a psychopath, there is an absolute lack of empathy for others. Ayers buried a girl he raised without blinking an eye. Oh, both can be intelligent, which is the truly frightening part. Cunning. And Ayers is that," Patrick said. "I think Megan is on the right track. Whoever you need to call, whatever we need to do, we must get Letterman out of here. Not just for any help he might give us, but because we are human beings. And I believe Megan's instinct that he's in danger."

Ragnar nodded and put another call through to Jackson.

If Jackson couldn't handle a transfer, Adam Harrison would.

A minute later, a guard Ragnar had known for years, Langdon Gear, walked in with Letterman.

"He's fine; he doesn't need to be shackled to the table," Ragnar told him.

"Up to you. I'll be outside until Morris picks up his post," Gear assured him.

Ragnar nodded his thanks.

Letterman sat at the table. He looked scared. And when Gear was gone, he didn't need any questions—he started talking.

"You've got to get me out of here!" he exploded. "Carver is dead. Dead! They killed him in the cafeteria. And you should see the way they look at me. I know it. They're going to kill me!"

"So, Carver did communicate with you somehow?" Ragnar asked.

"What? I—no! He didn't communicate with me. I know why he was arrested; it was all over the news. And he might have won in court—"

"Did Rory Ayers communicate with you?" Patrick asked.

"Rory Ayers… I don't think so. Wait! Who are you?" Letterman asked Patrick.

"Doctor of psychiatry," Patrick told him.

"You think I'm nuts?" Letterman asked.

"I just met you," Patrick said. "I don't have enough information to form an opinion."

"Shrink talk. I'm not nuts. Wait, maybe I am nuts. Is it good if I'm nuts? I mean, the girl…that woman, Grace…she didn't die. She was kinky." He laughed suddenly. "Maybe she's nuts? Have you thought about that? Stark raving mad." He leaned forward. "She's the kind of party girl who wants it really rough, but she doesn't feel right about it. She's at war in her own mind. Some friend of hers was killed, right? I think I read or heard something about a witness coming in to identify a girl who was buried. So, she's crazy. Maybe she wanted to know what her friend went through," Letterman said eagerly.

"And you just happened to have a coffin for her?" Ragnar asked.

"I…well, I admit, I like stuff kinky. I was going to save her— yeah!" He laughed suddenly. "Yeah, that's the ticket! I like being the warrior kind, the knight in shining armor. I go and get her—after she asked to be in there—and the sex is really hot!"

"That's your defense?" Ragnar asked him skeptically. "Well, if you've got it all figured out, I guess there's not a whole lot you can give us. Oh, and if that was the case, why would you be frightened of Rory Ayers? I'm imagining you'd be just fine here."

Letterman turned to Patrick. "You have to help me. I am the battiest bat in the belfry!"

"All right," Patrick said. "I'd like to help you because the girl did live. While you attempted murder, I wouldn't want to see a death penalty for you."

"Death penalty!" Letterman said. "No, no—"

"You told us about the notices, and we're grateful," Ragnar assured him.

"What?" Letterman asked, surprised. "I mean, you saw...the notices? You understood them?"

Ragnar didn't elaborate. "Some," he said simply. "I think you meant to give us something, right?"

"Oh, yeah, absolutely," Letterman said.

"What we don't know is how the communications are going out to create the notices," Ragnar said. "You saw a notice and you acted on it. How did you know to act on that particular one?"

"I...didn't know if it was real or not until I went to the corner," he admitted. "Until I asked if there was a 'Grace' working that night because I heard she was hot as hell. And if I had succeeded in...oh, you know, digging her up, playing the knight—"

"We know that's a crock," Patrick said gently.

The man's face wrinkled up painfully. Ragnar thought he might shed tears.

"Are you going to get me out of here?" he whispered.

"We are going to get you out of here," Ragnar said. "And we can keep you safe. We can help you. But only if you help us."

Letterman looked down, grimacing.

He mumbled something.

Ragnar glanced at Patrick, who shook his head.

"What are you saying, Mr. Letterman? I can't hear you," Ragnar said.

Letterman looked up. "The dark web. But the site I found was gone after I saw the encryption that alluded to the fact that not only was 'embracing love' something that was sexually rewarding, but it could increase a man's financial gains as well. The site disappeared. If you don't know how the dark web works—"

"We have general knowledge," Ragnar said. "But when I asked you before about Ayers and Carver—"

"Well, they are in here as Embracers, right?" he asked. "That man was burning angry at his wife, from what I've heard. He wanted her dead. And if women were killed once he and Carver were locked up, the more their court defenses might work, right?" he asked hopefully.

"The site already went down?" Patrick asked.

"The night I went out," Letterman said. "They disappear like that right away so law enforcement doesn't have a way to trace them. They're routed all over the world, encrypted, and…well, I wasn't worried…"

"And they pop right back up," Ragnar muttered.

"How did you know where to look?" Patrick asked politely.

Letterman winced again.

"We are getting you out of here. But if you want real help from the people where you're going to be, it would really behoove you to help us," Ragnar said.

"Is that a threat?" Letterman asked. He didn't sound belligerent just pathetic.

Ragnar shook his head. "It's a simple statement. When officers, guards, wardens, whoever, hear someone has sincerely tried to cooperate, they just like you better. And you are a likable guy, so if you give us any information, I think they'll see to it you are safe."

"I don't know how much it will help you," Letterman said. "I was at a strip club in Fredericksburg, and I was complaining about the lack of...activity in a lap dance. There was a guy and I guess he had been in the back room. When I was at the bar, he told me there could be all kinds of fun—that might even come with financial gain—out there if I knew where to look for it. He gave me a code. I logged on. The site was...well, it had all kinds of sex."

He stopped talking. Ragnar glanced at Patrick, who nodded. Ragnar asked, "Including snuff films?"

"Well, you know most of those are faked."

Some were.

Some were not.

"But how did that lead you to the notices?"

"There was a voice-over that told those on the site where to look for what could be loving, cocooning, and rewarding in so many ways. We were to get out there and start reading. There was a page that explained terms. And the voice-over was...well, good at making it a puzzle, a game, that only the most elite of men might discern. Then there was another page that explained certain terms. Then there was a page about dogs and about why certain 'bitches' had to die."

"Did you know the man at the strip club?" Ragnar asked him.

"I had never seen him before," Letterman said.

"Old, young, what was he like?" Patrick asked.

"Dignified—maybe forty-five, more likely fifty-ish," Letterman said. "He had a full head of hair, a silver-white color. And he was dressed in a suit. An expensive one, I think. At least, he made it look expensive."

"I'm going to have you speak with an artist. She'll do a rendering. Are you willing to go to that extent?" Ragnar asked.

"I—uh. Yeah. I mean, that will help me, right?"

"Yes," Ragnar said.

"Then, uh, you bet."

"All right," Ragnar said. "What do you think? Do you believe Ayers or Carver might have had something to do with the website, or were they just a part of it?"

"Oh, I think one of them might have been in on it," Letterman said.

"And why is that?"

He grimaced. "I don't think there was ever a notice Ayers should kill his own daughter, or the man should think he did such a good job he called the FBI. All that was in the news, you know. And there's been a big thing about the plans of the business, the wife's efforts to get her divorce through fast... I mean, you don't just accept another man's decree to kill your family, right? I was supposed to embrace Grace. You know that. Yeah, I think Ayers is in on it. Don't you?"

"All right," Ragnar said. "If there is anything else, anything you can think of, report it to the warden."

"Wait," Letterman said.

"What is it?"

The man shrunk in his seat. "There's more to me believing Ayers was in on it. Although I can't be sure. I saw the man on TV a few times; the press has followed him. And before that, he would be talking about repair on a federal building or the creation of a new project, and..."

"And?"

Letterman expelled a long breath and said slowly, "Ayers wasn't in any of the films I saw on the site—not that I could recognize or see anyway. You know, sometimes you see a lot of one gender's anatomy and not so much of the...lover. I never saw his face in the films, that's for sure. But..."

"But?" Ragnar prompted.

"I believe he did the voice-over."

Ragnar stared at the man. He didn't think Letterman was lying, although he was anxious to get himself moved to another facility. Ragnar was glad both Patrick and Megan were listening as well. He'd like their opinions on the matter.

"Interesting. Thank you."

"Very interesting. How many people were in the films you saw, do you think?" Patrick asked him.

Letterman shook his head. "Twenty? And I guess you had to have someone with a camera and a microphone. Those films come with a lot of panting, you know?"

"All right. Thank you," Ragnar said. "You have been helpful. And remember, if you think of anything—no matter how small a detail you think—tell a guard to get the warden; and he'll get hold of us right away. I'm going to try to set up a time with the artist this afternoon."

"But I won't be here, right?"

"You'll be transferred to another facility. There will be a warden there. And when you're situated, we'll be back with the artist, remember? This case is federal; some parts of it started off local, but all the accused in the case are now in federal facilities," Ragnar told him.

"Oh. Okay," Letterman said weakly. "But—"

"We aren't leaving until you're out of here," Ragnar assured him.

"And am I nuts?" Letterman asked Patrick hopefully.

"I will be going over my notes," Patrick told him.

"You didn't take any."

"I have an eidetic memory," Patrick said.

"Huh?"

"He sees or hears something and it remains complete in his mind long after he has seen or heard it," Ragnar explained. "We'll start with getting you moved to another facility. And that should happen right now. We'll also see that you're kept in solitary as a precaution until your trial date."

There was a tap at the door. Morris had evidently arrived to replace Langdon Gear. But he wasn't alone. Two federal officers had arrived.

"We're here for Mr. Letterman," the older of the two men advised. Ragnar nodded, glad to see the man who had arrived.

He didn't call Letterman by a number, but by his name. Prisoners were still human.

"When you're finished, Special Agent Johansen," the man said.

"We have wrapped up. I need you to be sure to inform our headquarters when Mr. Letterman has finished with intake," Ragnar said.

The man nodded.

Joel Letterman stood.

"There's not going to be an accident? These guys aren't going to kill me on the way?" he asked nervously.

Ragnar turned to the federal officers. They produced their credentials.

"I think your chances are far better with these men than stay-ing here," Ragnar said. "And I do need you alive."

"Right. He needs me alive!" Letterman told his escorts.

"Trust me. We'll get you to where you're safe," the younger of the two said.

Letterman still looked ill, but he went without a whimper as the federal officers escorted him out.

"That guy is…pathetic," Morris—who had stood silently, watching the exchange—said when they were gone. He shook his head. "He was trying to kill a woman, and he's so damned scared himself."

"Well, Carver was just killed in this facility," Ragnar said.

"Yeah, well…" Morris said, shaking his head. "It started as a food fight! A simple food fight. They've interrogated every man who was in the cafeteria that day, and no one is sure how it started. And as you know, there was a pile-up, and no one could see who was on top of Carver. Well, there were tons of men on top of Carver…and others. He was just the only one dead. Strange. You have to know how to defend yourself. I would have thought Carver would have seen what was com-ing, but then…" He shrugged. Then he looked over at Megan. "Self-defense! It's everything."

"Not to worry," she said cheerfully. "These guys have been taking me to the gun range!"

"That's good. Practice makes perfect."

Patrick looked at Ragnar. "I think we should speak with the men who were pulled out of the pile—even those on top."

"We were grabbing people off people fast," Morris said. "I don't know if I could tell you who was where when."

"We'll study the security footage," Patrick said. "But that's for another time. Thank you." He seemed ready to leave. But he had more to say.

But just to Ragnar and Megan.

Ragnar thanked the officer as well and nodded to indicate they were leaving. He went out ahead of them but waited to see them through the gate to the entry.

Megan brought Hugo out of the observation room, knowing it was time to leave.

She, too, thanked Morris, and they retrieved their weapons from Brendan Kent at the desk.

"You think that was really necessary?" Morris asked Ragnar. "I mean, moving Letterman? It really looked as if Carver was just, well, just the bottom man. I mean, seriously, we try to stop it, but you know in any facility you come up with all kinds of allegiances. And I guess when you're locked up in here, a food fight may turn into a real affront on a man, and even our less-violent offenders can get carried away."

"I think Letterman is just better off," Ragnar told him. "Anyway, thanks," he said.

They headed out beyond the gates and to the car. And he was glad; he'd wanted to get away from the facility. Or he had wanted Megan away from the facility.

He waited until he had driven a block away before he turned to Megan.

"Your thoughts?"

"I believe that everything Joel Letterman said to you—once he started telling the truth—was true. I also believe we'll never trace that website. It will be gone just as he said. I read an article the FBI spends as much—if not more—time on cybercrime than on organized crime."

"There are massive units dedicated to the task," Ragnar said.

"Morris wants Ayers to get the death penalty," she said.

"I imagine many people do," Ragnar said.

Patrick leaned forward from the back. "Ayers is one of the most frightening individuals I've ever come across. He is narcissistic to such a degree they'd need another term just for him. And listening to him, delving into his mind, he believes he's so important he will be seeing himself as a free man and sooner than later."

"There is someone out there," Megan said. "Someone with money, and Ayers believes with his whole heart this person is going to come to his rescue." She shrugged, turning to Ragnar. "I'm glad Jackson got someone to get Letterman other than Morris."

"Oh?"

She nodded. "He's... I don't know. I believe he thinks most of the people he 'guards' should be in prison and get the death penalty. If he was in that cafeteria and he did see anything, I don't think he would have stopped it. He would only do the least of what he had to in order to retain his position. He's just— well, I don't like him."

Ragnar looked at her intently.

"Someone close to Ayers has been getting his messages out. Angela hasn't found anything on Morris, and she's good at what she does, but so are these guys. I'm going to have him watched. Get Jackson to have someone undercover become a new guard at the facility."

"Well, Letterman will be out of it."

"And Ayers will still be there," Ragnar said.

"Right. But thankfully, Letterman won't," Megan told him. Her eyes held such a shimmering honesty. Letterman had tried to kill Grace. But she was the kind of woman who believed in justice.

She wanted him to have his day in court.

Prison, yes.

But alive.

He nodded and looked ahead again. He really wanted her off the case. He wanted her in a high tower—like Rapunzel—except there would be no wicked witch, no one, anywhere, who could hurt her.

For now...

Things between them were...for now.

But Patrick had seen something. In him and maybe even in her.

He inhaled deeply. They had to get through what they needed to get through. Then there would be time to think about the future.

He couldn't just let her go again. He had found himself dreaming about waking beside her every morning, seeing that beautiful emerald color in her eyes, watching her smile...

He gave himself a mental shake.

They had to finish the case.

"I can tell you this," Patrick said suddenly. "Letterman is terrified, and he wants to live. Megan is right. Once he started telling the truth, he was telling the truth."

"Did Rory Ayers do the voice-over for the website?" Ragnar asked.

"I believe he did—or at least Letterman sincerely believes he did. I think he was frightened to tell you that. And I think the only way he believes he'll ever be safe is if Ayers is dead," Megan told him.

"Where's he being moved?"

"DC—and he'll get there. Jackson handpicked the men who came for him. What I'd like to do is get to headquarters and see if Maisie is available. She's the best at listening and understanding what someone sees in their own mind or remembers."

"She's good," Megan said. "Her likenesses almost seem to leap off the page!"

"We'll contact her, and head back."

"Okay. We have a little time, right?" Megan asked.

"Lunch would be good," Patrick said.

"I'd like to get back to the gun range," Megan said. "Just for half an hour, okay? I may not like Morris, and I may be suspicious of him, but he was right about one thing. Practice makes perfect. I'd like to feel better about my ability when it comes to my defense."

"We're with you!" Patrick reminded her.

"And I'm grateful. But I do want to improve my own ability!" Megan said.

Ragnar turned the car, heading in the direction of the range. He didn't think Megan honing her skills was a bad idea at all.

Patrick sighed. "Well, they do have a snack bar."

They parked at the range, and went in. Paying at the counter, Patrick asked whether it was okay that Hugo came inside, and then about the food.

"Limited," the clerk admitted. "Burgers, hot dogs, and a yucky vegetarian burger." He lowered his voice, as if afraid the owner was lurking nearby. "I never said this! Dale Barrie would have my as—my job. The hot dogs are fine," he said. "My recommendation, and the fries are okay, too."

"A hot dog, it is," Patrick said.

They all headed to the snack bar area. Hot dogs and fries were ordered all around. There was a wall separating the little food counter from the range, but even there the sound of gun-fire carried through. They'd picked up earmuffs for their time at the range slots but didn't put them on as they ate.

"Okay, the hot dogs are edible," Patrick said. "Even decent."

"And quick," Ragnar said.

He felt someone coming from behind him and he turned. It was Dale Barrie, the owner of the range.

"Hi there. Happy to see you gracing us with your presence again so soon," the man said.

Ragnar stood and they shook hands. Barrie had been a cop before he'd retired and purchased the range. He'd served in the army as a sniper, and at sixty, he still had a remarkable, deadly aim. He also stood as straight as a pillar; and while his face was lined, he retained a good thatch of iron-gray hair.

He was happy to meet Megan and Patrick, telling them he knew their sister, Colleen.

"Remarkable woman," he said.

"We like her," Patrick said.

Barrie grinned. "Well, of course. Hey, enjoying the hot dogs?"

They didn't get a chance to answer. His phone started ring-ing. It looked as if he would just draw a line across it and let it go to voice mail, but he frowned at the caller ID, muttering, "Now?" Then he excused himself. With a nod to them and a smile, he walked away from the table.

"He's afraid of whoever called," Megan said.

"Yep," Patrick agreed.

Ragnar frowned. "Dale Barrie? The man served in the mili-tary and then the police force. I can't imagine—"

There was suddenly a loud scream that penetrated the explosive sound of bullets and made its way through the separating wall.

"Get down, under the table!" Ragnar ordered, jumping to his feet. "Patrick, stay there with Megan, no matter what!"

He all but shoved Megan beneath the table, glared at Patrick, and carefully went to the door that separated the snack bar from the range and looked out.

Chaos reigned.

People were armed but terrified. Many of them were just armchair enthusiasts, with no combat training, and quick to pull the trigger at anything. The shooting range bullets were soft or flat, but they could still kill.

People were cowered down, seeking shelter, looking about as if desperately trying to discover where the shots were coming from, and many of them were shooting wildly themselves.

A woman was screaming her husband had been hit. The young man who had recommended the hot dogs was down flat against his desk, desperately calling 911.

Now?

Dale Barrie had said, "Now?"

Could the man be involved?

"Ragnar!"

His name was shouted just as he heard Hugo growl and whimper—all in a few seconds.

Megan was his concern. Her safety. He had to get to her...

She was no longer under the table.

It was Patrick screaming for him. Trying to scream for him. Ragnar ran back to the table. And as he reached it, he knew the event had been planned.

Just like the food fight in the cafeteria at the facility.

When he reached Patrick, he thought he might be dead. Then he realized Patrick was struggling to speak.

And there was no sign of Megan.

Hugo was curled up and whimpering next to Patrick on the right.

And Dale Barrie lay by Patrick's left side.

And he *was* dead. No question. He had been shot. A dark red stain bloomed over his entire chest.

"Megan!" Ragnar screamed her name, searching the panicked crowd.

Patrick tried to reach for him.

"Needle!" Patrick gasped. "Both of us… Hugo…that way…"

He pointed to the exit.

"Morris! Patrick, was it Morris?"

Patrick tried to shake his head. Tried to form words. He managed to mouth a name.

And beg, "Megan!"

Ragnar started to move, dialing for help as he did so, aware sirens were already sounding—the clerk had gotten through to emergency services.

Hugo was whining, trying to stand. Ragnar had no idea how someone had drugged the dog, Patrick, and probably Megan so quickly. Patrick was all but paralyzed as he lay on the floor. But Hugo was trying to move.

Ragnar swept the big dog into his arms, still careful with his Glock, and raced out of the facility for his car. He had to think.

Where?

And he prayed, somehow he would be able to find Megan in time.

And what he needed desperately now was to hear Megan's voice in his mind.

CHAPTER SIXTEEN

Megan woke in a coffin. She didn't know it at first; she woke to stare at darkness. She tried blinking furiously, and she knew her limbs and her mind were both groggy.

What had happened?

The shooting had started. She and Patrick had dragged Hugo with them under the table. Then they had seen someone about to accost Dale Barrie. Patrick had pulled his weapon and started out from beneath the table. Then he'd spun around, getting a shot off before he'd plummeted to the floor—a needle stuck in his arm. Hugo had whined and she realized the dog had been hit first—with a dart.

Then she'd seen the man in the hoodie. In disguise…

Same old disguise. Bad theatrics. The same bulbous nose.

She started to reach for the gun secreted at her ankle. But she didn't make it. The needle slammed into her arm, hard, and the world disappeared, the sound of gunfire fading last.

She should have known. Maybe she had known; she'd just

been getting to the truth, a truth that had been just beyond her reach…

Why?

Even in her fogged state, she knew that, to some, money did make the world go around. Some people killed because of the sexual rush they achieved from their act. Some practiced necrophilia, some got off on torture and pain.

The human monster truly made evil space spiders seem tame.

She thought of Patrick. She had to believe that her brother was alive, that he'd just been drugged.

Like Hugo. Fury burst into her fear—her dog! *They'd hurt her dog.* And whether she made it out of here or not, she had to hope that Hugo…

Stop. Think. You made it through a situation like this before!

She tried to move. Her limbs were unwilling. But she could breathe more easily, think, figure out her position, and…

She could hear conversation. Not because she had her sister's acute hearing.

But because people were talking right above her coffin prison.

"We need to do this—fast," a voice said.

"That wasn't the deal," another voice replied urgently. "I'm supposed to get to—"

"No, dammit, I killed a man to get her here!"

"I hope you killed the stinking brother and the wretched dog!"

"I killed Barrie and I wish to hell I had killed the brother instead. The brother, a doctor? Doctor? A shrink? Seeking to save lives? The asshole is quicker on the draw than a damned gunslinger. I'm bleeding like a stuck pig! That's what we need to take care of—now! And killing the brother wasn't the point, was it? I was told to get her the hell out of there and screw anything else. And there isn't time for you to do any kind of play-ing around. Did you get the hole dug?"

That had been said by the man with the "bulbous" nose.

"Yeah, the hole is dug. I want to see her again. I want to..."

"You can dig her back up when some time has gone by."

"I like them fresh!" She knew the one voice. The other she couldn't quite place. It was familiar, too, and something about it just wasn't quite right.

She stopped listening for a minute. She tried concentrating. Tried reaching her sister or her brother through the power of her mind. It might not be real; it was worth attempting. Noth-ing that they had was supposedly real, but there was no reason to give up on something that might work. Colleen had heard her once. She cried out in her mind for Colleen, Patrick...

Ragnar.

They have me in a coffin. I don't know where. I don't know how long I was out. I'm trying to get my strength back. They don't seem to know that I have a gun. I can still feel it at my ankle, so I know that they didn't take it away, though they may know that I now own a gun. I don't think we went far; there is a little bit of light slipping into the coffin.

"I want to see her again!" the more plaintive voice whined.

Megan snapped her eyes closed. The coffin lid opened. Light poured on her.

She dared to carefully crack her eyelids, imperceptibly.

She tried concentrating again. Desperately.

We couldn't have gone far. It's still daylight. There are no windows on this thing. It's barely walls. I can even hear trees rustling outside.

"I want her. Before I bury her. That was the deal."

"I can shoot and kill you now, too. Damn, man, this one took everything. I've risked everything!"

"With that nose? This is really ridiculous. We do *his* bidding?

I don't think so. We take all the chances; he promises things that may not happen!"

Keep fighting with each other, keep fighting, Megan prayed.

She thought that she heard something. An answer in her mind.

Wishful thinking?

But she felt it with her mind, heard it in her mind, and believed it in her heart.

I'm coming!

It was Ragnar, promising her that he was close on her trail.

"She's so beautiful!" the man went on.

"She's been a thorn in his side. He wants her buried! Come on!"

The lid of the coffin was going to close again. She let her eyes fly open. She stared upward and knew she had to talk and play for time. It had saved her once.

She could only pray that it would save her again.

She forced a smile.

"Come on! I know you like to play! Puzzles, pretense. Come on now, win this argument with…"

She looked around the room and, momentarily stunned, she went speechless.

Logic? Or something else? Ragnar wondered.

They hadn't taken her far. He could swear that he heard her whispering, saying just that thing. It was still daylight; if they had traveled a long distance, it would be getting dark.

Well, it wouldn't be dark for several hours. But they still wouldn't have taken her far; she was too valuable a commodity. They would want her dead and buried quickly.

Or rather, buried and dead quickly!

He called Jackson, then Mark and Colleen. They were already out on the road, too, but he felt that between him and the other members of the Krewe, he was closer.

To what, he wasn't sure. He was gambling, but there was no choice. The Krewe was a large unit, and dozens of other agents would be searching in every conceivable direction.

He was heading to the closest place he knew about, a state forest.

Just twenty-two miles, toward the north, toward the east. He would find a rich state forest. And he was counting on making the right decision. But Hugo had leapt out of his arms before he had reached the door. And while a dog couldn't possibly follow tire tracks or a vehicle that had taken off while in a vehicle himself, Hugo *had* found where the vehicle had been parked, and he'd barked like a maniac, stumbling a little as he'd returned to Ragnar, where Ragnar had helped him into the car.

They couldn't be far ahead of him—if he was traveling in the right direction.

He was. He had to be.

Hugo—sitting next to him in the passenger's seat—barked.

And, looking ahead, he saw that one of the entrances to the forest loomed before him.

Would they have used the legitimate entrance?

Yes—from there, they would have wound around until they came to the wildest, thickest part. They would have abandoned whatever car they had stolen. They would have carried her in, knocked out. It was amazing that Hugo had fought off the drug so quickly, but he thought that he had seen a dart by the dog. Maybe the dart hadn't delivered its full dose. Maybe they had underestimated the size, strength, and abilities of the animal.

Or maybe they hadn't cared. They'd just needed to get Megan away.

He was certain Ayers had maneuvered this episode. He'd demanded it after they had spoken with him and left the facility. He wanted his wife dead; he wanted Megan dead more. And he was the kind of man who would demand that his followers take any risk.

And now Ragnar knew what they should have seen all along. Except that it was painful to accept. He didn't know it all...

Was there a partner? Someone waiting with a coffin—prepared for Megan. Or had the preparation been there all along?

From the first, he thought. Ayers had wanted Colleen because she was one of the agents who had discovered his daughter, Deirdre, buried in the woods. One of two agents who had saved her life. But he had also taunted Ragnar, telling him he'd have been just as happy with the sister.

Ayers had never stopped plotting to kill Megan. He saw her as easier prey, a woman not trained in law enforcement.

Ragnar drove on into the park, thinking of the massive number of acres it encompassed.

He needed a smaller trail. One that barely allowed a vehicle. Deep in the park, probably.

He asked his voice system to bring up a map of the state park on his phone, and he slowed to a crawl, studying the map.

A narrow trail led far to the northeast of the park.

No activities were listed in the area. No real trails led to it.

"There, Hugo," he muttered.

The dog barked. He drove on, putting through a call to Mark, letting him know he'd advise him as soon as he found out if he was right and to keep Jackson informed.

He had to be right.

He drove on.

And he almost missed the rusty little foreign car that had been pulled tightly into the trails along a root-strewn dirt and gravel road.

He shifted his vehicle into Park. And then he either heard or thought he heard her voice again.

The coffin is open. I'm talking...talking... I pray you hear me!

His phone rang and he answered quickly, but also turned the volume off on incoming calls.

It was Colleen.

"I can hear her, Ragnar. I can hear Megan. She's alive and she's doing all she can to stay that way! But she doesn't know where she is!" Colleen told him urgently.

"I think I've found her," he said, stepping out of the car and waiting for Hugo.

Hugo sniffed the ground and barked, looking anxiously at Mark, running into the trees and then running back for him. He needed to follow.

"Mark has my location," he told Colleen. "Get here. I'm trusting Hugo to take me to Megan."

There was no one else in the room.

Just her captor.

Using two different voices, he'd been arguing with himself.

Had he been playing? Or had he been suffering a serious delusion?

"I need to bury you," he said.

"Why? Because Rory Ayers said so? Because Joel Letterman is spilling all the beans, and Ayers will wind up executed? Were you always one of them—or did he promise you something?"

"Ayers won't be executed."

"I think he will. And let me ask you this—just how much of what you've been promised have you received?"

"I will receive it. And I've got you, don't I?"

"Because someone is controlling Ayers? Someone else really calls the shots?"

"There's a money man. Ayers calls his own shots."

"Trust me. We learned enough from Letterman to find what we need. If you stop now, you won't be guilty of murder. I could even say you rescued me from the shoot-out in the gun range."

"You would never say that."

"You don't know that."

"I know I have to move quickly. They'll be looking for you. This has to be done. I can't let you go! I need my job, and my reputation is clean—"

"We know," Megan interrupted dryly.

"I do like you."

"Aw, that's sweet. I always thought you were cool. Handsome. And you wore a uniform really well. And you have a sense of humor! You just don't know what a plus that is in a man."

His voice changed slightly. "There is time! I want to play—"

"No!"

Patrick would have a field day with him… He seemed to be the true definition of split personality.

"You hit my brother with the same stuff you gave me?" she asked. She prayed he was alive.

"He shot me!"

"But you intended to dose him anyway."

"Had to—him and the damned dog. I knew superman Johansen would have to rush out to see what was happening, to save what lives he could."

"How did you manage that?" she asked.

He started to laugh. "It's a gun range. Shoot a few people with the right kind of weapon in a shooting gallery and the crowd goes wild shooting back. It was the easiest part of the whole thing. I tried to warn Dale Barrie, but..." He broke off and shrugged. "A sniper in the military! And the guy was a wuss! I guess he hadn't believed I'd really try it."

"Now?" she heard Barrie say. And he had been dismayed. Whatever deal he had made with the devil, he hadn't wanted to pay his due.

"Bury her!" he suddenly roared.

"Wait! Look at her, those eyes, that smile!"

His expression changed oddly with his voice when the good and the bad took over. She wondered how he had managed to go about his work—day after day—and still appeared to be perfectly normal. He didn't even have a sealed juvenile record.

Or a parking ticket.

Her limbs were coming back to life. She reached out and touched his face. She couldn't let him get her into the ground.

"So clever!" she said. "You arranged for Amelia Ayers to be taken and buried. And you arranged for the fliers to go up that alerted the acolytes as to what women needed to be taken."

He shrugged. "Easy enough."

"Well, for you, yes, of course it was. Another man wouldn't have done so well."

His face took on a hardened expression. "Kill her! She's playing you!"

"We're having a conversation!" Megan snapped.

Again, the face change. "Yeah!" The softer expression was back.

"So, Ayers is promising money and a lot of it, I take it," Megan went on. "And he conned you into doing all his dirty work for him. So, who killed Carver?"

That brought out a laugh—and a face change again. "I did!"

"What?"

"It was easy. We went into lockdown-all-hands-on when the food fight started. I rushed from my post to the cafeteria and made sure I was the one digging people off Carver. And luckily, there were a lot of them. I had the shiv. And that's why it was never found. They didn't search us!" He started to laugh again.

"But who started it all?"

He laughed again, truly enjoying himself.

"Carver started it."

"Carver?"

"Ayers told him a lie about another prisoner. Through me, of course. Ayers pretended to be fuming about a man who he believed had been on the website and betrayed him. Carver believed he was starting the fight for a man to be killed—he just didn't know *he* was the man who was to be killed!"

"A very cunning man, indeed," Megan said. She needed to get the "nice" personality back. "You're bleeding!" she said, concern and sympathy dripping in her voice.

"I told you—your brother shot me!" the angry personality said.

"Let me help you, please. That's a lot of blood, and where you were hit in the arm... I don't know that much about blood vessels, but I think you need a tourniquet at the very least!"

This time, though, she didn't get the "nice" guy back.

"Enough! You're stalling, and I have work to do! Now get in there!"

She had sat up in the coffin to talk. He pushed her shoulder. She desperately tried to think of a way to shimmy down and reach the gun at her ankle within the narrow confines of the box. It was impossible. She could fight, but he might knock her out and that could make matters worse once the lid of the coffin was closed.

And she was already beneath ground level.

"Wait, please, I'm telling you—"

She broke off.

There was a noise at the back of the cabin.

He drew his gun, heading in that direction.

"FBI!" came a roaring voice.

Ragnar.

Her captor swirled, drawing her halfway out of the coffin and against him, placing the nose of the gun at her temple.

No more Mr. Nice Guy.

"Show yourself and then go. Or she gets a bullet in the head!"

Hugo was about to go bounding in.

Ragnar stopped him, catching his collar, looking quickly at the dog, and bringing his finger to his lips.

"You're surrounded, Brendan Kent, and everyone knows who you are and what you have done. Let Megan go, and I'll speak with the judge and at your trial. I'll tell them Ayers had control over you. But you have to let her go right now!"

"Liar!" Kent screamed. "You're just saying that. You'll do everything in your power to get me the death penalty!"

"No. The death penalty is for men like Ayers," Ragnar said. "If you let her go—"

"My life is over. My job is gone—can you imagine me in a facility in the general population? I'd wish a thousand times that I'd been shot."

"No, you can help us. Like Letterman. And we can see you're kept safe, in solitary confinement, away from anyone who might want revenge on a man like you."

"Show yourself!"

Ragnar stepped into the bones of the old cabin with his gun aimed at Brendan Kent's head. He was good, and he knew it.

Megan was alive. She had kept herself alive—and kept Kent from going through with the burial. She was frozen in the man's hold, but she looked at Ragnar, and he knew she was grateful he had arrived.

Whatever the outcome might be.

Could he shoot Kent?

Ragnar was fast, but he might not be fast enough, not when Megan was being held in Kent's grip.

He figured Brendan Kent was good, too. Good enough to squeeze the trigger in a split second.

Someone had taken down Dale Barrie, and Barrie had always been armed—an old sharpshooter who owned a gun range.

"It seems like we're at a strange impasse here," Ragnar said.

Megan had played for time. Maybe he had to do the same. Mark and Colleen and others would be heading to the location. They knew how to handle a situation, sneaking around, finding positions...

Could they get here fast enough?

He was accustomed to making split second decisions. The way Kent was talking, he had decided this was his endgame.

And Megan would be going with him.

She was staring at him with those emerald eyes he had come to know, and she may or may not have moved her lips.

But he heard, "Hugo."

He released his hold on the collar. Hugo leapt forward.

Kent swung his gun toward the dog.

Ragnar shot...

And less than a second later, another shot rang out.

When Kent had turned to face Hugo, Megan had grabbed the gun strapped to her ankle, thankfully and remarkably still there. She'd brought it up in a smooth motion and fired, just the way she'd been taught.

As Kent went down, Hugo rushed him, snarling.

Megan called the dog back, and he loped over to her.

Just then, Colleen burst into the room, followed by Mark and Jackson Crow.

Colleen flew to her sister, cradling her in a fierce hug.

Mark knelt by Brendan Kent. He looked at Ragnar and shook his head. "May or may not make it—he was bleeding already. His gun hand is about blown off. And Megan caught him in the right shoulder."

Jackson called for EMTs.

"Patrick?" Megan cried.

"Patrick is all right," Colleen assured her quickly. "I'm amazed he drugged Patrick and Hugo instead of killing them."

Megan rushed to tell them. "He's like two people! I thought there were two men here. His face, his voice, everything about him changed when he took on his various identities and talked to himself. Patrick will know!"

"Split personality?" Colleen asked. "Is that real?"

"There's so much he could say," Mark muttered.

"There's so much he did say, and I've had my phone on Record," Ragnar told them all.

Megan looked at him. "How long were you out there?"

"Long enough to try to figure out how to play it," he admitted.

"I knew you would come," she whispered.

Colleen had finally released her sister. And Ragnar didn't care who saw what or what they might think.

He strode across the room to her, drawing her into his arms. Holding her.

Hugo joined them—once he was certain the man who had taken Megan was not getting up and was barely breathing.

Ragnar was still holding her when the EMTs arrived. Brendan Kent was taken away on a gurney. It was decided Mark would ride with the ambulance, and Colleen would get their vehicle and follow along with Jackson.

Right now, they had to see if the man was going to live or die.

There was much to be sorted out.

A forensic team arrived; every location was thoroughly searched in hopes of discerning if it had been used before.

If there might be a coffin buried nearby.

Once Megan had been given a once-over by the paramedics and they were all cleared to leave, Ragnar, Megan, Colleen, and Jackson walked back through the woods to their vehicles, Hugo padding along happily behind them.

Jackson paused at his SUV, looking sternly at Colleen. "We'll have to sort this all out tomorrow. But you and Mark—you're on your honeymoon. Could the two of you please go back on it? And you two!" he said, glaring at Ragnar and Megan. "Yes I know, tomorrow you'll want to talk to Ayers. But then you are hereby ordered to take a few days, agent and consultant. You fired your weapon, Ragnar, and you know protocol. But I know as well, you'll want to speak with Ayers. It will happen." He got into his car, leaving no room for discussion.

"Well, getting back on the honeymoon would be nice," Colleen said. "But—"

"Colleen, we will talk to Ayers with Patrick again," Ragnar assured her. "It will be a new game—because we caught his right-hand man. We'll have to make sure no one else in the facility has been in on it. But from the way he was talking—and we can all listen to the recording—he was as proud of being Ayers's main man as Ayers is of being…Ayers." He hesitated and then smiled. His arm was still around Megan. "And you two can go back on your honeymoon. I promise you I will never leave Megan's side again."

Colleen grinned. "It's probably a good thing you did, or you could have been down with Patrick and Hugo."

Megan cleared her throat. "I think I did pretty well myself."

"You were amazing," Ragnar assured her.

"Yeah, you were," Colleen admitted. "Okay, well, I'm off to the hospital."

"And we're…off," Ragnar said.

Finally, they were back in Ragnar's car. Darkness was coming on. As he started the vehicle, Ragnar looked at her and asked anxiously, "Are you really okay? Are you feeling ill from the drug he hit you with? Did he hurt you?"

"Ragnar, I'm fine. More than fine!" she told him. "The drug has worn off. I'm sure he wanted me awake and aware when I went in the ground. Or at least half of him did. He didn't hurt me; he must have just carried me in and set me in the coffin and closed the lid, but then he got into a fight with his two halves. That was so strange! I could have sworn there were two people there, but both were him."

"It is unbelievable he went to work and appeared to be a normal person by day. I don't know enough about psychiatry to understand, but I do know hard-core killers like BTK went years without their families having any clue. This is really different—but it will take someone like Patrick to figure it out and explain it. I just… I have never been so…"

"Frightened?" she asked softly.

"Yes, frightened."

"Because you're not frightened for yourself; you are frightened for others."

"Never like today."

She smiled and turned toward him as he drove out of the narrow trail.

"I'm alive and well," she said softly.

"And you really did great. You...you knew how to keep him talking and arguing with himself."

"I knew you would come," she said. "I couldn't maneuver myself to reach the gun without him seeing, and I was afraid if he took it from me, that would be it... Because of you and Hugo, I had a chance. And I knew you would come!"

"I heard you," he said.

She smiled, nodding. "Because we're close," she whispered.

"You know...you can go back to New York now. It will be safe."

"I could."

"Or—"

"I love what I do. I'm glad I can be helpful here. But I really love what I do."

"I see," he said quietly.

She laughed, turning to him.

"No, you don't see," she told him.

He glanced her way quickly, maneuvering across the road.

She was smiling, so alive, and he was so grateful, and he was...

In love.

But she loved her job. And he knew something inside him wouldn't let him leave his job.

"Megan, I—"

"Would you like it if I was here on a more permanent basis?" she asked him.

"What?"

"Well, many people are working remotely these days. I think I could speak with my publisher and make an arrangement." She laughed. "Half the time, we have to leave the office and go home to actually edit a book anyway. Oh, but wait!"

He drew the car off to the side of the road, slammed it into Park, and reached across to the passenger's seat, drawing her into his arms again.

He kissed her, and the kiss became long and filled with promise.

And when they finally broke, she looked at him mischievously.

"It's one of those nights, Ragnar!" she said.

"One of those nights..."

"We saved a life! Mine. And it feels so good. Well, you know me! I just love to celebrate!"

He smiled and revved the car.

"I just love celebrating," he assured her.

"And, Ragnar," she said, her voice barely a whisper.

"Yes?"

"I love you," she told him.

He drove to the side of the road again and took her into his arms.

"I love you. Madly, deeply—probably a little insanely. I want to see your face every night when I go to sleep and every morning when I wake up. For the rest of my life!"

They kissed again.

Hugo woofed from the back.

Megan pulled away from him and smiled. "Okay, we'll keep

it casual so we can get home—or home to the safe house—and celebrate!"

He drove as quickly as he could, just within legal limits.

They barely made it into the house.

And they celebrated. All through the night.

EPILOGUE

Patrick was fine, and Megan had seldom been quite so happy to see her brother.

Though he wasn't terribly happy with himself.

"Hey, you got a shot into the man!" Megan reminded him. "And you never know. He might have moved faster if you hadn't. He was suffering and bleeding a great deal."

"Before you and Ragnar shot him," Patrick said.

They were seated at a table in the conference room with Jackson, Angela, Colleen, Mark, and Red and Hugo.

Brendan Kent remained in the hospital. Because of his condition and blood loss, the doctors had put him into a medically induced coma. They would see how he did.

"Was all that real?" Megan asked her brother.

"Split personality or Dissociative Identity Disorder is certainly a recognized diagnosis. Usually, however, those suffering from DID are more likely to hurt themselves than others. Of course, this is a different case. And I admit, I didn't see it in the man. Not that I had any long conversations with him. I believe it is real in his case. His one personality has empathy and remorse. I think it was hard for him to try to pull off taking you. Before, he never had to get his own hands dirty. Interesting."

"And," Jackson said, "he does name Ayers as being the main man."

"I think that as far as he knows, Ayers is the main man. But the timing suggests that this is far reaching and that there are still other players we don't know about. Because Ayers hasn't been in prison long—although he could have gotten to the man in another way. Right now, I don't know. But I can say this with certainty—Ayers is a dangerous man. And whatever his position in the empire or enterprise, he has power."

"However he pulled it off, I agree. He is a very dangerous main man—one who could coerce a man with Kent's reputation. I believe that from wherever and however, Ayers saw something in him he could play upon. And Ayers used Kent well. Except, of course, he didn't know what he was up against when it came to gifted triplets," Ragnar said.

"Oh, he arranged it all!" another voice said.

Sergeant Alfie Parker had swept in to join them. He was greeted warmly.

"I did what I said I was going to do, and I haunted the facility," Alfie told them. He might be a ghost, but he apparently wanted his chair at the conference table, too. Taking a seat, he added, "I hate to admit I was suspicious of Morris. I thought he was taking too strong a stand against the man, talking about wanting him to get the death penalty all the time. I knew it was someone there, but I only saw Ayers near Kent once, and that was when he walked in to talk to another guard about an attorney appointment and stopped and stared at Ayers. Of course, even a ghost isn't everywhere at every time. Thankfully, you pulled it off!" he said gently.

"And, hopefully, the Embracer murders are really at an end," Angela said. "What's left for us is to find the names of the victims we know about, and hope we've discovered most. They all deserve justice." She let out a little sigh. "At least, if we can really silence Ayers, there will be no promise of financial gain for anyone."

"We may never solve all of the past," Megan said. "What's important is the future."

"And the future is the thing, of course," Alfie said, rolling his ghostly thumbs. He shook his head. "I still wonder..."

"If there is someone who was above Ayers?" Ragnar asked him.

Alfie nodded.

Patrick spoke up. "Hey, Alfie, I've decided to practice down here a bit. We'll need to do more work with Ayers, and if Brendan Kent makes it, well...yeah. He's an intriguing subject. I am definitely fascinated and interested in working with the man, and seeing what else we can get out of him. There may be more. And maybe now with what we already have from Kent, we'll get that 'more' from Ayers."

Alfie nodded. "I thought I'd be more helpful. But I am impressed the living did so well. And, Megan—you're usually an editor!"

"And researcher," she reminded him.

Patrick said sincerely, "We will find Susie."

Alfie looked at him. "I believe you will. And..."

"And?"

"I have the strangest idea this might all be connected."

"As well it may be," Ragnar said.

"Something to work on in the future," Jackson said. He glanced at his watch.

"We've all listened to the recording, worked with all we could. Oh, I got Maisie on a call with Joel Letterman. She did a likeness of the man he met at the strip club. Angela, would you bring it up on the screen, so everyone here is aware? We'll be sending it out widely."

The image lit the screen.

Alfie Parker stood. He stared at the screen for a moment, and then around the room.

"I believe," he said, "that man there is John Smith."

★ ★ ★ ★ ★